I0785047

A Widow's Whim
By,
Julie Morrill

Acknowledgments

I am deeply grateful to the many people who helped bring
A Widow's Whim to life. My thanks to the residents of Etna
and Scott Valley who so generously shared stories,
photographs, and memories of our valley's past.

Special thanks to historian and author Gail Jenner who
encouraged me to keep writing and offered more insight
into Etna's fascinating past.

To Pastor Wendell and Mrs. Marilyn Seward, whose
faith and kindness helped inspire the heart of this story, I
owe deep gratitude.

To my friend and fellow history and English teacher,
Katie Morris, whose roots in Scott Valley run deep, and
whose encouragement of my writing never waned.

Dedication

For my husband Pete — Thank you for your endless
patience, encouragement, and for being the inspiration
behind my hero's humorous personality and steadfast spirit.

CHAPTER 1: Elopement

Philadelphia, Pennsylvania – August 1893

Vivian Garrett had always dreamed of a grand wedding—
her mother in tears, her father reluctant to give her away. The
reception would be luxurious, she'd wear a meticulously
designed gown, and her friend Sarah Carlisle would be at her
side as her maid of honor. But tonight, Vivian stood in a
small, dimly lit church she didn't recognize. Beside her was
Draven, her fiancé, and before them, a minister with an odd,
twisted expression that edged on a smirk. No witnesses were
present, an allowance of Pennsylvania law, but the intimacy
was beginning to feel less like a daring secret adventure and
more like a dazed fog.

She tried to catch Draven's eye, seeking reassurance, but
he seemed more interested in rushing the ceremony than in
his bride. Doubts scratched at her mind. She pushed them
down, trying to focus on the minister's words and the shine
of the gold band on her finger.

"I now pronounce you man and wife," the reverend
intoned, his voice echoing in the empty space. Draven's kiss
was perfunctory, a mere brush of the lips. He mumbled a
quick thanks with a wink to the minister and, with a firm grip
on her arm, spirited Vivian out of the church into the waiting
carriage.

As their conveyance rattled along the cobblestone streets, Vivian gazed at the city passing by. Her heart pounded with a mix of excitement and anxiety. She smoothed her fingers over her wedding dress, the satin cool and smooth under her touch. The gown felt like a hollow victory—beautiful but unseen by beloved friends and family. She nervously twisted the ring on her finger.

They arrived at an elegantly furnished cottage by the Delaware River, their honeymoon retreat. Moonlight danced on the water, and Vivian did her best to drink in the beauty around her, but Draven's detachment gnawed at her.

He laughed suddenly, breaking the silence. "Father will disapprove of you," he said, imitating his father's stern expression. He meant it as a joke, but it felt like a blow to Vivian. She forced a smile, determined to win over the Randalls, the elite family to which Draven belonged.

As night turned to dawn, Vivian lay awake, her mind spinning. The marriage she had imagined—the loving connection, the shared joy—was absent. She felt deceived, unsure of what she could trust about Draven's intentions.

Draven stretched beside her, yawning as he stared up at the brocade canopy above the bed. "You needn't worry about your parents finding out," he said casually. "They will never know how easily you agreed to this."

A knot tightened in her stomach. "What do you mean?" she asked, her knuckles white, twisting in the quilt pulled up to her chin.

Draven's smirk was unsettling. "Let's just say this ceremony was arranged to suit my purposes," he said lightly, as though discussing the weather. The words felt like a slap. "It's time for you to run along back home to your mother and father, my dear," he said, stretching his arms and clasping them behind his head. "You see, we were never actually married, sweetheart. The man in the church was only a friend of mine. He's performed such ceremonies for me before." He snickered.

Vivian's gut felt hollow as she rose, her legs wobbly and twisted in her long, white peignoir. Her dream of a joyful wedding had been replaced by deception and betrayal. She stuffed her corset into a carpetbag and fumbled with her dress as she buttoned it over her nightgown. Without another word to Draven, for fear she might give him the satisfaction of crying, she drew a determined breath and left the cottage, slamming the door behind her and hearing his snide chuckle inside.

She had told her parents she was spending the night at Sarah's house. They would never know the humiliation that weighed heavily on her heart.

As she stumbled into the dawn light, her steps blurred along the stone path home. Shame and sorrow clung to her, and she whispered a broken prayer, asking God to forgive her dreadful mistakes. Abandoned and humiliated, she had never felt so foolish and alone.

"I love you, Vivi, but you can be so headstrong and impulsive sometimes." Sarah's voice was soft but firm as they sat together on a garden bench in Philadelphia's Fairmount Park.

Vivian's eyes were downcast, and her entire body trembled. "I know, Sarah, and I hate that about myself. This horror has forever changed me into a more sensible person, I promise you."

"Why do you always have to do such unconventional things? Like when you said you wanted to run your own business and be mayor of a city someday. It frightens me sometimes," Sarah chided gently, concern etched in her voice. "When your father taught you bookkeeping, he gave you wild suffragette ideas. Sometimes you take risks without thinking of the consequences. Eloping with a stranger, Vivi, that was dangerous and reckless."

"You don't need to remind me of my wrongs, Sarah," Vivian bit back angrily before burying her face in her hands. "I thought he loved me," she whimpered. "He was so handsome and charming."

Sarah squeezed her hand. "Charming should have been your first clue."

"Don't I know that now?" Vivian's tone was bitter. "We first met here in this very park."

"Why didn't you tell me about him?" Sarah's voice was hurt.

"I'm sorry," said Vivian. "It all happened so fast. One minute we were meeting here; the next, he was proposing. The next, we were married. I couldn't wait to surprise you with the news."

"It's a surprise, all right," Sarah shook her head. "Married less than twenty-four hours before it ended."

Vivian shifted her weight on the bench.

"You have to tell your parents," Sarah insisted. "You can't keep the biggest event of your life a secret from them."

"I will, and you will too," Vivian warned, her eyes fierce.

"What if you're pregnant?" Sarah asked, her voice barely above a whisper.

Vivian's heart skipped a beat. "Don't be ridiculous." She stood and smoothed her skirt, allowing one hand to rest on her abdomen for a half-second.

Sarah rose and rested a hand on Vivan's shoulder. "You're my dearest friend, Vivi. I'm just worried about you. I don't want anything bad to happen to you."

"Something bad has already happened to me."

CHAPTER 2: Crisis

*T*wo weeks had passed since Vivian's regrettable encounter with Draven Randall. The summer breeze rustled the leaves as she and her friend Sarah strolled along the banks of the Delaware River.

"I'm very troubled about something," Vivian whispered as she placed a trembling hand on her abdomen. "If this worry is true, what should I do?"

Sarah stopped abruptly, clutching a hand to her bodice. "What? Oh, no. Vivian, you need to tell your parents."

"I cannot and will not do that," said Vivian, her voice firm. "I don't want to alarm them or dishonor them."

Sarah squirmed. "You need to find a husband fast."

Vivian frowned, wringing her hands. "I can't rush into another mistake. I don't trust my judgment anymore."

Sarah pondered for a moment. "You could pretend to be a widow."

Vivian looked at her friend in surprise. "A widow?"

"It would buy you time," Sarah suggested. "And you wouldn't have to hide your pregnancy."

Vivian sighed. "But where could I go? No one here would believe it."

"Go to Izza, then," Sarah said.

"My sister Isabel? In California?"

Sarah nodded. "It's a thought."

Vivian fell silent, walking on ahead of Sarah. The idea of pretending to be a widow and moving to California swirled in her mind. She'd have to tell her sister everything, but it would give her a fresh start.

"What are you thinking?" asked Sarah, catching up to her.

"I'm thinking of what it would be like to be a widow in a small western town in the mountains of Northern California," Vivian mused.

"I'd miss you terribly," said Sarah.

"I'd miss you too. But maybe this is what I need. A fresh start."

"I suppose." Sarah exhaled a jagged breath. "Better to cut all ties and be a widow. It frees you to remarry if you want."

"But my parents," Vivian sighed. "They'll eventually know everything."

"They'll understand. You were wronged, Vivian. And besides, you thought you were legally married. Whatever comes of this, there's a way forward, and you're not alone."

Vivian's heart ached with the weight of her decision. She knew Sarah was right, but the thought of leaving everything behind was daunting.

"If I can get Izza to agree to the plan," Vivian said, "I'll need to find a husband. Quickly."

Back home, the tension was palpable. Vivian's mother, Eliza Garrett, paced the floor, sobbing and wringing her hands. "How could you do this to us, Vivian? How?"

Mr. Garrett sat stoically on the settee, his countenance stern, yet his eyes brimmed with sympathy.

"Well, aren't you going to say anything, Clarence?" Eliza demanded, hysteria rising in her voice.

Vivian watched her father's chest slowly rise and fall. He closed his eyes and rubbed a hand across his forehead. "My first thought is the legality of all this," he said. "If

Draven is the father of your child, he must be held accountable to do the right thing, which is to marry you properly."

"But he's a horrid man, Father," Vivian cried. "You can't make me marry him!"

"Your father's right, Vivian," Eliza squealed. "You're with child out of wedlock. It's a complete scandal!"

"What to do? What to do?" Clarence mumbled. He took a deep breath.

"Do something, Clarence," Eliza whimpered. "This means utter disgrace and ruin for us."

"We're going to pray about this, get some sleep, and see what ideas come to mind tomorrow," said Vivian's father.

He stood and walked to his quavering daughter, drawing her close in an embrace. "It'll be all right, Vivi," he reassured her. "I'm not sure how just yet, but it will all turn out right in the end."

"In the end?" Eliza declared. "What about between now and the end? It won't be all right, I assure you."

"Hush now, Mother," said Clarence. "We'll talk about this in the morning."

A week later, it was all settled. Sarah's idea proved to be a good one after all. It couldn't be confirmed medically at this time, but there was a high probability that Vivian was with child out of wedlock. Clarence managed to obtain a forged marriage certificate from a lawyer friend. Though not legal, it provided evidence that Vivian had been married before she became pregnant. They also created a false death certificate for a faux husband, a Mr. Oscar Wendell Smith. Vivian, now the unfortunate widow of Mr. Smith, was to be sent west on a train to California, where she'd live with her sister Isabel.

With tears streaming down her face, Vivian hugged her parents and Sarah at the station before boarding her railway car, knowing her life would never be the same and, as the train lurched and chugged away from the station, she waved goodbye from her window, the weight of her decision heavy on her soul. But there was also one tiny glimmer of hope in the darkness. California beckoned, offering a chance at redemption and a new beginning. And, if she wasn't pregnant, she could always go back home.

CHAPTER 3: The West is Calling

Chicago, Illinois

The bustling sounds of the railway station filled the air as Blue Ryan and his fellow stevedores hoisted a large wooden crate from a train car onto the waiting flatbed. The summer sun bore down on them, making the task even more grueling. Blue wiped the sweat from his forehead, his muscles straining with the effort.

"Hey, Michael!" Blue called, waving to a homeless beggar huddled in the shadows of the depot.

"Why do they just sit around and beg?" grumbled Butch, Blue's partner, as they heaved another crate.

"Most are sick, weak, or injured," Blue replied, his voice steady. "I've talked to them. They'd work if they could, and they'll work as soon as they can."

Butch scoffed, "You're too trusting. They're all just lazy bums. When I move to California next year, I'll make twice as much as I earn here. I'll find me a pretty little wife and build a nice home for us."

California. It was all Butch ever talked about.

"You should seriously think about goin' with me," Butch continued. "You grew up on a dairy farm, and you're a hard worker. Anybody in their right mind would hire ya. You said yourself no churches or schools around here need preachers or teachers. Maybe you could find a position in California."

Blue hoisted another crate and wiped the sweat from his eyes. "What about all these poor beggars? They're like my congregation."

Butch shrugged. "Are ya really usin' the teachin' and preachin' gifts God gave ya, or are ya just yammerin' and givin' 'em food?"

The question pricked at Blue's conscience. Butch had a point. His incessant talk about California was starting to get to Blue.

"Think of all those carnal, selfish whoremongers out west who need a preacher, not to mention all the poor, uneducated country bumpkin children in need of a teacher," Butch said, a grin spreading across his face.

Blue sighed. He didn't like change and rarely did anything without a great deal of prayer and thought. But months of waiting, praying, and searching for ministerial work and teaching jobs had proved fruitless. He didn't want to be a stevedore forever. Maybe it was time to do what God had truly called him to do.

At the end of the workday, Blue trudged home, his stomach rumbling and his mind churning with ideas. He bought a newspaper and carried it to his rented room. After hanging his hat on a hook, he slumped into a chair and ate a meal of cold chicken and leftover potatoes from the icebox. He flipped through the paper, his eyes catching on an advertisement:

Move to California! Hard-working, able-bodied men needed in mining, logging, ranching, farming, construction...

California again. It couldn't be a coincidence. Even as a minister, he'd likely need to do manual labor on the side to earn a decent wage until he found a school where he could teach. That would be fine with him.

The article listed dozens of cities and towns. Blue pored over a map and studied California's geographical features. Mount Shasta, towering over 14,000 feet tall, caught his imagination. He matched nearby towns to the list in the article. Etna, California. Nestled in a farming and cattle ranching valley, it seemed like a promising place to live, explore, and meet new people. He might even meet his future wife. But what if he couldn't find a wife there? He chuckled to himself. He was living in one of the nation's most populous cities and hadn't found a wife. Maybe he should just trust God with his marriage prospects.

Standing, he paced the room, then walked to the window. He breathed out, fogging up the glass, and traced a question mark on the pane. Rain pelted the street below, and there was ol' Tommy Bob on the corner, huddled under his umbrella, panhandling. The sight tugged at Blue's heartstrings.

He practically sprinted to his bed. Crouching, he reached beneath the frame and pulled out a small trunk. Opening it, he found his .45 Colt revolver in its leather holster, along with several rounds of ammunition.

"I hope I'll never have to shoot anything but wild game," he said aloud, the weight of the gun feeling foreign in his hands. "But you never know. It's the Wild West, after all." Excitement rumbled in his chest, and his eyes shot upward. "Well, Lord, if I'm headed in the wrong direction, please redirect my path. I'm headin' to California."

He packed the gun away, closed the trunk, and sat back on his heels. He could hear the rain pattering against the window, a soothing sound that eased his mind.

With renewed determination, Blue stood and walked to his desk. He pulled out a piece of paper and a pen. He began drafting a letter to his parents, explaining his decision.

"Dear Ma and Pa,

I hope this letter finds you in good health and spirits. I've been doing a lot of thinking and praying lately, and I've come to a decision..."

He wrote about his struggles to find work as a preacher and teacher in Chicago, about the people he'd met and helped, and about Butch's constant talk of California. He described the ad he'd seen and the pull he felt toward the West.

"I believe this is where the Lord is leading me," he concluded. "Please keep me in your prayers. Your loving son, Blue."

Satisfied with the letter, Blue folded it carefully and set it aside to mail the next day. He then sat down to make a list of things he'd need for the journey: sturdy boots, durable clothing, a Bible, and a few keepsakes from home.

As he packed, his thoughts drifted to the adventures that lay ahead. The promise of wide-open spaces, the challenge of new work, and the hope of finding a community where he could truly make a difference filled him with anticipation.

That night, as Blue lay in bed, he felt a mix of nervousness and excitement. The idea of leaving everything he knew behind was daunting, but the opportunity to start anew and fulfill his calling was too compelling to ignore.

He closed his eyes and offered a silent prayer. "Lord, guide me on this journey. Help me to be strong and faithful. Let your will be done."

CHAPTER 4: Far from Home

*W*idow Vivian Smith stepped gingerly from the stagecoach onto Etna's Main Street, her black dress and bonnet a stark contrast to the vibrant bustle of the small town. Her face was hidden beneath a sheer veil, masking her fatigue from nearly two weeks of travel. Wiping dust from her eyes and chapped lips, she longed for a hot bath and a heartfelt conversation with her sister.

The driver heaved her trunk down, and it thudded onto the boardwalk outside Tanner's Telegraph Office. When the trunk struck the ground, the clasp came undone, spilling its contents. At the same time, a mischievous dust devil swirled past, catching a stack of leaflets and scattering them down the street.

"Oh no, no, no!" Vivian cried, scrambling to gather the flying papers. The stage driver helped a little, but several leaflets were beyond saving, flipping and tossing like white doves on the breeze.

"Sorry, ma'am," the driver said, glancing at the pages in his hand before handing them to her. "Votes for women?" He raised a bushy eyebrow.

"Yes, thank you," she replied curtly, snatching the leaflets. "Do you oppose women's suffrage, sir?"

"I don't have an opinion, ma'am," he said, tipping his hat before clambering back onto the stagecoach.

Vivian turned and waved at a familiar figure. "Isabel!"

A primly dressed young woman glanced round before focusing on the stagecoach driver. "Where's my sister, Vivian Garrett? She was supposed to be on this stage."

"No one by that name, ma'am," the driver said. "Only passenger was this widow here," he added, jerking a thumb at Vivian. With a snap of the reins, the coach moved off. There was a look of bewilderment on Isabel's face.

"Isabel, it's me," Vivian called, struggling as she lugged her trunk from the street and onto the boardwalk.

Isabel's eyes were wide with shock. "Vivian? What happened? Did someone die? Who died? Are Mother and Father all right?"

Vivian bit her lip. "Oh, dear. Mother and Father didn't tell you?"

"No," said Isabel, her voice quavering as she grabbed Vivian's hands in hers. "Tell me what? What has happened?"

"I'll explain everything, but first, can you help me with my trunk?"

Together, they lifted the heavy container, grunting as they hefted it toward a stone storefront, perspiration gathering on their foreheads and in the pits of their arms. "What have you got in here, Vivi? Solid gold?"

"Surprisingly heavy clothes are all."

Two Chinese brothers, working in a room on the building's first floor, offered to help the two ladies, and they were kind enough to carry the trunk up a flight of stairs to Isabel's apartment. Inside, the flat was small but tidy, with a parlor, a dining area, and a kitchen with a wood stove and hand pump sink. Vivian tried to tip the two gentlemen, but they refused, bowing politely as they made their departure.

As soon as the door closed, Vivian laid a crumpled suffrage leaflet on the coffee table and collapsed onto Isabel's couch. "I'm so glad to be out of that confounded stagecoach," she said, whipping off her black hat and veil.

"Vivi, don't swear," Isabel scolded, opening an ice box and chipping a few chunks of ice. "Now, please, tell me what happened. Why are you in mourning?"

Vivian bit her lower lip. She could lie and say she was an actual widow or tell Isabel the truth, which she would find out anyway. She decided on the truth, but there was no easy way to tell the story without her sister overreacting.

Isabel settled on the sofa and took Vivian's hand, stroking it gently. "I'm trying to be strong, Vivi. Please tell me who died."

Vivian broke loose from her sister and rose to her feet before wringing her hands and pacing.

"Stop moving and fidgeting, Vivi. You're making me nervous."

Vivian stopped and faced her sister squarely. "I married a man named Draven Randall III."

"What—?" Isabel squeaked.

"Please don't interrupt me until I'm finished."

Isabel pressed her lips together and stared with eyes wide as saucers.

"Do you remember the Randall family, Izza?"

She nodded.

"Their son met me, proposed to me, and we eloped."

Isabel's mouth dropped. "How--? What? Vivi, how could you?"

"Please don't interrupt me. And then, after one…" Vivian's voice tightened. "…*solitary* night with that wretched ogre of a man, he humiliated me and told me our whole marriage was a counterfeit. He faked the whole thing. The minister wasn't even a real minister. He was just a paid friend." Isabel opened her mouth to speak, but Vivian held up her hand. "Two weeks later I missed my monthly."

Isabel inhaled sharply. "Do Mother and—?"

"Yes, Mother and Father know all about it. It's why I'm here." Vivian exhaled and scrubbed her eyes with her fingertips. "But there's more. Father arranged for a forged marriage and death certificate, so that I could come here as a widow. A pretend widow."

Isabel returned to the kitchenette and poured tea over the chips of ice she'd placed in two glasses, her hands trembling so that she nearly spilled the tea. She spoke in a hushed tone, "So, you're here, possibly pregnant, unmarried, pretending to be a widow, and now we're both living a complete lie?"

"It's the best idea we could think of, Izza. It was mainly Father who thought of it, and my friend Sarah. We didn't know what else to do."

It was Isabel's turn to wring her hands and pace the floor. "You always act on impulse, Vivi."

"I can't deny that," Vivian admitted.

"Mother and Father must be in shock."

Vivian's shoulders drooped. "They were. They've gotten over the worst of it by now."

"They nearly jumped out of their skin when I said I was coming out west," said Isabel, "because it was out of character for me. I'm not typically the adventurous one, but you..."

Vivian could only nod.

Isabel finally settled on the sofa next to her sister. "I suppose you're not completely to blame. Your real mistake was trusting that scalawag. You must find a husband immediately--especially if you're, you know..."

"With child," Vivian said. She shook her head. "The last thing I want is another husband. I think all men are scoundrels. I'll stay a widow. I'll be free and single. I'll be fine. *We'll* be fine."

"But you'll need support. How will you manage with a baby?"

"I have you, Izza. Besides, I might not be pregnant."

"But if you are, you desperately need a husband. I can't support you and a baby. Even if I got a job as a teacher, my paltry salary wouldn't take care of the two of us, much less a baby."

"You still haven't secured a teaching position?"

Isabel shook her head. "I was about to write letters to other school boards in California and Oregon before--"

"Before you heard I was showing up?" Vivian asked meekly.

Isabel didn't answer.

"I'll find a way to support myself."

"You're my sister, Vivi. We'll figure this out, so help us God." She blew out a puff of air. As she did so, the suffrage leaflet on the coffee table fluttered to the floor. Isabel retrieved it. "What's this?"

"Not now, Izza," said Vivian, snatching it from her hand.

"Vivi, promoting women's suffrage will never help you find a husband!" Isabel squeaked. "Not in this town! Oh, Vivi, you and your radical ideas!"

"What if I find a husband who supports women's suffrage?" Vivian challenged.

Isabel laughed wryly. "You won't find a husband like that anywhere in America, much less here in California."

The corners of Vivian's mouth tugged downward. "I can dream, can't I?"

"You can stop dreaming and start dusting off those bookkeeping skills Father taught you." Isabel made a "tsk" sound with her tongue. "I don't need the embarrassment of you bringing women's suffrage to this town, Vivi. You'll ruin my reputation."

Vivian crumpled the leaflet and tossed it onto the coffee table.

There was an uncertain silence before Isabel spoke again. "So, you're a widow."

"I'm Widow Smith," said Vivian, "and my husband's name was Oscar Wendell Smith."

"A completely made-up person?"

Vivian nodded.

"And he left you with no money?" asked Isabel.

"Not a cent, the scalawag." Vivian sighed. "I'll search for work straightaway."

"I'll help you," said Isabel, "and we'll work it out. Between you and me and God and your future husband, we'll work it out."

CHAPTER 5: Imposter

"*Hello*, I'm Mrs. Smith—*Widow* Smith," Vivian said to no one, curtsying slightly. It was early morning, and her sister was dressing for work. "My late husband, Oscar, was a man of great virtue and kindness, though our time together was regrettably short." She laughed and blew her nose. Pressing her forehead against the cool windowpane, tears blurred the view of the bustling street below. She clutched her stomach, feeling a hollow ache as if a part of her had been ripped away.

She straightened and slapped her hands together as though dusting them off. "I need to find work," she declared resolutely.

A second monthly flow missed last week was convincing her she was pregnant. Then again, she'd missed her courses before, so maybe it meant nothing. Maybe she still had her whole life ahead of her to do as she pleased. If she were pregnant, would any man want to marry a pregnant widow woman or a widow with a small baby?

She took in Etna's Main Street through the glass. Back home in Philadelphia, an economic scare had dampened all industry, including her father's businesses, but there was no sign of recession here. Two schoolgirls in pinafores and bonnets skipped hand-in-hand along the boardwalk, their laughter mingling with the distant clatter of horse-drawn carriages.

A wave of heartache fluttered through Vivian. Here she was in a new, wild outpost in the middle of nowhere, far from the comforts of everything familiar. She didn't know what she'd do without her sister. And the thought of her parents and friends back home wrung out her heart like a dried sponge. She missed her suffrage meetings, helping her father with his work, and his words of encouragement. She missed her mother and the way she fussed over her to the point of annoyance. She missed Sarah most of all.

She was ashamed to have been so deceived and then rejected and shunned by Draven and his family. Her one mercy in playing the part of a widow was that it allowed her to experience and even exhibit some of the pain she truly felt. "I'll find a husband if I must," she told herself, "but I'll be extra careful to find a decent man this time."

She followed the swarm of men's hats weaving up and down the sides of the street. Despite graduating from Mrs. Doebler's finishing school and numerous lessons in etiquette, Vivian was terrible at flirting. Still, if she'd been pretty enough to capture Draven Randall's interest, she could certainly catch another man's heart in this town where bachelors were in abundance.

A scrawny cowboy spat tobacco into the street. "Slim pickings," Vivian mused, wrinkling her nose. "No wonder Izza hasn't found a beau yet."

"You see what I have to choose from?" asked Isabel, making Vivian jump.

"Oh! Good morning, Izza!"

Isabel padded into the kitchen. "Will you ever tell your husband the truth or will you expect me to keep your secret forever?"

Vivian rubbed her fingers on her temples. "If I even marry, it all depends on whether I have a baby or not. I suppose he should know the truth. I'm just not sure when I should tell him."

"Hm," said Isabel as she lit a fire on the stove. "If you wait till after you're married to tell your husband, he'd have grounds to divorce you."

"But if I fall in love with a man again and tell him the truth before we're married, he'd leave me for sure. He might even tell everyone in town and ruin my reputation—and yours."

"Sounds like we're keeping your secret, then."

Vivian nodded. "Time to stop thinking about husbands and start looking for work."

Isabel set cups of tea and bowls on the table. "I think you'll find both work and a husband soon enough."

"You always cared more about gaining an education than finding a husband, Izza. Do you ever regret it?"

Isabel's eyes briefly clouded over. 'No, but things haven't turned out as planned,' she said, her voice tight with a hint of resignation.

"I'm sorry," said Vivian. "Any news of a teaching position opening up?"

"No. My work at the mercantile is all right for now, though, and the school will need another teacher eventually."

The sisters ate breakfast before Isabel headed out the door.

"Thank you again for letting me stay with you, Izza."

Isabel smiled back. "You know you're always welcome."

After a few hours of scrubbing laundry, Vivian was surprised when the clock struck half-past eleven. If she didn't hurry, the post office would close for lunch, and her letter wouldn't go out with the day's post. She wrapped a light shawl across her shoulders, wrapped her purse strings over her wrist, grabbed her envelope, and examined herself in a mirror beside the door. Her reflection in the mirror revealed tired eyes and a sad expression. She pinched her cheeks, trying in vain to bring some color to her pallor. She patted the gold, braided bun on the back of her head and left the apartment, descending to the main floor, past the Chinese brothers hard at work.

A bluster of dust met her on the boardwalk. She closed the door behind her and leaned against it, blinking in the bright sunshine. Hasty clouds swept across a sapphire sky and her black wool skirt whipped about her ankles. She smoothed a strand of butter-gold hair behind an ear and lifted her chin with aplomb.

Etna was a clattering, clamoring boomtown of foreign faces, shouts above the dusty squall, ladies walking arm in arm carrying parasols, baskets or brown-papered parcels. Men stomped and clomped up and down the boardwalk, jogged across the street, galloped their horses, drove creaking, rattling wagons with whistles and whoops. Disheveled construction workers labored in propping a skeleton wall. Hammers rang. Sweat and dust blended with the odor of horses and freshly milled pine boards. There were people everywhere, but mostly men. Lots of men.

A swirl of grit peppered her face, and she knuckled her eyelids. New town, new people. Now was Vivian's chance to start making a good impression. Her heels clicked on the wooden boardwalk and, when she reached the post office, she stared at a large, shaggy dog lying on the stoop. She crouched beside the heap of fur, her hand trembling as she gently patted its head. 'You're just tired, aren't you?' she murmured, her voice softening with genuine concern. The dog didn't move.

"Whose dog is this?" she shouted. "Hello? Anyone?" People pushed past and she crouched at the dog's head.

She stepped gingerly over the lifeless pile of fluff and twisted the doorknob, gusting into the post office with a loud clanging of a bell. She pressed herself against the door to close it and rotated into the quiet room, where a portly postmistress was assisting another customer.

Vivian cleared her throat. "Um, there's a large dog lying outside. Does he belong to either of you?" Neither postmistress nor customer responded, and Vivian resigned herself to standing and waiting. The minute hand on the clock clunked forward—five minutes to twelve.

The bell above the door jingled again and a young brunette blustered in. The intruder's thick, ambered perfume assaulted Vivian's nostrils and stung her eyes. "Confounded wind!" the brunette complained, readjusting the rosette brooch nestled in the vee of her low neckline. She was about the same age as Vivian. She slammed the door and stood behind Vivian, arranging the gaudy, pheasant-feathered hat atop her fluffy, rounded, messy Gibson. While her hair had probably been stylish before the tempest hit, it was a bit of a disaster now.

The girl offered no response to Vivian's friendly hello and comments on the weather. A civilized Philadelphian woman would at least reply with a "Good day." Then again, a civilized Philadelphian would never wear such a revealing costume in public in daylight hours and she'd wear far less perfume.

Vivian tipped her eyes to the clock again and tapped her foot quietly on the pinewood floor. The customer at the counter finally departed so she could step forward to take his place. All at once, the odor-drenched girl brushed past and claimed the counter ahead of her.

"Excuse me, ma'am," Vivian protested.

"Good morning, Samantha! What can I do for you today?" the postmistress greeted cheerily.

Samantha. Vivian wrinkled her forehead. "Excuse me, miss. I've been waiting and I—"

"I'll be with you in a moment, ma'am," said the postmistress.

Vivian pursed her lips. She was here to make a good impression on people, not create a scene.

"Hello, Barbara," said Samantha. "Wait till I tell you the latest news."

Vivian groaned inwardly and dabbed at her eyes that still burned from the sticky perfume. She watched the clock and fumbled with the envelope in her hand.

Samantha leaned over the counter. "Tessie says she's been thinking."

"I hope she doesn't hurt herself," Barbara snorted.

The two ladies giggled and the feathers on Samantha's hat swayed. Vivian's jaw clenched. Three minutes to twelve. Her letter would miss today's post.

"So, what has Tessie been thinking?" asked Barbara.

"*Who* has she been thinking of, you mean?"

Barbara adjusted her spectacles and affixed a stamp to an envelope. "Who, then*?*"

"Matthew Wright."

Barbara clucked her tongue. "Don't you worry about him, Samantha. That boy would never settle for the likes of Tessie Blackman."

"But Matthew's character isn't so pristine, and you have to admit she *is* pretty."

"If you like ill-bred, loquacious, earsplitting tarts," Barbara winked. Her earbobs shook in rhythm with the folds of her chin and Samantha cackled.

Vivian rolled her eyes. *Who's the tart? Samantha forgot to look in the mirror before she left the house this morning.*

"But what if he's looking for a little jam with his tart?" Samantha asked.

"Oh, you're a naughty one," said Barbara. "Better to let Matthew be and you set your sights higher."

"Pardon me," Vivian interrupted again. "It's nearly noon and I just want to make sure I can mail—"

"In a minute, ma'am," said the postmistress.

Vivian tapped her toe again. These two ladies were so gossipy that she'd have to be careful, or she'd end up being the brunt of ridicule and shame like this Tessie girl, whoever she was.

"She's such a terrible flirt, I wouldn't doubt she could win over Matthew Wright," said Samantha with a sulk in her tone. "He doesn't even notice me anymore."

You'll only catch a man who has a dull sense of smell, Vivian smirked to herself.

"Tessie flirts with all the boys and not one of them cares for her a whit," said Barbara.

"Truth be told, I wish I had some of her skill when it comes to flirting," said Samantha.

"You do well enough with your natural charm and beauty without throwing yourself at men, Samantha dear."

"If only that were true." Samantha's voice was flat. "The fact is, I can't seem to attract the men I *want*."

"Because you're too particular," Barbara scolded.

"Have you seen the men here? I'm waiting for someone decent to come to town and sweep me off my feet."

"Well, don't wait too long," Barbara advised. "You don't want to end up an old maid."

I'll be an old maid if you don't hurry. The clock ticked on. One minute to twelve.

At last Samantha plunked a coin on the counter and wished Barbara a pleasant afternoon, sweeping past Vivian as though she were invisible. The clock's minute hand clicked to twelve as Vivian approached the postmistress and placed her envelope on the countertop.

"The mail goes out at noon," said Barbara with a surly stare.

Vivian kept her irritation in check. "I'm well aware, ma'am. I would have mailed this sooner if someone hadn't cut in front of me to chat with you for the past five minutes." Fearing she had said too much, she changed her tone. "Is there still time for this letter to go out today?" she asked sweetly.

"We'll see," Barbara glowered.

Barbara examined Vivian's envelope. "Philadelphia, Pennsylvania," she said in a brusque tone, a glint of suspicion in her eye.

"Yes, ma'am." Vivian glanced at the return address and her name. She'd written "Vivian Smith" on the envelope. What had happened to Vivian Garrett? She had vanished, and she missed the carefree, fun-loving girl she'd been just a few weeks ago.

"That'll be a penny," said Barbara.

A blast of air invaded the room as the bell above the door jingled.

"Top of the mornin' to ye, Babs Mitchell!" said a voice thick with a Scottish burr. He removed his broad hat to reveal a shock of thick, tousled, gray hair.

"Afternoon's more like it, and don't call me Babs, Cocoa Joe McGovern. I'm Mrs. Mitchell, the mayor's wife to you."

"Ha! Ha! Haaaaa!" laughed Mr. McGovern, slapping his thigh. "Ye really know how to tickle me funny bone!"

Barbara scowled. Vivian bade her a good day and Cocoa Joe bobbed his head as she skirted past.

"You just missed your daughter, Cocoa Joe. She was here just a few minutes ago."

"I saw her outside," said Mr. McGovern.

"Is your mangy mutt outside?" Barbara asked.

Vivian rested her hand on the doorknob.

"He ain't no mangy mutt," said Cocoa Joe.

"Is that your dog, sir?" Vivian inquired.

"Yes, ma'am. Me faithful Bobo."

"Oh, sir, I'm so sorry, but I think he's sick. He may be dying."

Cocoa Joe burst out a snort and Barbara joined him.

"Bobo ain't dyin'," said Cocoa Joe.

"Oh," said Vivian, "but I think he might be hurt—"

"You must be new in town," Barbara cut in.

"Where ye from, lassie?" asked Cocoa Joe.

"Pennsylvania?" asked Barbara.

They were asking too many questions. "It was nice to meet you both. I'm sorry about your dog, Mr. McGovern, sir."

Joe and Barbara laughed heartily, and Vivian's face burned. She left and nearly tripped over the dog as she closed the door behind her. "You poor thing. Rest in peace," she said, stepping over the dog. It was sad no one cared for him, but Cocoa Joe would realize the truth soon enough.

Vivian took a deep breath, grateful for the wind that cleared her eyes and nose of the remnants of Samantha's perfume. Wagons clattered, loaded with lumber or hay. An Indian couple crossed the street. Construction workers perched atop a high beam on a skeleton frame. One man balanced on a joist and catcalled to her. She ducked her head. Couldn't they see she was in mourning?

She cast her eyes southward. Just past the post office was the neat, newly built telegraph office with its plain walls and stark wooden benches that doubled as a stage stop. Next to it was the unpretentious Paystreak Delicatessen on the corner, a dull contrast to the tall, flashy, red brick walls of the modern Parker Campbell Store across the street.

Eager calls from the construction crew increased in volume. Not wishing to encourage the uncivilized bunch, she peered upward and glared at them, surprised to find them gesticulating wildly. "Go! Run!" they shouted.

She froze, confused.

"Afternoon, ma'am!" a voice shot into her ear.

The construction men shook their heads. "We tried to warn you!" One man shouted.

Vivian backed off a step to confront a man whose body and face were far too close to hers. She put a hand to his chest to block him. "Stop right there!" she directed.

The man halted. "You new in town, ma'am?"

"Maybe," Vivian faltered.

He held out his hand. "Name's Hiram Planter. What's yours?"

"Ladies don't shake hands, Mr. Planter." She was in need of rescue, but there was no one. The construction crew shrugged sympathetically.

"Leave the lady alone, Hiram," a worker hollered.

"I welcome you to Etna, ma'am," said Hiram, unabashed. "Now let me tell you about my brother. We live together and we hate each other."

"Mr. Planter," said Vivian, "I really—"

"Hiram, go home!" shouted another construction worker.

But Hiram was oblivious to everyone. "His name's Hubert. My brother. Isn't that lucky? He was the lucky one. He got the normal name. I wish our parents had named me Hubert. I got Hiram. You know what people say about me? There's Hiram. Don't hire 'im!" He guffawed noisily.

"I really must go, Mr. Planter," Vivian interrupted. "Good day." She twisted around, jumped down from the boardwalk, and ran into the street's busy traffic. A man on horseback tore past. It was the mail courier on his way out of town.

"I see you met Hiram Planter," a man's voice broke through the ruckus.

Her focus snapped to a kindly older gentleman who held out his hand and helped her back onto the boardwalk. "You must be a newcomer to these here parts if you got stuck talkin' to Hiram," he said consolingly. "Nearly got yourself run over in your escape, though."

"He's gone?" Vivian asked anxiously.

"Yep. You had it easy. Your exchange lasted only a few seconds. Most people can't escape Hiram for at least half an hour." He raised his eyebrows and pointed to the construction crew. "My men tried to warn ya. My name's Silas Bowman."

"Oh." Vivian glanced up at the construction workers. "I'm Vivian Ga—I mean I'm Widow Smith."

"Welcome to Etna, Widow Smith," he said, tipping his hat. "I'm sorry for your loss, ma'am."

"Thank you, sir," said Vivian.

"I've gotta run. Good day to you and welcome to Etna." Mr. Bowman scuttled down the boardwalk.

"Time to look for work," Vivian said to herself. While she spent plenty of time trekking about town in search of work, she found no one who needed a bookkeeper. Tired and a little dejected, she decided to end her day with a visit to the Wildwood Café. She placed her hand on the doorknob and stopped. A poster in the window caught her attention:

Etna's Annual Harvest Ball
Saturday, September 30th
Seven o'clock P.M.
at the Beehive Dance Hall

Vivian's heart skipped with excitement. Would it be appropriate for a widow to attend a ball just weeks after her husband's passing? She'd ask Izza later.

The Wildwood Café was busy. Vivian approached the cashier and introduced herself to Miss Darcy Meyer, proprietor of the café. Unfortunately, she wasn't hiring either.

"I heard someone was lookin' for a bookkeeper a while back," said Darcy. "Now who was that?"

Vivian waited expectantly.

"Cocoa Joe McGovern!" said Darcy, snapping her fingers. "Yes! You can talk to him. He comes in a lot." She stood on tiptoe and skimmed the room. "Not here now, though. You know where his ranch is?"

"No," Vivian shook her head, wondering if she could work for Samantha's father.

"Yonder, down China Hill, past Chinatown and the livery," she gestured. "You can't miss it."

"Thank you, Miss Meyer," said Vivian.

"Call me Darcy, Widow Smith," she said.

"Darcy, then. Is he an honorable man, this…this Cocoa Joe?" Vivian asked.

Darcy snorted. "He's a little rough around the edges, but as honorable as they come. No need to worry about that one."

Back home at Isabel's place, Vivian flipped the pages of a *Godey's Lady's Book* magazine. Ball gowns, hair accessories, shoes, corsets, wedding gowns. All caught her fancy.

The *Gibson.* Samantha was brave enough to wear the daring new hairstyle. She'd almost chosen it for herself before coming out west. Magazine in hand, she stepped across the parlor to the mirror. If it was at all proper for her to attend a ball while in mourning, she wanted to change her hair. The magazine sketches illustrated mounded and loose coiffures in the lovely Gibson fashion, and she hoped her thick, wavy hair was long enough to achieve the look. She loosened her hair from its bun and made several attempts at the style before giving up. She would ask Izza for help with it later—if there was any hope of improving her looks at all.

Footsteps stumped on the hollow wooden staircase.

"Vivian!" Isabel called.

Vivian raced across the floor, tossing the magazine onto a bookshelf and sliding in her stockinged feet into the kitchen, where she sawed through a loaf of bread and stirred the pot of cabbage and barley soup on the stove. A key clicked in the door's lock and Isabel entered to empty baskets of jars and other foodstuffs into the kitchen cupboards.

"What happened to your hair?" Isabel asked.

"Oh, this?" Vivian patted her head. "I was trying to style it. Guess it didn't work out so well."

"I guess not. You want me to help you with it after supper?"

"Yes, please," smiled Vivian. Her sister really was sweet.

"Supper smells wonderful, by the way," said Isabel. "How was your day, besides the hair fiasco?"

Vivian told her of the people she'd met, including the odd Hiram Planter and eccentric Mr. McGovern. "Strange name, *Cocoa Joe*. What do you think of him?"

"Hiram's an odd duck, but Cocoa Joe's all right," said Isabel. "He's on the school board. Barbara Mitchell and Samantha McGovern are busybodies, though." She yawned, sat on the edge of a chair, and unbuttoned her boots. "Mind what you do and say around those two or they'll go blabbing it all over town. It could even end up in Barbara Mitchell's column in the newspaper if you're not careful."

"A gossip newspaper writer?" Vivian shuddered. That reminded her: "They talked about a lady named Tessie Blackman. Who's she?"

Isabel walked in her stockinged feet across the parlor and nestled her boots onto a rack by the door. "Her father died, and she works at the saloon to make money to care for her sick mother. Some say she also works at the brothel above the saloon—" Vivian gasped. "—but don't believe it. I think some folks here just like to spread lies and make up sensational stories for the fun of it."

"Oh," Vivian relaxed.

"And something else about Tessie. She's a very pretty, flaxen-haired blonde, but she's ill-mannered and *dreadfully* loud. When you hear her voice, you'll know what I mean. Powerful enough to wake the dead!"

"I feel sorry for her," said Vivian.

"Don't go trying to befriend her. She has a bad reputation, and you have to think about your own image—especially in your situation."

"I looked for work today," said Vivian, changing the subject, "but didn't find anything. I heard Cocoa Joe might be looking for a bookkeeper, though."

"You could do worse. He really is a decent man, even if he's a little uncivilized." Isabel returned to the table. "I've been thinking, Vivi. Maybe you won't need to find work at all. If you find a husband soon enough, there's a chance he could think your baby is his."

"I could never be *that* dishonest, deceiving my own husband like that," said Vivian, setting plates of bread and bowls of soup on the table.

"You're already being dishonest by making everyone think you're a widow," said Isabel.

Vivian took a seat and poured cups of tea, carefully, quietly resettling the teapot and bowing her head as Isabel closed her eyes and said a prayer. They enjoyed their meal through a few beats of silence before Vivian spoke again. "There's a dance coming up. It might be a good place for you to find a beau, Izza."

Isabel grunted a little hum. "You're the one who needs a beau."

"Do you think it's too soon for a widow to attend a ball?" Vivian ventured.

"I'm not sure. You should know. You were always top student in Miss Doebler's etiquette classes."

"I didn't pay much attention to etiquette for widows," Vivian frowned.

Isabel pushed back her chair. "I have an etiquette book." She grabbed a book from a shelf and brought it back to the table to peruse the table of contents. "Here it is. Mourning for widows. For *young* widows."

"Yes?"

"Oh, dear," said Isabel.

"What is it?"

"It says here that widows must remain in mourning a full year."

"Does that mean no dances?"

"No dances for an entire year, Vivi," she repeated.

"But what about here? Out west, I mean? Could there be an exception to that rule?"

"You could ask Widow Butler. She might know. She's a widow who no longer wears black."

"When do I get to stop wearing black?"

Isabel rustled through the etiquette guide again. "It says you can wear gray, purple, heliotrope or lilac after six months of mourning."

"Ugh. Four more months. Being a widow is such a nuisance."

Isabel bit her lip. "Well, it's possible that western etiquette says you can attend the upcoming ball, so let's plan that way and have some fun," she said, closing the book and clapping her hands.

"All right," Vivian resigned with a smidge of hope.

"Let's start with that mop of yours," Isabel teased.

After washing dishes, they skimmed through *Godey's Lady's Book* for sketches of hairstyles.

"Look at this," said Vivian, pointing.

"Are you sure you want the Gibson?" asked Isabel. "You don't think it's too *avant-garde* for this backward little town?"

"Samantha McGovern's wearing it. And very well, I might add."

They took turns perching on a chair before the parlor mirror as they styled one another's hair.

Isabel's face pinked. "I have a confession to make." Vivian raised her eyebrows expectantly. "I have a sort of beau named Earl Boyce. He's just a friend, though."

"A *sort* of beau?"

"He's a scruffy, scrawny cowboy," said Isabel, annoyance in her tone. "He's nice enough, but I'm hoping to meet someone better looking."

"So, you're stringing him along?"

"Maybe." She shrugged. "I can't wait to get to the dance, where I can meet someone dashing."

"But you're using this Mr. Boyce to get there?"

"Don't judge or scold me, Vivi. We do what we have to do."

"Yes, we certainly do," Vivian muttered.

CHAPTER 6: Regrets, Cattle & Mourning Etiquette

$\mathcal{S}$unshine lit the room, and a melodious birdsong drifted from distant pastures as Etna awoke with a clamor of horses, rattling wagons, buggies, and stagecoaches. Vivian peered out the window to watch handsome young men working in the skeletal rafters of a new building across the street. She had awakened with regrets and homesickness, but as construction hammers pounded, a sense of anticipation rose within her.

Emerging from Isabel's apartment, Vivian encountered Etna's blur of swishing skirts, clattering wagons, and riders on horseback. She was on her way to meet Isabel's boss at the mercantile to see if he needed a bookkeeper. At first, she felt conspicuous, shrouded in her black mourning garb as she pushed her way along the boardwalk, dodging grimy cowboys, rugged lumberjacks, lean and weathered farmers and ranchers. Yet, as she peered about, she became aware of the diversity of the people around her—Indian women in calico dresses, Chinese men with their long mustaches and floppy-sleeved shirts. Alsatians hollered in French, while Scottish and Irish immigrants conversed in their thick accents. There was no need to feel self-conscious, after all.

She was just about to pick up her pace when the ground began quaking and she stopped abruptly. "What's happening?" she asked herself, gripping a porch column in front of the telegraph office. Her legs shuddered and a thundering noise sounded in the distance. Was this an earthquake? She'd heard of earthquakes in California.

People seemed oblivious as they continued to stream past her. Shading her eyes, she peered southward to see a low boil of dust rolling down from the hills and heading straight toward town. Others glanced back, unperturbed as the rumbling grew louder and the glass panes in the streetlamps began to rattle. Vivian fought the urge to panic. Why was no one afraid? Shouts, whistles, whoops, and an eerie bellowing rose from the looming cloud.

"Confound it all!" a logger swore from the seat of his timber-loaded wagon as he tied a bandana around his nose and mouth and urged his team to a gallop.

People scattered from the street and boardwalk, looking more annoyed than frightened. One woman dragged a child by the arm, hopped onto the boardwalk, and ducked into the lobby of the Schmitt Hotel. A pane of glass dislodged from a streetlamp and crashed to the ground and Vivian used both arms to hug the porch column. She thought of running, but a mixture of fear and curiosity glued her boots to where she stood. The clamor grew deafening, and dust soon darkened the street as haunted, white eyes appeared in the thick haze. Cattle! A cattle drive straight through the center of town. That's all this was. Hollers and whoops soared above her, and she squinted at the phantom forms of the construction crew across the street, waving their hats and smiling as though this was a parade. Vivian pulled a handkerchief from her skirt pocket and used it to cover her mouth and nose as the bawling beasts swarmed and trampled just a few inches in front of her beyond the edge of the boarded walk. Though dust stung her eyes, she didn't dare lose her grip on the column now.

A lumbering cow jostled her toe, and she slipped, hanging from the porch column, her feet swinging over the street. She yelped and tucked up her knees, squeezing them tightly around the wooden column as cows pressed beneath her. Strong arms wrapped around her. She opened an eye to see a man's face peering up from her shoulder and shouting, "Let go and put your arms around me!" as he gently yanked at her body in an attempt to pry her loose from the column.

A cow mooed inches from her. "No!" she screamed.

"Let go and I'll hold you," he said again.

"I'll wait till they pass," she protested.

"You could be injured, ma'am. Please let me carry you to safety."

Vivian peered up the street at no end in sight to the swarming mass of cattle. She reached out a tentative hand to the man while maintaining a tight hold of the column with her other arm. Taking her free hand, he placed it on his shoulder and tugged her until she pulled loose and clung to him with both hands. He carried her against his broad chest, and when she finally touched her feet to the wooden planks of the boardwalk, she managed to press herself to within an arm's length of the man and stood panting, trembling.

"Thank you," she said shakily. "You can release me now." She tilted her head upward and sucked in a quick breath when his tanned face and brilliant blue eyes swam into view.

"Steady now," he said, still not letting go.

She placed her hands on his, stunned by the electricity that suddenly pulsed through her arms. "I'm fine," she said, annoyed that he was having such an effect on her. When he finally withdrew his hands from her waist, the warmth of his hands remained in her. "Thank you again," she said, wishing her legs didn't feel like jelly. When she staggered a little, he cupped her elbow to keep her from falling.

"Let me walk with you," he said. But the whistling and shouting of cowboys riding the tail-end of the cattle drive cut off their conversation as they chased one last, white-eyed stray cow with a dog nipping at its hooves. As the bovine mass moved out of town and the dust of Etna began to settle, people poured out of buildings.

She hated to admit she needed help, but her body felt a bit wobbly, and she was still disoriented. "I suppose," she said. He offered his arm, and she hesitated, glancing about quickly. No one seemed to be watching. She took his arm and, though she didn't lean or put any weight on him, his strength steadied her. She felt the power in his arm and the tautness of his muscles, and another kind of weakness trickled through her.

They made their way along the boardwalk and across Diggles Street, pausing at the entrance to the Parker Campbell Store, where a mother parked her baby carriage and picked up a wriggling baby. A lump crammed her throat. If she were truly pregnant, that could be her in fewer than eight months. She slipped her hand away from her escort's arm and tipped her gaze to his face, swallowing a gasp as his tender, yet yearning blue eyes pierced hers.

"Have a nice day, ma'am, and stay safe," he said, touching the rim of his hat before he rotated and stepped from the boardwalk into the street.

"Thank you again," she called out. But he didn't hear her. The vague notion that he looked familiar niggled at her mind as she entered the mercantile. If only she knew his name. If only he'd look back at her again.

Vivian entered the store and spoke with Isabel's employer, Mr. Campbell. Unfortunately, he wasn't hiring. Resuming her search for work, she made several more unsuccessful inquiries at several businesses before plodding through Etna's streets of powdery dust to stop in front of a prim, tidy boarding house with slate blue paint and white trim. A sign on the gate read, "Butler Boarding House." The place belonged to Widow Butler, the woman Isabel wanted her to meet to ask about mourning etiquette.

Maymie Butler was warm and welcoming, yet very busy. While she worked on her sewing, Vivian explained the reason for her visit.

"I admire your spunk and spirit, Widow Smith. Believe me, I do, but I'm in no need of a bookkeeper right now. What I really need is a husband." She chortled to herself. "But my man needs a kick in the pants to get him to court me."

Vivian ventured onward. "My second question is about mourning etiquette in the West."

"What do you want to know, dear?" Widow Butler asked with a pin pinched between her lips.

"Proper etiquette teaches that a widow must wait an entire year to mourn her late husband before attending any dances or going courting again. Is it the same out here in the West?"

Widow Butler laughed out loud. "Certainly not! Things are much looser out here. No one would judge you a smidge if you changed out of that ghastly black thing and into something more colorful, if that's what you're asking. Unlike back East, a young widow in these parts couldn't make it on her own for long without a man to care for her. Unlike myself, most widows remarry within six months of losing their husbands." A frown tugged at her mouth. "If a certain someone hadn't dragged his feet, I'd have been remarried by now." She winked at Vivian. "If you're thinking of attending the Harvest Ball, you go right ahead but if you're a recent widow, don't dance. Just sit and watch. You're young and pretty enough that men will show some interest."

"You're sure no one would fault me?" she asked.

"Not a bit," Widow Butler assured her. "In fact, I have a couple of heliotrope mourning gowns—one for daytime and one right pretty lace gown made just for someone in your situation. I'd be happy to lend them both to you."

Vivian flushed. "That's very kind of you."

"Not at all. Take my advice, Widow Smith. You go ahead and mourn your late husband, but don't you dare let guilt stop you from saying yes to a handsome bachelor who comes courtin'. I'm sure your late husband will forgive you." She set her sewing aside and excused herself from the room. "I'll be right back with those gowns for you," she said, retrieving them from a wardrobe. "Here, try these on."

Vivian tried on the dresses and modeled them for the seamstress.

"They fit you well," said Widow Butler. "I could make a few minor alterations, but I don't think they're worth my time. You won't be needing them long." She wrapped the gowns in paper and placed them in a large box with a matching bonnet adorned with a dusty pink veil.

"Thank you, Widow Butler. You've been a great help to me."

"Oh, please, call me Maymie," she replied.

Overwhelmed by the woman's generosity, Vivian thanked her again. "Shall I pay you to rent the gowns?"

"I'd like to see you try," she said. "Keep them until you find yourself a husband. Oh, and about your bookkeeping work, why don't you try talking to Mr. McGovern down at his office at Big Valley Ranch? I hear he's looking for someone." She chuckled. "If he hires a woman, I'll be surprised, but you never know with Cocoa Joe."

It was getting late by the time Vivian left Widow Butler's place, and she had to hurry home to prepare supper, but she was both apprehensive and hopeful about paying a visit to Mr. McGovern the following day. She was also excited about the blessing of being able to attend the Harvest Ball and the chance to extricate herself from her black mourning dress. Puce and heliotrope might be less than fashionable, but they were a sight better than black any day.

Blue Ryan spent the rest of the day in search of work. His first stops were at a couple of Protestant churches in town. The pastors were welcoming enough, but they were well-established and in no hurry to move on or retire anytime soon. As Blue meandered through Etna, he was pleasantly surprised to discover that almost every business was in need of a hired hand. In talking to folks about town, he learned that he could earn a good wage as a cowhand for a Scottish immigrant called Cocoa Joe McGovern. The work was hard, but the rancher offered free room and board and treated everyone with respect. It certainly was worth looking into. Finding work wouldn't be any trouble in this town, but he knew he'd better take some time to seek God for wisdom.

He also needed to talk to God about the prepossessing young widow he'd held in his arms that morning. He couldn't stop thinking of her. Thin and light, he could still feel the bones of her ribcage in his hands and the softness of her bosom against his chest. The scent of her skin reminded him of his mother's flower garden back home, and her hair was the color of golden honey fresh from the comb. He'd gazed into her frightened green eyes, and her trembling pink lips had been only inches from his own. He would have been tempted to kiss her if there hadn't been people watching.

Vivian didn't tell Isabel about the cattle incident in town that day and hoped she'd never hear about it. As she lay on the sofa in her sister's apartment, watching the light from the streetlamps flicker through the lace curtains onto the ceiling, she shivered at the memory of her body pressed to her rescuer's chest. If she wasn't careful, she'd do something impulsive, like fall in love with a total stranger—again.

CHAPTER 7: Sunday

*V*ivian stood in a jumbled line that made its way stutteringly into the Congregational Church. She adjusted her hat, content with its mauve veil that covered her face. Though sheer, it made her feel safe and protected from the overwhelming newness of this town and all the people in it—especially when she heard a little girl ask, "Mama, is that the lady who was hanging from the post when all those cows were running past?"

Once inside the nave, Isabel disappeared in the crowd and a low cough rumbled above Vivian's head. Looking up, she beheld a rather dashing young man.

"Pardon me, ma'am," he said, fidgeting with the hat in his hands. "I'm Cade Ranson."

"It's a pleasure to meet you, Mr. Ranson. I'm Vivian Gar—I mean, Smith. Widow Smith." There was an awkward silence. "I suppose you're working on the building on Main Street?" she asked.

"Yes, ma'am," Cade nodded.

Another pause. Vivian was formulating a new question when Cade ventured to speak again. "Are you…are you widowed, ma'am?"

"Yes, I am," Vivian replied.

"I'm sorry for your loss, ma'am," said Cade.

Vivian thanked him and the two fell into silence again. At least this man wasn't mentioning her embarrassing cattle drive incident. He was a little inept but made a respectful attempt to be polite. He was also handsome with his sandy brown hair and light scruff of a beard on his chin. "How long have you worked in construction?" she asked.

It took some effort, but she managed to drag some answers out of Cade as she longed for the service to begin and spent more time looking around the nave at other congregants, hoping for a glimpse of the handsome man who had rescued her the previous morning. She spotted Samantha from the post office. She was hard to miss with a gaudy contraption on her head the size of Texas. And her dress sleeves were so large they looked like two ticks about to pop and nearly knocked over her pew companions.

Piano keys plinked and the crowd hushed. Rescue from Cade Ranson hadn't come too soon. Vivian bade him a good day and weaved her way through the crowd to Isabel, where they stood to sing the familiar hymn, *I Know Whom I Have Believed*. Despite the liveliness of the upbeat tune, her thoughts wound back to Draven and tears stung her eyes. The pain she felt fit her pretense of a widow's grief.

Following the opening hymn, Widow Fitzgerald moaned out a dreary solo and Elder Kopp's prayer was just shy of anesthetizing. When the reverend took his place at the pulpit, Vivian hoped his words would hold her attention. She was mistaken. Samantha McGovern sat in the pew directly in front of her, the sickening heaviness of her perfume swimming through the rapidly warming room. She gave up trying to crane her neck around the girl's sleeves to see the reverend while he preached. Though she had spied out the congregation for her mystery man, she didn't see him. With her luck, he might not attend church or have any faith at all.

It wasn't long before her eyes were drooping, and she was sure she permitted them to close for only half a second before Isabel's elbow dug into her ribcage. She straightened, yawned, and covered her mouth with a hand that got tangled in her bonnet's veil. Opening her eyes wide, she massaged her temples. She crossed her legs and swung one foot back and forth.

"Stop wiggling!" Isabel hissed in her ear. "You're like a squirming little child."

Vivian restrained herself from sticking out her tongue. At that moment a gift from Heaven swung daintily from an invisible thread above Samantha's puffed sleeves. Leaning forward, Vivian let out a long, gentle sigh. The tiny creature floated, swung. Isabel's elbow jabbed into her ribcage.

"What?" Vivian mouthed, gesturing toward the spider, but Isabel refused to look and missed the insect's climb up its thread and into Samantha's hat. The brief reprieve from boredom was over.

The watch pinned to her waist read half past eleven. Another wretched thirty minutes to go. Outside, the sky grew as dull and overcast as Reverend Patterson's sermon.

"The Lord preserveth the strangers; he relieveth the fatherless and widow," the revered droned, "but the way of the wicked he turneth upside down."

Vivian leaned forward and slumped her head on a hand. She'd probably be ribbed by her sister again, yet apathy was taking over. Others in the nave had their eyes closed. Why shouldn't she nap as well? Maybe this was why Sunday was considered a day of rest.

She peeped through her veil to find two men across the aisle grinning ridiculously at her. One wore a rough scraggle of mustache and he was missing a tooth; the other winked at her. In church! The gall! She sat up straight, slammed against the back of the pew, and shuddered. Isabel was right. Men here were completely uncivilized.

"Shall we pray?"

Vivian thought she'd never heard such wonderful words, since they signaled an end to the grueling sermon.

"Glorious air," she murmured once outside on the lawn of the churchyard. Other congregants gathered in the refreshing dampness from a recent shower.

A bespectacled, owlish gentleman bowed imperiously to Vivian. "Mr. Oswald Davis, at your service," he bleated, wiping steam from his glasses. He wasn't at all handsome, although his clothing was finer than most and his comportment indicated he had some measure of upbringing.

"Nice to meet you, Mr. Davis," Vivian acknowledged politely. "I'm Widow Smith."

"May I walk you home, Widow Smith?"

She consented reluctantly and shrugged to her sister. As rain began to fall again, Oswald stretched his umbrella into the air and held it over her head. However, since he was about an inch shorter than she, he barely kept the umbrella above her hat.

"I'm the town undertaker," Mr. Davis snuffled, pushing up his glasses and taking a step to nudge her toward town. Vivian wrinkled her nose at the idea of marrying a funeral man. She looked behind her for Isabel and saw her following close behind beneath a stranger's umbrella.

Vivian hurried her pace, keeping Oswald Davis jogging to keep up, while he rambled about his family in Ohio, his apprenticeship in Cleveland, his business success in Etna, and his newly built home for his future wife and family. Vivian's eyes rolled. She'd just survived the most boring sermon in history and was now subjected to hearing this man's pomp and swagger.

Splashing through puddles, she hopped from beneath his umbrella into the rain, dashing across Diggles Lane to the covered boardwalk. At the same time, Isabel dashed past her and down the walk to their apartment faster than a runaway jackrabbit. What horribly offensive thing had Isabel's escort done or said?

Unfortunately, Oswald caught up to Vivian then and civility obligated her to walk with him to the doorway of their building, where they stopped, and Vivian formulated an excuse to duck inside.

Oswald stood beneath his umbrella and readjusted his spectacles. "May I call on you tomorrow, Widow Smith?" he implored.

"I'm so sorry, Mr. Davis, but I'm new in town and everything is still so overwhelming to me. I need more time to settle in and adjust to my surroundings." She hoped she was refusing him courteously, yet firmly enough.

"Of course, of course." He twitched like a fidgety squirrel. "Tuesday, then?"

She would have to play her widow's card. "Oh, Mr. Davis, I'm just not ready to go courting again so soon after the passing my dear late husband. I'm sure you understand." She pretended to dab at tears with her handkerchief.

"I see, I see." He jerked his head up and down in what might have been a nod; she wasn't sure. He pushed his spectacles. "Aha!" he exclaimed, startling her. He held a finger in the air. "The Harvest Ball. May I escort you there, ma'am? Perhaps by then you will feel somewhat…somewhat less bereaved?"

"Oh, no, Mr. Davis," she sniffed. "If I can possibly muster the courage to attend the ball, I'll probably go alone. It's all just too soon after my poor husband's untimely death, you see."

"Well, if there's anything you need, Widow Smith, anything at all, my business is right around the corner and, in fact, directly behind this building. You could probably peer out a window and see right down into Pig Alley and the back of my shop." He laughed nervously. "It's the one with the coffins. Nice coffins. Well-made. I work right beside the Chinese laundry service. They do their washing in the alley out back." He sniggered uneasily, jerking his head again in his strange manner.

"Oh, no," said Vivian, pretending to stifle a sob. "How could you speak of coffins to a woman so recently widowed?"

"Oh, I'm begging your pardon, ma'am. Perhaps I'll call on you after the ball is over?"

He was not taking the hint. "Mr. Davis," Vivian spoke bluntly, "your insensitivity toward me as a widow is utterly appalling, especially for a man in your profession. I cannot abide your company a moment longer. I apologize for having to be so forthright with you. Good day, sir." She ran inside and shut the door behind her; then leaped up the stairs. Once inside the rented room, she peered out the dining room window and watched Mr. Davis as he slunk away like a dog with its tail between its legs.

Isabel had changed out of her Sunday dress and stood in the kitchen, stirring a pot on the stove. "I'm so sorry for leaving you alone, Vivi," she said. "I just couldn't bear that Sprat for one second longer."

"Whatever happened to Earl?"

"He had to go home early, but he wants to meet me for supper tomorrow night," said Isabel.

"Are you still leading him down the garden path, Izza?"

"I'm afraid so," she admitted. "Don't make me feel guilty."

"So, you were stuck with this Sprat fellow?"

Isabel nodded.

"Funny name. What did he do to make you run?"

"He put his hand on my waist," said Isabel.

"Is that so bad?"

"It is if it's Sprat."

"You could consider Oswald Davis," Vivian suggested. "He has money."

"He makes money from dead people, Vivi. Now change your clothes and come help me peel apples."

Vivian obeyed and returned to the kitchen, where the two worked together as they talked and enjoyed a light lunch.

"Vivi," Isabel said after some time had passed. "I wonder if you might have any news for me about a recent cattle drive through town."

"What have you heard?" Vivian demanded sharply.

"Something about a widow woman dangling from a porch column as a herd of cattle nearly trampled her to death. Does that sound familiar?"

"Oh, my goodness, Izza," Vivian whimpered, her face fiery. "I can't believe people are talking about me. How utterly humiliating."

"Embarrassing, not humiliating," said Isabel, shaking her head and suppressing a smirk.

Vivian told herself that, as embarrassing as the incident had been, there really was no need to be humiliated.

"Of course," Isabel said slowly, "I've also heard talk of a certain black-clad widow woman clinging for dear life to a dashing young man who rescued her from this herd of stampeding cattle and threw her over his shoulder like a sack of potatoes."

"What?" Vivian squealed. "It wasn't like that at all!"

"Wasn't it?"

"No, I swear it wasn't."

"Well, don't go swearing—especially on a Sunday, Vivi." Isabel's mouth twisted. "What a sight that must have been. I'm just sorry I missed it."

"And I'm sorry you're more concerned with missing the show than the fact that I could have died."

"Except that you didn't die, because you were rescued by a handsome stranger."

"He didn't have to rescue me. I could have held on until the cattle passed."

"I'm sure," said Isabel.

They were quiet for a spell while they washed dishes and cleaned the kitchen.

In an effort to find a new topic, Vivian asked, "What does your ideal man look like, Izza?"

Spreading spice-scented peach filling into pie crusts, Isabel answered wistfully, "Brown hair like mine, I guess. But his looks don't matter as much as manners and attentiveness. How about you?"

Vivian's forehead crinkled. If her baby were to look like its parents, she'd probably need a man who looked like Draven. She shivered. "I guess I'd like a tall man with black hair," she said. "He doesn't have to be handsome, but I want him to be kind and good. That matters more than anything."

"Did you happen to see your handsome hero at church this morning?" Isabel asked.

"No, I did not," said Vivian defiantly.

"Was there anyone at church who struck your fancy?"

"There was Cade Ranson."

"Oh, he's a talker, isn't he?" Isabel giggled.

"Do you know him?" asked Vivian.

"How could anyone really know him? He can hardly put two words together and he usually attends the Methodist Church."

"He's probably an outlaw," said Vivian.

Isabel snorted. "And has robbed several banks and has a stash of gold buried up on Forest Mountain Pass."

"He's handsome, though," said Vivian.

"He is that, if you like the idea of being married to a corpse."

"How insensitive of you to talk about corpses when you know I'm a widow in mourning." The sisters giggled. "Speaking of which, Izza, Widow Butler says it's all right for a widow to attend a dance and go courting!"

"Oh, I'm so glad, Vivi! We can attend the ball together, then." Isabel slid a couple of pies into the cookstove. "Do you think you're getting used to Etna?"

"I've survived an earth-shaking cattle drive, a dead dog, Hiram Planter, Oswald Davis, the world's most boring sermon, and endless gossip and humiliation, so, yes, I suppose I'm getting used to it."

The soft fragrance of rain swept through the open window, cooling the hot, peach-scented apartment. After canning and baking, Isabel was napping in her room, while Vivian restlessly paced the parlor floor. She scratched out a note to Isabel, donned a jaunty, green-veiled toque, picked up an umbrella, and went downstairs.

Aside from the tinny plinking from a saloon, the Sunday afternoon street was empty and quiet. She walked down the boarded walk, slowing her pace at the shuttered saloon door to risk a sidelong glance into its interior, where saloon girls were dolled up in low-cut dresses and wore rouge on their lips and cheeks. She removed herself quickly when a man caught her eye and winked. She shouldn't be on the street alone, especially as a widow, but she wasn't wearing mourning attire and, in her ivory linen skirt and white blouse, she was happy to break from widowhood and avoid being recognized as Widow Smith. Keeping her head hidden beneath her umbrella, she was glad to be an anonymous, nondescript woman enjoying a Sunday stroll.

When the light rain shower burst into a downpour, Vivian sought shelter in the Schmitt Hotel, hoping she might once again run into her handsome cattle drive stranger. There, lounging on a sofa, was a handsome gentleman with brunette hair, brown eyes, and the barest hint of shadow on his clean-shaven face. He sat by himself in the lobby's sitting room, reading a newspaper and smoking a cigar. She was a little sorry it wasn't her hero, but this man wasn't bad-looking.

He rose. "Good afternoon, ma'am," he greeted.

She explained her ducking in to avoid the rain.

"You're welcome to take a seat," he offered, folding his paper and setting it aside. "You could keep me company."

"Well, I suppose there's no harm," she said, removing her cloak. The gentleman hastened to assist her. "I'm Martin Graver," he said.

"I'm Miss—I mean, I'm Widow Smith. It's a pleasure to meet you, sir."

Martin expressed sympathy for the loss of her husband and asked a few polite questions about her dearly departed Oscar before sharing an inordinately large amount of information about himself. He was from Boston and shared about his family, his work for his father, and his search for work out west. He made Vivian laugh and before she realized what time it was, she and Martin had talked for two hours, although he had carried most of the conversation. He surprised her by inviting her to dine with him later that week.

"As a widow, I'm not sure if it would be proper for me to be seen in public with you," she hesitated. She also wouldn't want her blue-eyed stranger to see her courting another man. It might make her look unavailable.

"I don't see the harm in it," he said. "Even widows go courting after a spell."

"I would need to find a chaperone," Vivian suggested, not knowing how to politely say no to him after their pleasant exchange.

"Fair enough," said Martin. "Well, when you procure your chaperone, leave a note for me with the hotel's desk clerk, letting me know what evening would work best for you. I suggest dining at the Wildwood Café."

The sky was darkening, and the rain had subsided by the time she bade him goodbye. Martin Graver seemed nice enough. He even looked a little like Draven Randall, which was somewhat disturbing. If he were a decent human being and Mr. Blue Eyes wasn't interested in her, this gentleman might make a good husband and decent father, should she have to consider remarrying.

CHAPTER 8: Procuring a Chaperone

The previous day's brief rain shower passed, and Monday arrived with a cool hush of mist and a fresh, earthy aroma of mushrooms and moss. Walking down the bank to Etna Creek, Vivian was happy to be hidden in the fog and out of her mourning clothes. When she reached the lowland fields, she fancied a stroll through the grass, but after her recent experience with cattle, she was apprehensive. Instead, she climbed onto a fence and sat watching the docile creatures who paid her no attention at all. Tomorrow she might try walking through the pasture, but today she was content to watch and think.

In the short time she'd been in Etna, Vivian had observed women, foreigners, and native Indians enjoying more freedom than expected. Some women, like Darcy Meyer, Widow Butler, and Barbara Mitchell, worked, owned property, and ran businesses. Indians appeared to be welcome in town. And there were a lot of industrious foreigners. All these things encouraged her plans to work as a bookkeeper. She might even rent an office someday and have her own clients.

But Vivian's true passion was to make a difference in the lives of other women. In such a progressive town, she could spread word of the suffrage movement and probably get more women involved politically. Having worked to organize rallies in Philadelphia, she knew she could do the same in this small town.

Energized with hope for the future of America, Vivian hurried home, changed into Widow Butler's heliotrope mourning clothes, gathered an armful of her precious suffrage pamphlets, and was soon standing in front of the Wildwood Restaurant on the corner of Main and School Streets. She wasn't shouting or being obnoxious. She was peacefully, quietly handing out the papers to women who passed by. Most were polite and grateful. Only a handful shook their heads and returned the papers to her. "My husband would never approve of such a thing," they said. She'd heard that plenty of times before. A few women stopped to talk with her, two to argue against suffrage, one to ask more questions. By mid-morning, only three leaflets remained in her hand, and she ceased with her campaign, satisfied with the marvelous start to her day.

Next on her agenda was to find a chaperone and, since widows often took on the role, she paid another visit to Widow Butler. Upon entering the boarding house, she found Maymie busy sewing and another pang of guilt shook her. How could she pretend to be in mourning when real widows were suffering?

"What's that you have in your hand there, Widow Smith?" Maymie asked.

"Women's suffrage leaflets," said Vivian, giving one to her. "I was handing them out today and saved one just for you."

"Oh, my," said Widow Butler, asking Vivian to set it on a nearby table. "I'll get to reading that later when I've finished my work for the day, but I have to warn you that folks have been talking about you already. First, I heard you nearly lost your life in a cattle stampede; today I heard about you getting onto your soapbox and screaming about votes for women."

"I didn't scream or stand on a soapbox," Vivian protested. "All I did was hand out leaflets."

"There's no need to be defensive. If you ever decide to organize a meeting or rally, you can count me in, and I'm all for helping women. As widows, you and I understand the need for suffrage more than most, but folks here are stuck in their ways and could even get violent, so you'd best be careful and not go around stirring anymore hornets' nests. Start small and quiet and establish a good reputation before you go standing on anymore street corners. You're lucky you didn't have rotten eggs or tomatoes thrown at you. It may not seem like you've done much, but you've gone and stirred the pot and, like it or not, you're already the talk of the town."

"All I did was hand out pamphlets," Vivian muttered again. She changed topics. "How are you doing since your husband passed? Has it been terribly difficult for you?"

"It's been five years since, and I've had my up days and down. I daresay I'm fortunate, though, in that my husband left me money and property when he died. Even so, my experience has opened my eyes to the needy and you can bet I'm happy to support my church's widows and orphans' fund." Vivian nodded, feeling guiltier and understanding a widow's predicament more clearly than ever. "I'm sorry for your loss, Widow Smith, I truly am. Until we have those votes that we need, you'd best find yourself another husband, which reminds me, are you planning to attend the ball?"

"Not yet," she replied, "but a gentleman asked me to dinner, and I need a chaperone. Would you be willing to play the part or recommend someone who can?"

"I'm awfully busy," Widow Butler apologized. "Widow Fitzgerald might be interested, though. She lives on Center Street. You won't find her there now, though. I heard she was planning to have lunch at Etna's Main Street Bakery with Barbara Mitchell, Mrs. Miller and the McGovern ladies today. You could try meeting her there." She paused and smiled. "Now that's an interesting group. I wouldn't be surprised if they're already oiling the cogs of the rumor mill where you're concerned. Don't go giving them any of your pamphlets. At least, not yet. Wait until another scandal pops up to divert attention away from you."

Vivian thanked Maymie again for allowing her to borrow the mourning gowns and walked back into town. The day had warmed considerably, and she shed her shawl, draping it over her arms as she walked. Was it only her imagination or were people staring at her? A few seemed to shake their heads at her, but she hoped she was mistaken.

Inside the French-Alsatian bakery, the aroma of freshly baked bread made her hungry. She ordered a croissant sandwich and extra croissants and cheese to take home to Isabel for supper. Locating a small table at the back of the dining room, she sat facing the entrance, keeping her head down and hidden behind her hat and veil and wondering how she'd speak to Widow Fitzgerald without interrupting her luncheon party.

As patrons came and went, the bell above the door jangled merrily. Vivian finished her sandwich and was sipping the last of her beverage when Widow Fitzgerald bustled in with Barbara Mitchell and another woman wearing a lace cap. Clucking like hens and cooing like pigeons, they chose a table by a window.

Barbara's brassy tone rose above the others, "Yes, I think the article turned out rather well."

"You made me sound like a world traveler and explorer," laughed Widow Fitz.

"Well, you are, Mabel," said the lace-bonneted woman.

"You're certainly more adventurous than most people in little, old Etna," said Barbara.

"I liked your article on a woman's behavior, Babs," said the lace woman.

"Thank you, Melinda," Barbara said with mock humility. "If only certain young ladies would read my advice and take it to heart. And if only you'd stop calling me Babs."

"Something about brazenly choosing to be stupid, was it?" asked Widow Fitzgerald.

"She who knows the correct way to behave but brazenly chooses against intelligent refinement is the most miserable of creatures," Barbara quoted.

"Yes, brilliantly worded," said Melinda.

Vivian lost track of the conversation as the shop's door bell clamored with the coming and going of more customers. Voices rose and fell. Teacups, cutlery and china clinked.

"Supposedly, she understands bookkeeping," said Barbara.

Vivian nearly choked on a swallow of milk.

"I admire a woman who can make her way in a man's world and, Fitz, as a widow, you certainly must agree with the importance of a woman having a profession."

"I do," said Widow Fitz. "I'm grateful my late husband left me with a house and some money. "

"And you're not too proud to take any odd job that comes along," Barbara added.

Widow Fitzgerald nodded. "That I do. I've done some extra mending for Widow Butler lately, and I bake a dozen pies a week for Darcy Meyer at the Wildwood. I've even done some housekeeping for you on occasion, Babs."

"That's right," Barbara nodded. "And you made enough money to travel to New York."

"That I did," said Widow Fitzgerald.

"I suppose a woman's ability to work is important," stated Mrs. Miller, "but to go shouting on street corners is another thing entirely," she clucked.

I wasn't shouting, thought Vivian.

"Yes, I heard about that. Maybe it's the only way to get some folks to pay attention," said Barbara. "I, for one, would like to get my hands on one of those suffrage pamphlets.

And, if she ever decides to organize a meeting, I'll gladly attend, if only to gather news for my paper."

The door's bell jingled, and a thick, sickening sweetness blew in. Samantha and another woman greeted their friends before approaching the counter to order their lunch.

"Good afternoon, ladies," a woman greeted. Perhaps Samantha's mother? "What's all the news today?"

"We were discussing that clumsy suffragette widow lady who fell in the street and nearly got trampled by the stampede the other day," said Barbara Mitchell.

"And threw herself at some gentleman who rescued her," said Melinda Miller.

I never! Vivian almost said aloud.

"I heard what a spectacle she made of herself in public with that young man," said Samantha.

"And I hear she was standing on a soapbox in front of the Wildwood this morning, telling folks about votes for women," Widow Fitzgerald added.

There was no soapbox, Vivian spoke in her head.

"Oh, Father's looking for a bookkeeper, isn't he, Mother?" said Samantha.

"Well, yes, but a suffragette?" asked Mrs. McGovern. "You know how your father will react to that."

"I think he'd do better to hire a man," said Melinda Miller.

"Unless a woman's better for the job," Barbara huffed.

"Thank you for that," Vivian mumbled.

"I hear she's very young," said Mrs. Miller. "What references could she possibly have?"

"Quite right," agreed Mrs. McGovern. "A woman's place is in the home."

For pity's sake, why do women have to limit their own advancement? Vivian thought.

"Speak for yourself, Sammy Lass," Barbara gruffed. "I'm a suffragette myself. My place is certainly *not* in the home—at least not entirely."

"You're the exception, Barbara," said Melinda.

"But I don't have to be," said Barbara.

There was a commotion in the shop as more patrons crammed in, forcing Vivian to discontinue eavesdropping. When she was able to hear the group again, the topic was the upcoming ball and Samantha was whining about her failure to steal Matthew Wright's heart.

"Forget Matthew, dear," her mother begged. "There are plenty of other eligible young men available."

"Not when another pretty, young widow waltzes into town," said Samantha.

"I've seen her, and she is pretty," Widow Fitz agreed.

That's kind of you to say so, thought Vivian.

"But did you see how men were ogling her in church yesterday?" Samantha sulked.

Vivian held her breath as the others nodded.

"But if she's a proper lady, she won't be courting just yet and she certainly won't be at a ball," said Mrs. Miller.

But Widow Butler said I could go! Vivian protested internally.

"This is the West, dear," said Mrs. Sally McGovern. "Rules are different here."

Vivian relaxed a little.

"True," said Widow Fitzgerald. "I know what it's like to be a widow, trying to make it on her own. I haven't remarried, of course, but this widow gal can't possibly remain single for long, even if she doesn't go courting."

"Well, she'd better stay away from Matthew Wright."

Vivian waited for the luncheon party to leave before venturing out of the café to follow Widow Fitzgerald. Rounding the corner onto Center Street, Vivian jogged to catch up to her and introduced herself.

"Well, if it isn't the infamous widowed suffragette," Widow Fitzgerald smirked.

"Yes, it's me," said Vivian, blushing, "and, since everyone seems to have either heard or seen what a maladroit clod I am, I'll have you see now that I am rather lighter on my feet when I'm not around herds of cattle."

"That's the way, my dear," the elder widow tittered. "Laugh at yourself and others can't help but laugh along with you."

Vivian slowed her pace and fumbled in her drawstring purse for a suffrage leaflet. "And, as for women's suffrage, I have this for you, Widow Fitzgerald."

"Thank you kindly, my dear. I will surely read it and share it with my friends. In fact, would you happen to have any extra? I know someone who'd like a copy."

"I do," smiled Vivian.

Widow Fitzgerald thanked her as she accepted the papers. "Lord knows how challenging it can be as a widow in this world. Until my husband died, I had no idea just how important a woman's vote could be for our entire sex. And, my dear Widow Smith, let me offer my sincere condolences upon the loss of your husband."

"Thank you. And my condolences to you too, Widow Fitzgerald."

"Now let me get one thing perfectly straight before we speak any further. You simply must call me Widow Fitz like everyone else."

"Yes, ma'am," said Vivian.

Widow Fitz pushed open her garden gate and marched up the walk ahead of her guest. "Sit here on the porch while I fetch glasses of lemonade for us," she directed, pointing to a table and two chairs. When she returned, she cocked her head to listen as Vivian broached the topic of mourning etiquette with regard to dances and Widow Butler's advice on courting.

"Proper etiquette dictates that you wait a full year before going courting again," Widow Fitz explained, "but it's not inappropriate for a young widow, such as yourself, to come out of mourning to pass the time with a gentleman caller if you're in need of a husband."

"I see," said Vivian. "And would it be appropriate for me to attend the upcoming ball, do you think?"

"You may certainly attend, but you mustn't dance."

Vivian's shoulders slumped slightly. She consoled herself, however, with the fact that she was lucky to attend at all. She mentioned her need for a chaperone, explaining how she felt a certain camaraderie with other widows in town, and the sympathetic Widow Fitzgerald promptly obliged. They agreed to meet on Friday evening at the Wildwood Café.

As she walked home, Vivian smiled with relief. It had been an emotional day with people describing her as a screaming suffragette and a clumsy buffoon. However, she felt as though she'd made friends with both Widow Butler and Widow Fitzgerald and not all the gossip about her was negative. Some people admired her suffragette ways—as long as she wasn't shouting about them. Which she certainly never would.

After his first day of work, branding calves at Cocoa Joe McGovern's Big Valley Ranch, Blue Ryan trudged back through Etna on his way home to the Schmitt Hotel. It hadn't taken him long to find work, and with cowhands in high demand, he was happy his new position would pay well. Eventually, housing would become available at the ranch and, with free room and board, he'd be able to save money too. In the meantime, he was in dire need of a hot bath.

"Evenin', Mr. Ryan," said the bellboy as Blue wiped his boots and entered the lobby. "I've got a tub already full of hot water for ya."

"Sounds perfect," said Blue, his grin shining in his grimy face. "Thank you kindly."

As Blue settled into the steamy water, he hummed a tune and thought of nothing. Just what he needed after a day of intense manual labor until visions of his damsel in distress broke into his mind. Young, golden-haired, rosy-cheeked, nicely shaped, the girl had taken his breath away and sent shockwaves through his body when he'd hugged her to himself in his rescuing embrace. She'd also been dressed in black, and he wondered how long she'd been widowed. He was still on the lookout for her since they'd been separated, wondering where she lived, wishing he could see her again, and hoping she was ready to entertain the notion of courting again.

The turn of a key in the door lock awakened him from his reverie. He reached frantically for his clothes, his hat, anything, but the items were barely out of reach. He coughed to warn the intruder as a key jiggled in the lock, but the knob continued to turn and a drab, middle-aged frump of a woman with mussed hair stepped in.

"Excuse me, there's somebody in here," said Blue, sitting up and leaning forward to protect his modesty.

The woman carried a stack of towels into the room and laid them on a bench beside the tub. "I'm Darcy Meyer. I believe these towels are for you, sir, if yer name's Blue," she said gruffly.

"Yes, ma'am," he said curtly, "that's me. Thank you."

"What kind of a name is Blue anyhow? Is it on account of yer eyes bein' blue?"

"Um, sure," Blue squirmed. "Would you mind if I finished my bath in private?"

"Oh, honey, I'm the oldest of ten children in my family. Ain't nothin' I haven't seen," she cackled.

Blue couldn't believe the woman was still there, chatting.

"I've got to git myself back to my café, Mr. Blue. I'm just doin' a friend a favor helpin' ya with yer towels. My place is the Wildwood Café on the corner. Come on over for the best grub in town."

Blue thought he'd rather dine at any other restaurant in town after this encounter.

"Well, have a nice bath and welcome to Etna," said Darcy, closing the door behind her and forgetting to lock it.

Blue sat frozen for a good minute, holding his breath, while he waited to hear Darcy's footsteps fade. He whistled slowly, rose, toweled off, and dressed. "Well, that was different," he said to himself. "Welcome to the *Wild West,* Blue."

CHAPTER 9: Fairy Ghost

Etna Gazette Advice and Society Column "The Etiquette of True Beauty" By Mrs. Barbara Mitchell ETNA, Calif., Sept. 1893 --- Comeliness is without merit when possessed by the uncultured. Like a ring in a pig's snout is the pretty young lady devoid of manners. She who knows the correct way to behave yet brazenly chooses against intelligent refinement is the most miserable of creatures. She will never find true happiness. She will never find a higher position in society. Follow the laws of etiquette and good manners and so save yourself and your reputation, for physical beauty is only skin deep.

It was still early, before sunup. The dining table was bathed in candlelight. Vivian laid aside the prior day's newspaper and plunked a lump of sugar into her steaming cup of tea. So, this was Barbara's "brilliant" article? She flipped the pages of the *Gazette* to read about leg three of the upcoming English Triple Crown and a lengthy story of Widow Fitzgerald's recent trip to New York, where she'd attended the Barnum and Bailey Circus.

Vivian slathered butter and peach jam onto a thick slice of freshly baked sourdough wheat bread and scanned an advertisement for the Chicago World's Fair. The devastated city had risen from the ashes of the great fire of 1871 to offer a stunning display of architectural wonders and miraculous inventions. There would be amazing electrical exhibits and

Mr. George Ferris' gigantic wheel in which people could actually ride. She'd love to be there. Too bad it was over 2,000 miles away in Chicago.

On her way out west, she had glimpsed Chicago's skyline with its tall buildings etched against a clear blue sky. She'd also seen the grand station, where the train stopped. There had been crowds of people, women and children begging for food and money, men holding signs, begging for work. She also remembered one handsome young gentleman, probably a pastor or a Salvation Army volunteer, walking from person to person, handing out loaves of bread, placing his hands on shoulders, peering into faces.

Outside the apartment window, down on the street, a flash of white caught her eye. She jumped up and tugged back the lace curtain. A lantern's glow floated in the dark, milky fog. She snuffed out the candle and watched an ethereal figure with long, white hair disappear around the corner of the newspaper office.

Vivian ran to the door and wrapped herself in a plush, velvet cloak, shrugging the hood over her head. She ran down the stairs and across the street, trailing the specter in her long, flowing gown. The fairy ghost floated over a steep bank to the creek and gray pasture beyond. Vivian followed, picking her way carefully along a trail and over a footbridge, where she paused a moment to catch her breath. She heard the dull echo of cows chewing their cud. Her heart pounded harder. Still, she resolved to push onward across the field of bovines.

Shoving down her anxiety, she negotiated the gate and sprinted breathlessly through the herd, dodging the patties strewn across the damp grass. A cowbell rang and heavy hooves thunked dully. The lantern light disappeared. She stopped to listen to soft, invisible footsteps as they padded across the dewy grass. Straining her eyes, she spied the pale figure again as it slipped through another gate at the north end of the pasture and drifted gracefully across Horn Lane.

Vivian followed, chasing the specter over the road and past a livery stable. She crept to another fence and watched as the pale figure swung onto the shadowy bulk of a horse and disappeared, consumed in a shroud of pink as the first glints of daylight broke through.

Vivian headed home in a wash of yellow sunlight that sparkled on every dewdrop. The melody of a Grosbeak and the honking of geese floated in the dissipating mist and a southerly wind ruffled the leaves of alder trees.

When she arrived back at the apartment, Vivian stopped. She'd forgotten to tell Martin that she'd procured a chaperone. She walked to the Schmitt Hotel, entered, and scribbled a quick note.

Upon exiting, she ran smack into a gentleman pedestrian and jumped back. It was the handsome man who'd rescued her from the cattle stampede. She felt her cheeks go hot.

He touched the brim of his hat. "I was hoping to run into you again."

"Though not so literally, I'm sure," she replied.

He chuckled

Something like a rock stuck in her throat. His cream-colored shirt fit too tightly over his muscular torso and his rolled-up shirtsleeves revealed well-defined muscles with veins that stood out like sculpted cables through his tanned skin. She looked down, suddenly ashamed of how she'd been staring at his physique.

"Any more run-ins with cattle?" His eyes remained fixed on her face and didn't drag below her décolletage the way most men's did. Not that men paid much attention to her understated breasts anyhow.

"Not really, but I've stopped swinging from porch columns," she said. A dimple appeared in his cheek. She hated to make him into a hero, but she swallowed her pride and thanked him again for his rescue.

"It was no trouble, ma'am," he said. "I could think of worse things than holding you in my arms." His lingering gaze and sly smile tingled through her and the strength drained from her legs. She could think of nothing to say. "Have a nice day, ma'am." He shuffled away on his boot heels.

Dagnabbit. She still didn't know his name.

****

The apartment was empty when Vivian changed into her drab mourning clothes. Isabel had already left for work, and Vivian headed out to face another day.

The sun was high, and the temperature had gone from shiveringly cold to extremely warm in a short space of time. Dodging horses, wagons, pedestrians and chickens on Etna's busy Main Street, Vivian proceeded toward China Hill on the north end of town toward Mr. McGovern's Big Valley Ranch. Just as she was passing Kappler's brewery, Hiram Planter waltzed into her view and she jolted, tugging her hat and veil further over her face and making a wide, circuitous detour around the man. She snickered with relief when he cornered another victim.

Tramping down China Hill, she passed a small bevy of dark-headed men wearing straw hats, loose trousers, and baggy tunics—a songlike staccato of voices mixed with the pungent aroma of exotic spices. Two small terriers yapped noisily, chasing one another in the dusty road. On the porch of the largest shack, a Chinese woman rocked in a chair, puffing on a long pipe.

She'd heard of the famous "China Mary." Peering through her veil at the mysterious woman, Vivian was met with a broad, toothy smile and nod. Although disdained by some for her pagan ways, there were rumors that Mary had a regular flow of patients in and out of her hut and was secretly esteemed for her herbal remedies, compassion, listening ear, and confidentiality. It didn't hurt that her fees were more affordable than those of other doctors in Etna, including the veterinarian, Doc Severson. She wondered if she should pay the Chinese woman a visit. Perhaps she could verify whether or not she was pregnant.

A wide iron gate marked the entrance to Mr. McGovern's ranch, and she crossed the farmyard to an expansive barn with an attached office. While in the midst of preparing a condolence speech for Cocoa Joe's dog, the shaggy beast bounded through the office door to her, barking and pressing his slimy, wet nose into her skirt. She stumbled backward, but there was no escaping the probing muzzle. So, Cocoa Joe had been right; his dog wasn't dead or dying. Bobo had been resurrected.

Cocoa Joe McGovern appeared in the doorway of his office. "Bobo, ye rascal, let the poor lass be!" he scolded, while making no real attempt to correct the dog's behavior. Instead, he rewarded Bobo with pats on the head and a scratch behind the ears. "I remember ye, lassie," he said. "Ye are the one who thought me dog was dead." He bellowed a loud, "Ha! Ha! Haaaaa!" that made her jump.

"I see he's doing well," Vivian answered, removing the veil from her face. "I'm so glad."

"What can I do for ye this bonnie mornin', lass?" he asked.

Vivian introduced herself, told him she was Isabel's sister, and explained that she was looking for work as a bookkeeper. Mr. McGovern paused for a long while. Too long. She set her jaw and shifted her weight slightly.

"A female bookkeeper?" he asked, stroking his bearded chin.

Vivian pressed her lips together.

He stared at the ground and kicked some gravel with his boot. "I see ye are new in town, eh, lassie?"

"Yes, sir."

He snorted softly. "Ye are the suffragette widow lass who met me cattle face to face the other day, are ye not?"

Perspiration began to soak her bodice beneath her arms. "Yes, sir, your cattle and I are now well acquainted." No need to mention anything about suffrage.

He chuckled. "Folks 'round here call me Cocoa Joe. I suggest ye do the same."

"Yes, sir," she said, surprised at his response. She wrinkled her brow. "Do you like hot cocoa?"

He slapped his thigh and let loose another roar of laughter. "Folks call me Cocoa Joe on account of a little trick I played on me friends." He ran calloused fingers through his wild gray hair. "A wee bit o' whiskey in our cocoa made us all real happy one cold winter's mornin' while a-muckin' stalls."

She was about to launch into her experience as a bookkeeper when they were interrupted by a couple of ranch hands explaining how they'd cared for an ailing calf. When they left, Cocoa Joe asked, "Can ye spare a few hours a day to work for me? Mornings?"

She gaped for a split second before closing her mouth. "Yes, sir," she replied.

Bobo licked the boss's hand. "I'm not officially hirin' ye yet, but why don't ye step into me office where we can talk more?" He ushered her inside, plopped into a chair behind a large desk, and slid a ledger toward her. "If ye can make sense of this and prove to me that ye are savvy, ye are hired, lass."

She pored over the ledger. "It's clear enough to me, Mr. McGovern," she said promptly.

"That quick?" She nodded and he shoved a pile of papers to her. "Invoices, accounts payable, accounts receivable. Do ye think ye can take care of all this?"

She nodded, lifted her chin, and maintained a self-confident expression. "Yes, sir."

Cocoa Joe spat into a spittoon and Vivian hoped he hadn't notice her cringe. "Can ye start now?"

Her heart pounded. "Yes, sir."

"Folks will call me crazy for hirin' a female suffragette to do financial work," he said, "so don't ye go tellin' nobody, ye hear me?"

"Yes, sir," she agreed as indignant, smart retorts threatened to shoot out of her mouth.

Cocoa Joe stood, reached across his desk, and held out his hand. She stood and shook it heartily, shoving away the fleeting memory of Bobo licking his hand, and the fact that women didn't shake hands. "Ye can set yourself up at that wee desk over there in the corner," he said.

She thanked him and he gave her a jovial wink before ignoring her completely while he rifled through papers on his desk. She set to work, carefully and astutely reading through invoices and entering figures into a ledger. As the stuffy room warmed in the late morning sun, she removed her bonnet and golden strands of hair escaped from her bun, falling across her face. After an hour of productive industry with several noisy interruptions from ranch hands and cowboys, Cocoa Joe slammed a glass of iced tea on her desk, startling her. They sipped tea together while discussing various accounts.

"I've got a few dozen ranch hands ye might consider for a husband, Widow Smith," her boss said with a twinkle in his eye. Vivian's eyes widened and her mouth dropped. "Fine men, most of them."

"I'm…I'm only recently widowed, Mr. McGovern," she stammered

"No shame in husband prospectin', lassie. No shame at all."

She ignored him and went back to work. At noon, she straightened her paperwork, closed the ledger, discussed a schedule, and signed a contractual agreement. She would work from nine to noon for five days, at which time he'd assess her work to determine if he would hire her on a long-term basis. She gathered her belongings and was preparing to leave when Cocoa Joe asked her to sit a while longer. "Tell me more about ye-self," he prompted, leaning back in his creaky chair.

Vivian disregarded the clock and her rumbling stomach as she answered questions about her education, her manners, her upbringing, and her parents. At half past noon her boss was still interrogating her. She squirmed. He seemed gracious enough, but why so many questions?

"I want ye to meet me daughter Samantha," he said at last. "Ye look to be about the same age. Maybe ye could be friends."

"That would be nice," she lied. *Never going to happen,* she thought. "We met briefly in the post office the other morning," she spoke aloud.

"I think ye could help her, Widow Smith," said Cocoa Joe. "Me sassy Sammy Sassafras is a mite too eager when it comes to findin' a husband. She'd do well to tone down her charm, if ye know what I mean, but I can't say anythin' to her."

"I see," said Vivian. She couldn't deny that Samantha needed a few lessons in etiquette, but she couldn't be the one to help her.

One of Cocoa Joe's cowboys burst in, giving Vivian an excuse to make a polite exit and nearly tripping over Bobo where he lay on the stoop. She patted the dog's woolly head.

Passing by China Mary's hut again, Vivian peeked surreptitiously through her veil at the Chinese woman's mysterious, grinning face beaming at her through a window. Scalp tingling, she increased her pace through the shantytown. It was as though the woman knew her deepest, darkest secrets. She'd have to work up the nerve to speak to her. Eventually.

Over supper that evening, Vivian shared news of her job with Isabel, and the two celebrated the special occasion over glasses of cold lemonade.

"My biggest news is that Earl and I are no longer courting," said Izza soberly.

"What happened? Did he end it or did you?"

"He did," Isabel confessed. "I think he suspected I was stringing him along."

"Another bachelor is sure to ask you to the ball."

Isabel shrugged. "I'm not sure about that."

Vivian told Isabel about Martin Graver and her chaperone, Widow Fitzgerald. "Widow Butler says it's perfectly fine for me to attend dances as long as I don't actually dance."

"I'd like to see you attend a ball without dancing, Vivi." Isabel shook her head. "I know how much you love to dance."

"I hope to go, even if you have to tie me to my chair," Vivian laughed.

CHAPTER 10: Etna & Philadelphia

$\mathcal{I}$t was Friday. After a morning walk with only one brief, hazy glimpse of the fairy ghost, Vivian changed back into her drab mourning dress and hurried down China Hill for her first full day of work at Big Valley Ranch. When she arrived there, Bobo bounded out to meet her. "Don't you dare lick me, you slobbery beast," she commanded. The dog disobeyed and she used a handkerchief to wipe away the sticky slime from her skirt.

Cocoa Joe's Chinese cook bowed and greeted her as she entered the office, but her boss was nowhere to be found. "I am Li Wei," the cook said. "May I serve you tea or coffee, ma'am?"

Vivian accepted the offer of tea and commenced with her work. It didn't take long for the day to shift from shiveringly cool to uncomfortably warm. She stood, stretched, and unpinned the puce bonnet from her hair. Crossing to the door, she cracked it to let in a faint breeze. Bobo pushed inside and plopped at her feet, inviting her to scratch behind his ears, which she did before settling back to work.

The open door seemed to be a signal to ranch hands as a steady stream came and went from that point on into the morning. They politely offered their sympathies for the loss of her husband and did a great deal of inept flirting, while teasing her about cattle drives and grandstanding for women's votes.

"The stories about me keep getting wilder," she muttered to herself, more annoyed with the rising temperature than the bothersome rumors.

One wiry cowboy lingered in the office to converse and, since she couldn't concentrate on her work anyhow, she took a break and whisked a fan before her face.

"Indian summer, folks call it," said the cowboy, using his hat as a fan. "It's when we get a hot spell in the fall before the real cold sets in. Means last chance swimmin' weather. The boys and I are goin' up to the Johnson Creek swimmin' hole this weekend. Whew. Sure wish we could go there now."

A bead of perspiration trickled along Vivian's temple. "Do women ever swim there?"

The cowboy laughed outright. "Not that I know of." He sniggered. "But, you're welcome to come swimmin' with us, anytime ya want, ma'am." He shrugged on his way out the door.

Back at home, Vivian splashed water onto her face and flicked a fan in front of her nose as she stared at the letters on her sister's dining table. In one letter, she'd written to her mother and father about settling into Etna and working at Cocoa Joe's ranch. In a second letter, she wrote to Sarah about Martin Graver and told of her handsome mystery hero, adding a sketch of information about the cattle stampede. Of course, she neglected to mention anything about her suffrage efforts in either letter. Neither Mother nor Sarah approved, and she wrote nothing about her physical condition. She still wasn't sure if she was with child.

Most importantly, she'd written to Sarah, asking her to investigate Draven Randall's history. Had he faked other marriages in the past? Had he married and divorced other women? It was an alarming prospect, but she wanted to know if Draven was capable of being that nefarious.

Signing and sealing the envelopes, she settled them into her drawstring purse and scurried off to the post office.

Draven Randall III puffed on a cigar as he leaned on the veranda wall outside yet another mansion. About a month and a half had passed since his grandfather's death had set wheels in motion to ruin his life. The curmudgeon had made it clear that the only way Draven could receive any inheritance was to stop his philandering ways: no more elopements, illegitimate weddings, fake ministers, or forged marriage certificates. To make matters worse, no money would be released until his wife gave birth to a legitimate son born in wedlock—and he had to marry before the end of this very year! Draven blew a cloud of smoke from his lungs. His dead grandfather controlled his life even from the grave.

Week after week, he attended soirées and cotillions. And, as usual, every money-grubbing mother in Philadelphia thrust her sniveling, unattractive, overdressed, debutante daughter in his face. He despised the idea of being tied down. This was supposed to be his year to travel abroad, see the world, sow his wild oats. With the pressure of his grandfather's time constraints, his best option for a wife was Vivian. She was the most beautiful and, hey, if he was lucky, she might already be pregnant.

Cigar smoke evaporated in a gust of September's cool, damp wind as his eyes flashed to a girl stepping out onto the veranda. He groaned. Not another girl trying to corner him. But the girl saw him and immediately turned to go back inside. How perplexing. Why would any girl want to avoid him? If there was anything he hated more than being harassed by a flirtatious twit, it was being snubbed by one.

"Excuse me, ma'am," he called, crushing his cigar on the stone wall. She glanced back and grabbed the door's handle. Wait, he recognized her from somewhere. Church? Another ball? He sprinted to her. Ah, now he knew who she was. Vivian's friend. He'd seen them together several times. What was her name again? Sally? Suzanna? Susan? Sarah? Yes, Sarah. "May I ask you a question, ma'am?" he asked when he reached her side.

"I'm sorry, sir, but my chaperone is inside."

A choice swear word nearly burst from his mouth and he laid his hand on the door, preventing her escape. "Little girls and their chaperones," he snickered lightly.

"Please, sir, I must go inside."

Vivian would have taken the bait and bristled at being called a little girl, but not this compliant child. "You're a very beautiful young lady, Miss Sarah," said Draven in his sweetest tone possible. "Carlisle, is it?"

Her brows knit together, and her eyes were fiery. "Sir, you are no gentleman. I insist that you open this door and let me back inside."

"Not until you promise me a waltz," he said. "I don't want to miss out on dancing with the belle of the ball."

"Sir, your flattery is lost on me. Please open this door and let me back inside." He smirked and crossed his arms over his chest. "Mr. Randall, I know all about you, and I know you to be utterly insincere, so open this door now, or I'll scream for help and expose you as the beast you are."

Draven's clenched fists shook, and he fought the muscle tension in his face. "I don't know what Vivian told you about me, but they're all lies." He leaned against the door now, completely blocking her way.

"So, seducing innocent young women and faking marriages to them is a lie?" Sarah spat.

Draven felt his face contort and tried to remain calm. So, Vivian had told this wench everything. "I loved her," he said in strained voice. "I still do. She left me and I haven't seen her in weeks. She hasn't been to any ball or soirée." He feared his body language did not match his words.

"Oh, please," said Sarah, "you know where Vivian lives. You can find her any time you want."

"Do you think she'd want me?" asked Draven, hoping his face appeared eager.

"I doubt it." There was venom in her words.

"If you think there's the slightest chance, I'll call on her," said Draven.

"You don't have a snowball's chance in Hades," she scoffed.

Draven's eyebrows shot up his forehead. "A lady loses her beauty when she swears," he mocked.

"And maybe I don't care what you think."

"I'll pay the fair Vivian a visit this very week," said Draven. "We'll see what kind of chance I have with her. How about that waltz?"

"Remember that snowball?" asked Sarah.

Draven laughed and opened the door for her. "Pleasure meeting you, ma'am." *You impudent brat.*

Their hollow footsteps echoed on the wooden boards as Vivian and Martin strolled arm in arm in the glow of an orange sunset. Plinky piano music emanated from saloons. An owl hooted and a dry rustle of breeze-blown leaves skittered down the street. Martin shared how he'd been hired to work at the Johnson Falls Lumber Mill up Johnson Creek.

They met with Widow Fitzgerald in front of the Wildwood and entered the lively restaurant filled with patrons. Martin proved again that he was an easy communicator as they discussed their hopes, aspirations, and past achievements, as well as their happiest and saddest moments. Of course, Vivian didn't share her very saddest moments. All the while, Widow Fitzgerald played her role perfectly, remaining as silent as a fly on a wall and pretending to ignore them. And, though the evening was pleasant enough, Martin wasn't making her heart flutter. Even so, she could at least be content with him.

After a couple of hours together, Martin stood and crossed the dining room to pay the bill. It was in that moment that Vivian's feelings of contentment plummeted. There was something odd about his trousers. Were his buttocks oddly shaped? Were his pants stuffed with extra-long shirttails? She couldn't tell. She dropped her head and rubbed the back of her neck, hoping Widow Fitz hadn't caught her staring at the man's backside. Martin Graver might be a decent conversationalist, but she wasn't sure how content she could be with his strange derrière.

"Widow Smith, I wonder if I might escort you to the upcoming Harvest Ball," Martin queried as he walked her home. "Oh, dear," he said, clearing his throat. "Is it proper to ask a mourning widow to a dance?"

"I happen to know that it is perfectly proper for me to attend, Mr. Graver, but I'm afraid I can't dance."

"Oh, I see." He stroked his mustache and looked absently up the darkened street. "I'd still like to escort you, if I may."

"I'll have to sit there like a wallflower, watching you dance," said Vivian.

"If you don't mind, I don't mind," he said. "Even if we were to sit together and watch the dance, it would be an honor to have you by my side."

She agreed to attend the dance with him and said goodnight. After paying Widow Fitz, she climbed the stairs to recapitulate the highlights of the evening with Isabel, giggling when Vivian described Martin's strangely shaped buttocks.

"My, my, Vivi, two gentlemen suitors at once? I'm surprised, actually, considering all your impulsive and scandalous escapades of late."

"I know," Vivian winced. "I'm a little worried about appearances."

"A little? You should be *very* worried."

"Izza, you've scolded me enough about all the embarrassing things I've done lately."

Isabel took a deep breath. "You're right. Have you thought more about Mr. Ranson? Do you have any interest in him?"

"I would if I liked peace and quiet," said Vivian.

Isabel sniffed. "Just please try to be quieter and more subdued about things," she begged. "Try not to draw attention to yourself."

"Try not to embarrass *you* is what you're trying to say."

"Well, yes," Isabel admitted. "I have a reputation to keep."

An uneasy silence followed.

"Will you come with us?" asked Vivian. "To the dance, I mean?"

"I'd rather find a date," said Isabel.

"Maybe Cade Ranson could take you."

"I guess that would be all right. If he would ask me."

"Izza," Vivian sighed, "I'm thinking seriously of sticking with widowhood. Aside from having to wear such awful colors, it isn't all bad. I have my work and—"

"And maybe a baby to care for, don't forget," Isabel interjected.

"I don't think I really have any significant signs of pregnancy," said Vivian. "The truth is, I don't know what to expect. I've never been pregnant before."

"However, if you are pregnant, you're what? Two months along now?"

"I suppose."

"You should see a doctor."

"No, I don't trust the discretion of doctors here," said Vivian. "I'm thinking of going to see China Mary."

Isabel's eyes popped. "Oh, no, don't go to her. People say she's a witch."

"If she is, why do so many people go to see her?"

Isabel bit the inside of one cheek. "Well, I guess a lot of people say she's very trustworthy."

"Precisely. Trustworthy, confidential and helpful are exactly what I need right now."

"True. Too bad we can't find those same virtues in a man," said Isabel.

Goodness! Wasn't that the truth?

CHAPTER 11: Woods & Water

$\mathcal{S}$arah Carlisle braced herself and pushed through the gate of the Garretts' front garden in Philadelphia. She hurried along the path, climbed the porch steps, and took hold of the brass knocker, rapping on the heavy oak door.

"I'm afraid you're too late, dear," said Mrs. Garrett after Sarah warned the couple about Draven Randall's disagreeable character and potential visit.

"He was here earlier today, asking about Vivian," said Mr. Garrett.

Dread crashed into Sarah's gut. "What did you tell him?" Sarah asked.

"Oh, dear," cried Mrs. Garrett. "I'm afraid I said too much. I said she'd moved out to California."

Sarah's head began to swim. Best case scenario, Draven would never dream of going out west, and he'd forget all about Vivian. Worst case, he'd go to California in search of her.

It was a beautiful Saturday morning. Poplar leaves landed like golden coins upon the gentle gurgle of Etna Creek. Indian summer persisted, while mornings grew increasingly chilly. Embraced in a cloak of silent gray fog, Vivian searched again for the ghost girl. Having made her peace with bovines, she jaunted through the dewy grass, shoving down worrisome thoughts of Draven Randall and her possible pregnancy.

As she ruminated with the cud-chewing livestock, homesickness hit her again. Her father had always provided well for their family, but whenever she and her sister had asked for a luxury item, he'd made them work for it. He'd definitely taught her the value of a dollar. She'd resented her father at times; now she was grateful for all he'd taught her, since she had completed her week's trial period for her new boss and had been hired permanently.

The ghost girl suddenly appeared as an apparition on horseback. Her footsteps crunching over dried fir needles, Vivian broke into a run, chasing the girl for several minutes into the woods at the far side of the pasture. The girl couldn't have been more than fifteen years old. Vivian called out to her, but the specter melted into swirls of lavender mist.

Smack! She ran headlong into something tall, broad, and solid. "Tarnation!" she exclaimed loudly.

"Whoa, there, Missy!" a baritone voice spoke.

A tall man stood before her and her heart stopped. She took a step back, tripped on a rock, and tumbled onto her derrière. It was her blue-eyed rescuer—again! He offered his hand to help her up, but she refused, scooting herself backward. Accepting his help in public during a cattle stampede was bad enough, but they were alone in the forest now. It wouldn't be proper for her to take his hand.

"No, thank you, sir," she said, laughing nervously as she scrambled to her feet. "You really should stop rescuing damsels in distress."

"I would never dare call such a courageous suffragette a damsel in distress," he said, his ocean eyes twinkling, "though you do seem to have a knack for finding yourself in awkward situations."

She dusted off her skirt and avoided his gaze. "I'm sorry I swore," she said.

"I forgive you," he said. "I'm sorry I keep sweeping you off your feet."

"Oh, for pity's sake. You've done no such thing."

"That's arguable."

"I should be on my way," she said, commencing her walk past him.

"Don't you think it's about time you and I introduced ourselves?" he called to her.

"Perhaps another time," she shot back.

After walking only a few minutes, footsteps crunched behind her, and she spun on her heels. The man was several yards behind her. "Are you following me?" she asked, placing her hands on her hips.

He paused, slipped his hat from his head, and ran his fingers through his unruly dark hair. "Ma'am, I'm afraid we're headed in the same direction," he said, his tone apologetic. "Would you like me to wait a while and give you more of a head start?"

Vivian relaxed a little. "Fine. I'll turn back the way I came." She made a wide berth around him as she made her way past him again, pushing aside fir branches and twigs of underbrush. When her eyes glanced at his face, the sentiment emanating from his eyes was a startling blend of warmth, sympathy, and teasing. The intensity she sensed in him tangled her emotions. Perspiration crept beneath her bodice as she jogged away, hearing the stranger's voice singing as the distance grew between them: *All things bright and beautiful, all creatures great and small, all things wise and wonderful, 'twas God that made them all."*

Well, her desire to run into the man had certainly come true. But she hadn't expected it to be so literal and, though she didn't want to admit it, he really was sweeping her off her feet.

It was late afternoon. Vivian opened the parlor window to let in a breeze before seating herself at the table. She fanned herself and gulped a glass of iced tea. The noise of horses, wagons, and carriages made it hard to concentrate on the words of a story Isabel read aloud from the latest issue of *Strand Magazine*. Vivian peered at women twirling lace parasols and men mopping their faces with damp bandanas. All at once, pedestrians scattered like cockroaches and Hiram Planter rounded a corner. Vivian laughed outright.

"What's so funny?" asked Isabel.

"Hiram."

Isabel clucked her tongue. "Poor man." She sipped some iced tea and pressed the cool glass to her cheeks and forehead.

"Isabel, it's too hot. Let's go swimming."

"No, Vivi, it's not proper," said Isabel, "and it may not be safe. Some of the men around here are pretty rough."

"Don't be ridiculous," Vivian disputed. "No woman should be afraid to bathe in this dreadful heat. Besides, if you and I go together, we'll be perfectly fine."

"Splash some water on your face or take a cold bath," Isabel insisted. "Don't go doing anything impulsive again."

Vivian stood and stretched. "No, I'm sorry. I can't take it anymore. I'm going to Johnson Creek swimming hole."

"This is exactly the impetuous, foolhardy behavior that keeps getting you into trouble," Isabel reprimanded.

"You can remain in this oven, but I cannot. I'm going for a swim, Izza."

"What'll you wear?" Isabel asked reproachfully.

"My new bathing costume," said Vivian. "I'll wear it under my skirt and blouse to walk there," she said, lifting the suit from her trunk.

"It looks a little revealing, Vivi."

"To what? A few squirrels and maybe some fish?"

She changed and packed a small snack of a round of bread and some slices of cheese.

"Your clothes look a little lumpy," said Isabel.

"The local wildlife won't mind. You're missing out, Izza. I'll be cooling off while you're sweltering here."

"I'll bear it," said Isabel. "Besides, I don't have anything to wear for bathing."

"You could wear a camisole and bloomers."

"Not likely."

"I should buy you a bathing costume." She filled a canning jar with ice chips from the icebox; then filled another jar with tea before snugly wrapping both in dishtowels.

"You go and tell me all about it," said Isabel. "Maybe I'll go with you another time."

"There may not be another day this year," said Vivian as she pinned on her straw pancake hat. "Indian summer won't last much longer."

"What do you know about Indian summers?"

Vivian shrugged. "Do you mind if I take the *Strand* with me?"

"Take it," said Isabel, handing over the magazine.

Vivian's blouse was damp with sweat as she trudged up the dusty road to Johnson Creek. Even knowing how bedraggled she must look, she hoped to see her blue-eyed man again. She couldn't stop thinking of him. His sparkling eyes, his teasing smile, his clean scent of leather and soap. And his good manners and chivalry. He was kind and gentle too. He hadn't yanked her from the porch column that day. Instead, he had waited patiently for her to let go before gently carrying her, holding her in his arms. It was a shame she was going to the ball with Martin. And dagnabbit! She still didn't know her hero's name!

The vanilla aroma of sunbaked pine needles hung heavy in the hot wind that rushed through the conifers. Bright yellow maple trees lit the woods. A bear appeared on the road, and she froze, heart pounding in her ears as she watched it dart swiftly and silently across a meadow and disappear over a bank. She walked more warily from that point.

She rested on a log in the shade, water beading and dripping down her temples. She doffed her hat to swat the many gnats and flies that buzzed around her steamy face; then opened her tea jar, added a few ice chips, and swallowed the cool liquid. Cicadas buzzed and a woodpecker rapped on a tree. She tugged at her sticky blouse and seriously considered removing it. Wearing her navy-blue bathing costume would be so much cooler, and it was pretty and modest enough to wear as a blouse with its cunning striped sailor collar and short, puffed sleeves. She tucked her tea jar into her satchel and skimmed her surroundings before swiftly, gingerly unbuttoning her blouse, praying that no one would happen by and catch her in the act of disrobing. She made quick work of it and stuffed the blouse into her satchel. A soft, refreshing breeze touched her exposed skin, cooling it Instantly.

Resuming her hike, she left the road and followed a path to the deep crystal creek, where water splashed invitingly along the rocky edges. She was completely alone. She kicked off her boots and let her skirt fall like a puddle onto the sandy ground; then she exchanged her pancake hat for a white, ruffled cap. Dipping her stockinged feet into the water, goosebumps speckled on her arms. She wriggled her toes in the shallows and bent to splash her face and neck before plunging into the water that shot her body full of icy needles. When she adjusted to the shock, she swam across the pool and back, bobbing her head beneath the water for brief glimpses into the emerald depths of a sunken world filled with pebbles, twigs, minnows, and grassy moss.

Rotating onto her back, she viewed a canopy of yellow maples and azure sky overhead. A leaf broke and fell, spinning and twisting to land beside her like an island in her private pool. In a short time, her teeth began to chatter uncontrollably, prompting her to swim to the water's edge, where she touched bottom and sank her toes into the deep, soft silt before stepping onto the sandy shore. She grabbed a towel from her satchel and scrubbed her face, arms and legs, fighting to recover from the burning chill.

A faint scuffle of gravel startled her. Someone or something was walking through the scatter of quartz on the path above the swimming hole. She wrapped herself in the towel, stuffed her things into the satchel, and scrambled up a steep bank alongside the path, creeping deftly over smooth rocks to crouch in the shadows of an outcropping, where she held her breath and hid, waiting. A rumble of low male voices grew nearer, and her eyes darted upward. There was no means of escape. The slippery, rocky bank was too steep for her to climb. She was trapped on the ledge. Tucking herself behind the rocks, she touched the top of her head. Her cap was gone! She peeked around the rock to the creekbank. There it lay, a white smudge in the ferns along the creek's edge. Maybe no one would notice it. And maybe no one would notice her footprints either.

She leaned back into her hiding place again and brushed a cobweb from her nose. The deep, jovial, shouting voices grew louder. It sounded like much more than a few men. There must be at least half a dozen heading in her direction. As long as no one climbed onto her ledge, no one would see her.

Within seconds, baritone voices whooped and howled within yards of where she was hidden. This was followed by crashing splashes. She'd have to wait for the men to bathe and leave. She might be here a while.

The air was hot and, as her clothes began to dry somewhat, she folded her towel into a cushioned seat and made herself more comfortable. Though she made some noise in the process, the men were making such a racket that there was no possible way they could hear her. She also heard Cocoa Joe's unmistakable Scottish brogue and relaxed. Being found there by her boss would be mortifying, and he and others would probably tease her for the rest of her life, but at least she'd be safe with her boss there.

The men took their time, not seemi"g to'mind the bitter ice-melt. She dug through her satchel and bit into some bread and cheese; then she tried to read a story from the magazine. No, there was no way to concentrate on reading in a time and place like this. She took a sip of tea before stopping herself and capping the jar again. Drinking too much tea could put her in an even worse predicament.

She swatted a mosquito that tickled her ear and slipped her blouse from the satchel. Long sleeves would offer slightly more protection from the vile insects. Slowly, carefully, and with small, tight movements so as not to accidentally move outside the space of her hiding place, she put on her blouse and buttoned it with tremulous fingers. Next, she pulled on her boots and skirt before settling to wait.

Time passed slowly and, despite her towel cushion, her buttocks grew increasingly sore from the hard stone. She was also bored. Even worse, she was curious. She told herself not to be impulsive, but boredom and curiosity compelled her to take one tiny peep around the corner of her rock shelter. What she beheld burned her eyes more than juice from an onion. The image of bare-naked men would be forever sealed in her memory like an incandescent photograph.

Finding her breath again, she slammed back against the rock, dazed and in utter shock. Skinny dipping? What utter barbarians! She'd recognized Cocoa Joe, Silas Bowman, Cade Ranson, Martin Graver, and…

She peeked around the rock once more and gusted in a sharp breath. There was the back of what appeared to be her cattle drive hero. His tall, muscular torso was darkly tanned; the rest of him was stark white from waist to toes. She told herself to pull her eyes away, but she was frozen as a statue, barely able to breathe. Suddenly, all the men were in the water so there was no more immodesty. A great deal of splashing, kicking, wrestling, and dunking ensued. Someone threw a ball, and men teamed up to hit it back and forth across some imaginary line.

"It's your serve, Blue me boy," Cocoa Joe said to her mystery man, tossing the ball to him.

Was his name Blue or had Cocoa Joe given him one of his silly nicknames? Others called him by the same title. And how did Blue know Cocoa Joe?

When at last she released her gaze from the scene, she leaned back against the stone and placed a quivering hand to her pounding heart. This Blue gentleman was affecting her in ways she'd never experienced before. Even Draven hadn't made such an impression on her and she'd gone and married him.

"Howdy!" a voice spoke above her.

Vivian's heart choked in her throat. She looked upward. Crouched on the top of the smooth, rock embankment was a girl with long, thick, flaxen hair, her face pale, smiling, freckled. It was the fairy ghost from Cocoa Joe's pasture.

"Hello. I'm Tessie," the girl waved.

"Are you a ghost?" Vivian asked.

"No, you are."

Vivian put a finger to her lips. Even Tessie's whisper was too loud. The stories of her infamous volume were true.

"Sh!" Vivian warned.

"Here, let me help you escape your little prison there," said Tessie in what she must have thought was a whisper. "Collect your things and hand them to me. I'll reach down and pull you up."

"Please be quiet," Vivian begged.

"Oh, they're too busy splashing to hear me and they won't see you if you move fast. Of course, if they do see you, they won't see your face if you keep your back to 'em."

"What if you're seen?" Vivian asked.

"So what?" Tessie shrugged.

Vivian gathered her belongings and handed them to Tessie—all except her towel, which she draped over her head. Tessie reached and Vivian took her hand. "Are you sure you can pull me up?"

"I'm small, but I'm strong," Tessie promised.

"Hullo, there!" shouted a voice from the creek.

A surge of energy propelled Vivian as she scaled the rocky bank in one fell swoop, skinning a knee in the process. The two girls scrambled, crawling into a thicket of thimbleberries, where Tessie yanked her to her feet and, hand in hand, they ran, tripping, stumbling, and racing through the woods, not slowing their pace until the whistles, catcalls, and laughter died away behind them. They collapsed onto a log within view of the town of Etna. Tessie cackled uproariously while they took time to catch their breath.

"We can't stay here long," Vivian worried. "What if they follow us and find us here? I'll be eternally disgraced."

"They won't follow us," said Tessie.

Vivian cringed. How could such loud noise emit from such a small person? "You don't know that."

"So, you saw 'em?" Tessie twitted.

Vivian felt her face burn and didn't answer.

"You saw 'em skinny dippin'," Tessie guffawed, pointing to her. "I can tell by the look on your face!"

"Please be quiet," Vivian begged, clapping a hand over the girl's mouth. "What if they hear you?"

Tessie pried Vivian's hand away. "They can't hear a thing," she insisted, "but I know you saw 'em!"

"I saw nothing," she lied.

"Then why were you so anxious to hightail it outta there?"

Vivian was silent. She shouldn't admit anything to this girl. "I glimpsed a tad more than I should have, but I really didn't see anything."

Tessie roared. "You saw more men in the noodle than your eyes have ever seen."

Vivian groaned. "Please don't tell anyone about any of this."

"Who would I tell?" She lightly punched Vivian's shoulder. "Not bad lookin', some of 'em, eh?"

Vivian rubbed her arm. "You can't say such things."

"I can if it's true," Tessie argued.

"No, you cannot," Vivian reprimanded. "Where are your manners?"

"Lost 'em years ago," Tessie sniffed. "I went up there for a swim, but there they all was, crowdin' the swimmin' hole. It's so dang hot and I never got to swim. Looks like you had a good dip, though. And you had a better view than I did too."

"A *better* view?" Vivian gasped. "How can you say that? Were you watching them?"

"How could I not watch?" She rubbed her eyes. "I'll bet you'll never be able to wipe away the sight from your innocent virgin eyes as long as you live." She nudged Vivian in the ribs and laughed.

"I had no idea they'd swim without clothes," she admitted weakly.

"Pshaw!" Tessie exclaimed. "Did ya think they all had bathing suits or swimmin'?" She fanned herself with her hat. "It ain't fair they got to go swimmin' and I didn't. It's so goldarn hot."

Ignoring Tessie's swearing, Vivian opened her satchel and pulled out one of her canning jars. "Would you like some iced tea?" she offered.

"Sure would," said Tessie, lighting up.

Vivian handed her the jar and listened to Tessie gulp noisily. Everything the girl did seemed loud.

"Aren't ya glad I rescued ya?" Tessie asked, smacking her lips as she screwed on the lid again.

"Yes, very," said Vivian honestly. "Thank you."

"You're welcome," said Tessie. "Hey, so you're the ghost that's been chasin' me in the fields all these mornin's."

"And I thought *you* were the ghost," said Vivian.

They both laughed.

"I guess neither of us is dead or scary," said Tessie.

"I guess not," said Vivian.

"Except that I keep hearin' folks say you're goin' around tellin' people you want women sufferin'." She shook her head. "I don't mean no disrespect, ma'am but, for a widow, I think you'd know right well enough that we women already suffer enough in this world. We don't need any more sufferin'." Vivian tried not to laugh and was about to launch into an explanation when Tessie jumped up and stretched. "I gotta go. It was nice to meet ya and finally know you're not tryin' to haunt me." She flashed a grin before taking off at a sprint down the hill toward town.

"Wait for me!" shouted Vivian, grabbing her satchel and jogging to follow. But Tessie outdistanced her. She smiled to herself. She'd have to talk with Tessie and explain the meaning of suffrage. And, despite her lack of education, Tessie spoke her mind and didn't care what anyone thought of her. If only she could be more like that.

CHAPTER 12: Crystal Creek Church

*V*ivian sat perched on a pew at the Crystal Creek Methodist Church. It was a little nerve-racking to attend church alone, unsure of whether she'd recognize or know anyone. Cade Ranson noticed her walking and offered her a ride in his wagon, saving her from having to walk the two miles to the church. Not that she minded walking.

On their way to the service, she'd done all the talking, as expected. Even when she asked Cade questions about himself, his responses were largely incoherent, tempting Vivian to scream. What kind of parents allowed their child to grow up without learning to hold a conversation? He was handsome enough, but he was just too quiet. Nope. She could never imagine courting or marrying this man. It would never work.

Vivian scanned the sanctuary. Women held babies on their hips or in their laps as they chatted happily. That might be her soon. Would Mr. McGovern fire her? She couldn't think of that now. There was a man folks were calling Matthew Wright, which meant Tessie was probably close by, according to Samantha McGovern. Hiram Planter and Oswald Davis were also there. She ducked her head to avoid making eye contact with them.

"Excuse me," a woman beside her broke into her thoughts. It was Widow Maymie Butler. She introduced

Vivian to Mr. Garlan Segal. "He's my widower friend," she whispered in her ear.

"Ah," Vivian nodded.

Maymie also introduced her to a nice-looking Portuguese immigrant who didn't speak English. Maymie gave Vivian a clandestine wink, obviously hopeful she'd be interested in the gentleman. But did she want to have a courtship with a foreigner? It would be like courting Cade Ranson—lots of one-sided conversations. Widow Butler was pulled away and Vivian was left alone again. She scanned the nave. An Indian man and woman were conversing with another couple. How remarkably unusual that a Native American couple was accepted in church and treated like equals.

At that moment, a woman's voice resounded above the rest—the unmistakable voice of Tessie Blackman. While several people shook their heads and one woman covered an ear, she saw Cade Ranson sit up straighter and his eyes locked on the fairy sprite where she sat a few rows ahead of him. Interesting. So, all hope of Cade having eyes for her was gone. But all hope for her sister and Cade was also gone.

The minister approached the lectern, and the congregation hushed as he opened with a prayer. Afterward, he invited everyone to stand as a woman led the congregation in singing *Sweet Hour of Prayer.* As Tessie's voice rose above the rest and she leaned against the shoulder of the gentleman beside her, Vivian watched Cade stiffen. His prospects looked bad, but maybe she could persuade Tessie to consider him as a suitor.

The hymn concluded and there was a rustling of skirts and the creaking of wooden pews as everyone took their seats. Someone whispered the name "Martin," and she did a quick glance behind her. She didn't see Martin Graver, but her eye caught the handsome Mr. Blue looking directly at her. He smiled broadly and nodded in her direction, while she pursed her lips and looked away, pressing her back against her seat and willing her heart to cease its wild pounding. She clasped her hands tightly to keep them from quaking. The memory of Blue's naked, muscular body in the swimming hole flashed before her eyes and she reprimanded herself for entertaining such an image in church, of all places.

It took some time for her pulse to settle again. Draven had never had such an effect on her. No one had. What was so different about this man? Was it because he'd rescued her from the cattle stampede or was there some other reason?

"Wherefore be ye not unwise," Bishop Andrew Halley began, reading from the Book of Ephesians.

My heart is sure unwise, Vivian thought. *It has led me astray in the past and I can't let it do that to me again.*

Indian summer's heat quickly warmed the church, and Vivian opened her drawstring purse to withdraw her fan. She flipped it open and stirred it before her face while daring another peek at Cade. Sure enough, his eyes were still glued on Tessie Blackman.

"Be wise!" Bishop Halley admonished the congregation with a flourish of his arms. Vivian jumped. She should be wise and listen to this minister. At least he wasn't boring like Reverend Patterson." …but understanding what the will of the Lord is," the bishop continued.

The will of the Lord? How would she know what that was? God wasn't doing a very good job of revealing His will to her so far.

It was growing steadily warmer and people throughout the church were fanning themselves with whatever they could find—fans, hats, pieces of paper, hymnals. She peered over at Widow Maymie Butler. Despite the heat, she was situated awfully close to her Mr. Segal. Unfortunately for Cade, the same was true of Tessie with her pew partner. When Tessie leaned over and touched her lips to her gentleman's ear, Vivian slid her eyes to Cade and watched the muscles in his neck tighten. Yep, he was smitten.

Her thoughts slid to Blue again. He wasn't merely good-looking; he was stunningly handsome. She spent the rest of the service daydreaming of how it would feel to melt into his arms. And she ambivalently tortured herself with scenarios of how he'd react to hearing she'd been seduced into a fake marriage, was living a lie as a widow, and was maybe pregnant. It was too much for any man to bear.

The cracking of hymnals and rustling of petticoats woke her, and she stood with the rest of the congregation to sing the Doxology.

Vivian stepped into the churchyard, the scent of freshly cut hay trailing on a stifling breeze. She lifted a hand to wave at Tessie, but her friend was surrounded by four eager young men.

Nearby, Blue stood with the Native American couple, his deep, jovial tones weaving into a gentle hum of laughter.

With quiet resignation, Vivian scanned the crowd until her gaze landed on Cade. He stood apart, hands shoved into his pockets, shoulders slightly hunched.

She joined him and offered a sympathetic smile. "Mr. Ranson, what do you think of Miss Tessie Blackman?"

He watched his heart's desire surrounded by a passel of eager suitors. His fingers fumbled nervously with his tie. "She's nice."

"Nice?" Vivian echoed. "All right, well, that's something." She nudged him. "Who's she talking to?"

"Harvey Winslow," Cade muttered, his expression darkening. "She shouldn't be wasting her time with him."

It was the most words Vivian had ever heard him string together at once. "Are you worried about her?" she asked.

"Maybe."

"Do you care for Tessie Blackman, Mr. Ranson?"

He twitched yet said nothing.

"Yes, or no?"

His gaze lifted to meet hers. "Yes, I do." Then, as if surprised by his own admission, his eyes widened. "I do," he repeated, his voice a curious mix of wonder and certainty.

Vivian's lips curved into a grin. "I'm proud of you for saying so. Now, you need to tell her how you feel."

A flicker of panic flashed across his face. She laughed. "You can do it. You're talking to me, aren't you?"

"Widow Smith… maybe you could ask her if she likes me first?"

Vivian folded her arms. "Absolutely not. You must do it yourself."

"I can't talk to her unless I know I have at least the slightest chance."

Vivian released a sigh, planting a hand on her hip. "I don't approve of meddling. Nevertheless—"

"Oh, thank you, Widow Smith! Thank you very much!" Cade interrupted, his relief palpable.

"I haven't promised anything." He gave her another pleading look. "Fine," she said.

She would have talked to Tessie right then and there, but she could barely see the girl amidst her pack of admirers. Every attempt to reach Tessie was thwarted. Giving up, she shrugged helplessly to Cade, gestured to him to speak to Tessie himself, then turned to make her trek back to town.

Wiping her brow, Vivian whisked a fan before her face as she walked.

"May I offer you a ride, ma'am?" a deep voice resonated beside her. It was Blue. As she stared up at his crystal blue eyes and tanned, smiling face, for a split second, her heart forgot how to beat. He tugged on the horse's reins, pulled the wagon to the side of the road, and jumped down. "Sure is a hot day to be out walking," he said, presenting his hand to her.

"I haven't said yes to your offer," Vivian frowned coyly.

"Suit yourself, then," he said, dusting his hands together and walking back around the wagon.

Calling his bluff, she squared her shoulders and walked on ahead. He jogged to reach her and caught her by the elbow. "May I please have the honor of conveying you back to town in my wagon?" he asked. A slow melty weakness spread through her. She peered into his eyes and felt his gaze on her face like a gentle caress.

"I don't think we've been properly introduced. My name's Blue Ryan."

"I'm Vivian—I mean, Widow Smith. Pleased to meet you, sir."

"My condolences to you, ma'am. I'm sorry for your loss."

"Thank you, Mr. Ryan."

He walked her back to the wagon and assisted her in climbing up to the seat. "Vivian," he said, dragging out the word as though tasting it in his mouth. He climbed onto the wagon seat beside her and tapped the reins. "Pretty name."

The sound of her name on his tongue weakened her like fingers sliding over her bare skin.

"Are you visiting here in town?" she asked, all too aware of the nearness of him beside her.

"No, I think I'll be staying a while," he answered.

"Why's that?" she asked.

When he told her he'd found a job working for Cocoa Joe McGovern, she nearly choked but decided not to tell him she worked there too. It might be fun to see how he'd react to discovering her there.

"Why is your name Blue?" she queried.

"I was blue when I was born. After I survived the night, a blue eagle flew past the window. My half-Cherokee father streaked my cheeks with blue war paint and named me *Warrior Blue Eagle* on account of my strength and resilience in defeating death."

"Oh, for pity's sake," Vivan snorted. "Is any of that true?"

"I've found that spinning a yarn keeps people awake."

"Too bad you aren't a preacher, Mr. Blue Eagle. A few of your tall tales would keep your congregation awake."

"I am actually, and it's *Warrior* Blue Eagle."

"You're actually what?" she asked.

"A preacher."

"No, you're not," she said, laughing.

"I guess I deserve that. Now you won't believe anything I say."

"You're really a preacher?"

He nodded.

"And you're really named Blue because…?"

"The blue eyes," he admitted, tapping the corner of an eye. "But that's kind of a boring story."

"And it's your real name?"

"Yes."

"Tell me a less boring story, then," she said, fanning her face again, "but tell me a true story this time."

He told her of growing up on a farm in Illinois, graduating from seminary, and being ordained as a minister. He also told how he'd volunteered for the Salvation Army at the train station in Chicago while working there as a stevedore. The flicker of a memory juddered through her mind.

"Tell me about yourself, Widow Smith. Are you a native of California?"

She was about to speak when she caught sight of Martin Graver walking down the boardwalk with Samantha McGovern hanging on his arm. Just as well. Samantha could have Martin. He wasn't nearly as interesting as Blue.

"Ma'am, are you all right?"

"Oh, dear," she said, flustered. "I forgot what I was going to say."

"Well, it's a little early in our relationship to be calling me *dear*. I just asked if you were from California."

Vivian pushed a soft sniff from her nose before telling Blue a little of her life. Very little. Nothing about Draven, of course.

"I am so sorry for the tragic loss of your husband. It takes courage for a young widow to leave home and move across an entire continent like you have."

"I don't know about that. I have my sister here." She gave him directions to her sister's apartment, and he slowed the wagon to a halt, parking in the shade beside her building.

Narrowing his gaze, he asked gently, "Are you able to talk about your late husband?"

She pushed back the cuticle on a fingernail. She hadn't spent enough time rehearsing the story of her fake husband. "His name was Oscar Wendell Smith."

"Really? What—?" He stopped. "Oscar Wendell Smith?"

"That's what I said, yes."

Blue remained quiet.

"What is it?" Vivian asked somewhat nervously.

"Never mind. I'm sorry. I didn't mean to interrupt. Tell me about him."

"He was…." She should stick to something akin to the truth to help her remember her lie. "We eloped and were only married a day. He went away the morning after our wedding and was killed in the street by a horseless carriage in New York."

"Hm," he said. "Again, I'm very sorry."

"I should go," Vivian said abruptly. "Thank you for the ride."

Blue swiveled on the wagon seat. "Would you mind if I ask you a quick question?" His knees brushed hers.

"I suppose I don't mind," she replied hesitantly.

"What interests you, Widow Smith?" His tone was low, serious.

"What…interests me?" she stuttered.

"Yes."

She looked up the street. Something about him made her want to tell him everything. About life in Philadelphia, suffrage meetings, and how she believed women were equal in intelligence to men. Part of her wanted to tell him about Draven too, but that was impossible. It was all impossible. "My parents and friends back home," she replied at last. "I miss them very much."

"Hm," he said. "I miss family and friends back home too, Widow Smith, but that's not what you wanted to tell me, is it?"

Her mouth opened slightly, and she eyed him with suspicion. "You don't know what I'm thinking."

"True, but I can tell you're thinking of more than you're telling me."

The impertinence! "Thank you for the ride, Mr. Ryan," she said curtly. She gathered her skirts. How dare this man presume to read her thoughts?

"Wait," said Blue, reaching out a hand to touch her shoulder. "I'm sorry if I offended you. I only want to get to know you better." He withdrew his hand.

She gulped over a lump in her throat. "Oh," she said, the word hushed on her breath. She didn't know what to say. Should she tell him she wanted to get to know him better too? She peered back at him, and the expression on his face was caring and compassionate. "I…I thank you for the ride, Mr. Ryan."

"Let me help you down," said Blue.

"I can manage," she insisted, but he was already on the ground and jogging around to her side.

"Whew! It's hotter than blazes, isn't it?" he remarked, reaching up to take her hand. He kept a grip on her hand even after she'd alighted from the wagon. "Do you know how to swim, Widow Smith?" he queried, his eyes sparkling.

Her heart jumped. Did he…? Had he…? What if he'd seen her at the swimming hole? She forced a laugh and pulled her hand from his. "Hardly ever," she answered, twisting her fingers in her skirt.

He chuckled softly and climbed back onto the wagon.

"Thank you for the ride, Mr. Ryan."

"My pleasure," he said. "I hope to run into you again soon, Widow Smith. Literally."

Inside the gray light of the apartment vestibule, Vivian closed the door behind her and fought to steady her nerves. Her hand was still warm where he'd held it a little too long.

Blue. What an odd name. But he was a preacher. She'd never be able to lie to him and, once she told him the truth about Draven, he'd drop her like a hot potato. And if she was pregnant, he'd shun her forever. There was no future with Blue Ryan, unless she continued lying to him. If she was pregnant, there was no shame in being a widow with a child. But could she live her life lying to this man?

In the cooling, lamplit shadows of evening, a breeze rippled the lace curtains on the window as Vivian and her sister lounged in their nightgowns on the parlor sofa. Vivian told Isabel the events of her day—of her talk with Cade, about seeing Martin with Samantha, and of her ride home with Blue.

"For a widow, you sure are attracting the attention of a lot of bachelors in town," said Isabel. "You could be married sooner than you think. But you'd better be careful not to reveal the truth about Draven to anyone or you'll ruin your marriage prospects forever."

CHAPTER 13: Preachers and Cowboys

*I*ndian summer ended abruptly with a drizzly dampness that seeped into Vivian's bones as she slipped along the muddy path to Cocoa Joe's pasture. Balling her fists in her mittens, she quickened her pace to warm herself. All at once, nausea overtook her. She leaned against a willow tree beside the creek to vomit. Gulping deep draughts of fresh air, she choked on a sob and burbled a swear word directed at Draven. Nausea and vomiting were signs of her worst fear. Once again, she considered paying a visit to China Mary. Could she be trusted to keep a secret?

Wiping her mouth with a handkerchief, Vivian waited for her vision to clear before crunching through frost-tinged grass, balling her hands inside her mittens and puffing out a steamy cloud. Wobbling onward, she tuned her ears to the ripping of fodder and cows chewing their cud. From somewhere in the mist an echo of muffled hooves stomped. She froze her exhale until she saw Tessie astride a trotting horse.

"Mornin,' Ghost Girl!" Tessie called, shattering the stillness.

"Good morning to you too, Fairy Ghost," Vivian laughed.

Tessie slid to the ground and slapped the rump of her horse to send it galloping. "Are ya all right, Miss Vivian?" she asked. "You look a little peaked."

"I'm fine," she lied.

"Hm," said Tessie, sounding unconvinced. "Ya don't look like your usual self."

"I'm just cold."

Tessie harumphed. "Mind if I join ya on yer walk?"

The two ladies conversed as they walked. Vivian explained the definition of suffrage and Tessie shared her regrets of not finishing school and her displeasure with working at the saloon.

"Now that I know what suffrage is, I'm all for it and I'll gladly join your cause," said Tessie. "I was a fool to take the first job offered to me." She blew out, making her lips rumble like a horse. "The men don't treat me kindly at all. Even so, it pays for me to take care of me and my ma. She's been sick, ya know?"

"My sister told me," Vivian replied. "You have my sympathy, Tessie."

"Yes, well, if I were a man, I could find a decent job with a fair wage, but I had to go and be born a girl and get stuck workin' at a saloon, where I'm pawed at all day by drunken bast— Oh, excuse me. Drunken men. Too late to do anythin' about it now."

"I don't think it's too late," said Vivian. "Maybe you could go back to school."

"I'd love that, but I don't think it's possible." An impish smirk flitted across her face. "Ya know what I miss most about school?"

"What?"

"The boys!" Tessie laughed and slapped her thigh.

"Oh, Tessie." Vivian shook her head.

"No, seriously, I miss history and arithmetic. They were my best subjects." She vibrated her lips again. "But, speakin' of boys, not one has asked me to the Harvest Ball."

"I'm surprised. I saw you at church Sunday morning and you didn't look like you had any shortage of suitors."

"Those boys aren't serious. Not even Ma—." She clamped her mouth.

"Matthew Wright?" Vivian asked.

"That blamed boy's been flirtin' with me for years, but he has no plans to court me."

"Do you like him?"

"I don't know," she shrugged. "Iffen any man truly liked me, I s'pose I'd like him back."

"What about Cade Ranson?" Vivian proposed.

"That bump on a log?"

"It was only a suggestion," said Vivian, feeling discouraged for Cade.

"I thought you was with Cade."

"No, no," said Vivian, "I'm not interested in him."

"Probably 'cause the boy can't put two words together," said Tessie.

"No, it's because he has eyes for someone else."

"I'm not surprised," said Tessie, frowning.

The timing wasn't quite right for telling Tessie about Cade's interest in her, but there might be some hope for a little matchmaking.

Vivian peered out the window of Cocoa Joe's ranch office at Scott Valley's craggy peaks smoldering in a morning haze of pale, smoky blue. She leaned, touching her forehead to the pane of glass to watch a woman hopping as she dodged puddles in the farmyard. It was Samantha McGovern. A handsome young man crossed her path, and Samantha paused, standing arms akimbo, bobbing her brown curls.

"What are ye looking at?" Cocoa Joe's voice boomed, startling Vivian.

She straightened. "I believe it's your daughter," was Vivian's pert reply. She wondered what Cocoa Joe thought of his daughter's plunging neckline and the way she flaunted her buxom curves. Samantha certainly could turn heads and, although Vivian couldn't hear their discourse, she gaped as the handsome cowboy jogged to Samantha, scooped her up into his arms, and carried her through the maze of mud puddles and cow pies, settling her on the office porch.

Cocoa Joe chuckled. "That's me girl. She's a charmer, ain't she?"

Vivian hid her eye roll. She continued working as Cocoa Joe opened the door to greet his daughter. "Hello, me bonny Sammy Lass! What a surprise to see ye here." And to the cowboy, "Ye can get back to work now, laddie, and quit yer flirtin' with me daughter."

"Can't a girl come see her beloved father in his workplace now and then?" Samantha asked.

"Sammy Lass, ye wouldn't be a'comin' here unless ye wanted something. Now, come inside and talk to ye poor father."

Before stepping foot into the building, Samantha peered cautiously inside. "Where's Bobo?"

"I'm sure he's lyin' about somewhere, playin' dead or getting' his nose up some poor lassie's skirt." He snickered softly.

"Well, keep him away from me," Samantha ordered, stepping tentatively over the threshold and dragging in a cloud of noxious perfume with her. "I'm wearing a new dress."

"Ye are pretty as a picture, Sammy Sassafras." He twitched his nose, sneezed, and dabbed at his eyes with a handkerchief. Vivian sneezed too.

"Will you introduce me to some of your new hired hands?" Samantha queried, batting her eyelashes.

Her father's bushy gray brows lowered. "I've only one new lad who might suit yer fancy." He ambled across the floor to his desk, groaning as he eased himself into his chair.

Samantha cocked her head to one side and puckered her mouth. "Tell me about him, Father."

"Not now, Sammy Lass. I have work to do."

Samantha pouted and her father clucked his tongue. "Don't ye be getting' coy with me, missy. Ye know I'm busy." He waved toward Vivian in the far corner of the room. "Say hello to me new bookkeeper."

Samantha jerked her head around and Vivian saw her lips go from smiling to flat. "You hired a female bookkeeper?" she asked incredulously.

"Aye, lassie. Widow Smith, meet me bonnie Sammy Sassafras."

"Father, please don't introduce me with your silly nickname."

"Ha! Ha! Haaaaaa!" Cocoa Joe bellowed. "I'll come up with a nickname for Widow Smith to make it even."

"Oh, Father, your laugh is mortifying," said Samantha before turning to Vivian. "I apologize for your boss, Widow Smith. I'd like to say you'll get used to him, but I don't know anyone who does."

Vivian greeted Samantha and attempted to resume her work while the intruder paced the floor, wafting the pungent odor of perfume into every corner of the room. Vivian's eyes watered. Cocoa Joe sneezed and again blew his nose on a handkerchief. The odor was borderline toxic.

The voices of men talking, whistling, and laughing halted Samantha's pacing, and she danced to the window to watch her father's cowboys as they passed through the farmyard. Vivian kept her head down, clicking the abacus beads and hiding her face beneath the small brim of her hat, spying through hooded eyes.

"I'm here to meet your new hired hand, Father," Samantha said, casting a quick sideways glance to Vivian.

Cocoa Joe grunted. "Hm. That would be Blue Ryan."

Vivian fumbled and accidentally clattered her boss's abacus to the floor. She retrieved it with trembling fingers, whispering a quiet reprimand to herself. She was aware of Samantha's eyes on her.

Father and daughter continued their conversation as if Vivian were not in the room.

"It'll be hard comin' up with a good nickname for a fella who already has a moniker like Blue," Mr. McGovern chuckled.

"Blue." Samantha shook her head. "I don't know as I like such a strange name for a fellow, but I guess I won't fault him for that if he's handsome and earns a decent living. What else can you tell me about him, Father?"

"He's educated. Went to seminary to be a preacher."

Samantha arched her brows. "A preacher?" She touched a finger to her lips. "Hm. I wonder what that would be like. Does he want to be a preacher here in Scott Valley?"

Cocoa Joe shrugged. "I couldn't say. All's I know is he's eager to prove himself and he's a right hard worker." He spat into a spittoon.

"Oh, Father, please stop that awful habit. It's uncivilized." She paced the floor again. "At least a seminary man has more of a future than one who merely works on a ranch as a lonely, dirty cowpoke. No offense, Father."

"Me boys aren't mere ranch hands and cowboys, Sammy Lass. Ye know I only hire the best for me special cattle." He sniffed and used his kerchief to dab at his watering eyes. "Me good, ol'—"

"—Red Angus," Samantha and her father said in unison, laughing.

Cocoa Joe leaned back in his chair, put his arms over his head and spoke with a gleam in his eye. "I'm considerin' your mother's notion of sending ye back east to live with your aunt in Pennsylvania, where ye can meet a proper gentleman, Sassafras."

Vivian sucked in a breath. Not Pennsylvania! What if Samantha went there and learned about her sham marriage to Draven Randall and her fake marriage to…oh, what was her pretend husband's name again? Oh! Oscar Wendell Smith. She mustn't forget his name!

"Oh, Father, no," Samantha pleaded, "don't make me go back east."

Cocoa Joe sorted through paperwork on his desk. "I want only the best for ye, Sammy Sassafras. Now, let me get back to work. Daylight's a-wastin'."

Samantha took a seat in a chair facing her father. "I'll just wait here till Mr. Ryan stops in."

"Ye might be waitin' all day, lassie."

"I don't care," she said, leaning back and rooting herself to the chair. "The Harvest Ball is in less than a week and I still need an escort."

"Ye have plenty of suitors, lassie."

"And I haven't promised to go with any of them," she said. "I want to meet this Mr. Ryan first."

"Suit yeself," he said.

She leaned on her father's desk, settled her chin in her hands, and drummed her fingers. One minute passed, then two. The clock ticked loudly in the stillness of the room. In less than five minutes, Samantha stood. "Fine." She bade her father goodbye, waved a fleeting hand at Vivian, and left.

Cocoa Joe winked at Vivian and chuckled. "Would ye mind cracking open that window a smidge, Widow Smith, before we choke to death?" Vivian readily complied. "If me girl doesn't lighten up on that perfume of hers, she'll end up with nary a single beau to escort her to that dance."

As Vivian pushed up on the window pane, she watched Samantha stomp up China Hill and out of sight. No wonder the girl had such poor manners. Her father spoiled her rotten. *And now Miss Sammy Lass wants to steal Blue from me?* She thought. *How many suitors does a girl need?*

When noon arrived, Vivian gathered her belongings and stood to bid farewell to her boss when the door opened, and Mr. Blue Ryan gusted in. She did a quick inhale. With his disheveled hair and shadow of scruff on his face, how could he be even more handsome than he was when she last saw him in his Sunday best? Instead of saying hello, she hid her face beneath her hat. He didn't seem to have noticed her.

"Hello there, Blue Buckaroo," said Cocoa Joe. "Looks like a storm's a brewin' out there, laddie."

"Yes, sir," Blue replied. "I'm just checking in to say that a few boys and I are headin' out to round up some strays in your north fields."

"Best be getting' a move on before the storm hits, then."

"Yes, sir."

A trace of morality shot through Vivian as she watched Blue Ryan. He seemed like such a good, decent man. If they ever grew close enough to tell him the truth about Draven, her likely pregnancy, and her fake marriage and widowhood, he'd surely leave her. But if she kept her secret, her subterfuge would gnaw at her for the rest of her life.

Blue left and she craned her neck to the window. A whirlwind of dust whipped around Blue as he smashed his hat onto his head and tightened the stampede string beneath his chin. His head turned and his eyes caught hers through the window for a split second before she hastily dropped back into her chair. Her heart thumped wildly. Had he recognized her?

She waited until Blue and a few other cowboys rode away before she left Cocoa Joe's office. Trudging up China Hill with her skirt whipping about her legs, she slid an eye to China Mary's hut and saw the woman sitting on her porch, smoking a pipe. Much as she dreaded it, she knew it was more important than ever that she pay China Mary a visit. And soon.

CHAPTER 14: The Randalls

*T*wo weeks had passed since Sarah was cornered by Draven Randall at the September ball. Sarah could admit he was handsome and charming, but how could Vivian have been duped by such a man? He made her hair stand on end. The same shivers passed through her now as she set foot onto the red-carpeted lobby of the Randall & Randall Law Office. She dreaded seeing Draven and didn't want him to think she was chasing after him, but she had to help Vivian by completing this errand.

"My grandfather passed recently," Sarah fibbed to the secretary. "I've received a small inheritance, and I need some legal advice as to what to do with the money. A friend recommended that I consult with this office."

"The senior Mr. Randall is available," said the secretary.

"I need to speak to the younger Mr. Randall," said Sarah.

The secretary's mouth pursed reprovingly. "He's out of town and isn't expected back for at least a month."

Sarah's heart leaped into her throat. "He didn't go to California perchance?" she inquired.

"Miss," said the secretary, "this is a respectable business establishment, and we don't need young ladies harassing Mr. Randall."

"Can you just please tell me when he left for California?" Sarah pressed, ignoring the reprimand.

"About two weeks ago," the secretary answered snappishly, "not that it's any of your business."

"Well, then, I'll come back after the younger Mr. Randall returns," said Sarah, fighting to keep from running out of the office. She had quickly and easily gotten the information Vivian needed. Draven had gone to California in search of Vivian. She had to warn her—if it wasn't too late already.

Draven Randall's attempts to contest his grandfather's will had failed dismally. The old codger's sound mind and sharp wit were clearly evidenced in every sentence of the document, proving his astute mental competence. The legality of the will was unbreakable.

He didn't have to have a son right away, but Grandfather Randall insisted that he marry someone before the end of the year! The notion was inconceivable, but it forced him to think carefully about the woman he wanted for his wife and Vivian was the obvious choice. He would apologize for his bad behavior and woo her back. And if she were already with child, which was unlikely, it would be easy to convince her.

Swinging from the stagecoach, Draven landed in the muddy ooze of Etna's storm-darkened Main Street. Rain dripped from his hat and beaded on his wool overcoat. He worked the tension in his jaw and swore under his breath. So, this was where Vivian had escaped to? Could she have chosen a more drab, uncivilized, God-forsaken place? He needed a drink.

After checking into a room at the Blake Hotel, Draven swaggered across the rough-hewn, pine floorboards of the adjoining saloon and seated himself at the bar. Kerosene lanterns lent a slightly more cheerful air to the gloom, while a shoddily dressed man played a popular ragtime tune on the piano. Draven inhaled a hot meal, downed a beer, and studied the hoi polloi. Coarse, dusty men chawed plugs of tobacco. Weathered miners, lumberjacks, ranchers and cowboys drank, played cards, and flirted with barmaids. He observed that all the men wore hats, boots, spurs, and blue jeans, making him feel out of place in his felt bowler, starched shirt collar, and necktie. Even if he wouldn't be in town long, he made a mental note to purchase a "Boss of the Plains" hat and some spurs for his boots the following day. Fitting in with the crowd encouraged people to talk and he needed people to talk to him. When he'd finished his meal, he ordered a shot of whiskey.

A grizzled, old miner In dust-covered overalls hopped onto the stool next to him. "Where do ya hail from, young feller?" he asked, flashing his gapped teeth.

"Back east," Draven answered vaguely. "You wouldn't happen to know anyone in town answering to the name of Vivian Garrett, would you?"

The man threw back a shot of liquor. "No, sir, but if yer lookin' for fun, we've got some womenfolk 'round here who can show ya a good time, if ya know what I mean."

Draven ignored the man and looked across to the bartender. "Vivian Garrett," he said again. "Pretty, medium-blonde hair, seventeen. Have you seen her?"

"Nope." There was a drop of annoyance in the bartender's tone. "Don't sound familiar to me."

A beer mug slammed into the counter close to Draven's elbow. With great restraint, he managed not to react as a drunken, greasy-haired bloke leaned into his ear. "I hear yer lookin' fer a lady named Vivian," he slurred.

"That's what I said," Draven answered, repelled by the man's body odor.

"I might know where she is," said Greasy.

"Might ain't good enough."

"Knowin' fer sure will cost ya," Greasy said.

Draven refrained from making a snide remark and pulled a nickel from his vest pocket.

Wham! He was suddenly hit from behind and his chest slammed into the bar ledge. He swung round, his fist braced to pound whoever had launched the assault. Instead of facing a thug, he gaped at a petite, flaxen-blonde saloon girl, laughing uproariously where she sat in a tiny heap on the floor.

"Excuse me, mister!" the girl hollered with a shockingly ear-splitting volume. Patrons covered their ears. "I was doin' a little ragtime dance with this gentleman and lost my balance!"

"No need to shout, little lady," said Draven, still blinking in surprise.

"Oh, I'm not shoutin', mister. This is my regular voice. Ask anyone." She gestured to the nodding patrons and smoothed her mussed hair.

"Are you hard of hearing?" Draven asked.

"No, sir. I just talk loud." She chortled and displayed a coin. "Lookin' for this?"

Draven reached for the coin, but she pulled back her hand. "Be a gentleman and help me up first."

He tugged the girl to her feet.

"That's my nickel, Tessie," said Greasy.

"I don't think so," she said, handing it to Draven. "Here ya go, mister."

"Best get control of that dang voice of yers and keep out of other folks' business," Greasy bellyached.

Tessie pretended not to hear him. She adjusted her calf-length bar dress, revealing a good deal of skinny chicken leg.

"Best not try any more ragtime judging', miss," said Draven.

"I can dance just fine when I have a decent partner," she snorted. "And just who might you be, mister?" she asked, changing her tone to a coquettish purr that was still too high in volume.

"Draven Randall the Third, ma'am," he said, waving his hand above his head with a flourish.

Tessie made a half-circle around him, swaying her hips. "So formal and everythin'," she cooed. "Fancy businessman? Lawyer maybe?"

"Good guess," Draven allowed, leering. "I am indeed a man of the law."

"Tessie, do ya mind?" Greasy interrupted. "This gentleman and I was talkin' here."

"And you're from back east too, judging' from your accent," Tessie continued, ignoring Greasy. "What are ya doin' in these parts?"

Draven nodded to the empty stool beside him. "Join me for a drink, little lady. I'm doing a little business prospecting in Etna."

Tessie lighted onto the barstool. "Tell me more about this here prospectin', Mr. Draven Randall *the Third*. Are ya lookin' for gold?"

"Why don't you get back to work, Tessie?" Greasy urged.

"*I am* workin' here, Sneed," said Tessie irritably.

"Mr. Sneed, sir," said Draven, "I don't think I'll be needin' your assistance, after all."

Angry and swearing, Greasy stomped out of the saloon.

"Good riddance," said Tessie. "Now, where were we?" she asked in a sweeter tone.

Despite her decibel level, Draven was liking this little tart's attention. He put his elbow on the bartop and leaned into her face. "So, Miss Tessie, you wouldn't happen to know a young, East Coast dark blonde-haired lady in town by the name of Vivian Garret, would you?" he asked. "She's new in town, I hear."

"No, sir," she answered without a blink. "Iffen she's a real lady, I wouldn't know her." She laughed. "Ladies and me, we don't mix much."

"I see," said Draven, his insides beginning to salivate over the girl. "How about a woman named Vivian Randall?

"Randall?" Tessie's eyes popped. "Has your wife run away from ya or something'?"

"None of yer business," Draven growled.

Tessie slipped from her barstool and slunk around Draven, running playful fingers along his arm. "Can I interest ya in a game of poker with some of my friends?"

Tessie might be an impish child with an obnoxious set of lungs, but she was speaking his language. "I always like a good game of poker," he said, allowing himself to be led to the card table, where she introduced him to the other players: Silas Bowman, Earl Boyce, Oswald Davis, Harvey Winslow, and Matthew Wright. Draven seated himself and made another quick inquiry as to Vivian's whereabouts, but no one claimed to know her. He began to wonder if he'd come to the wrong town. He'd continue his investigation tomorrow. Tonight, he'd drink, gamble, and enjoy the captivating little Tessie.

CHAPTER 15: Warnings

Vivian awoke, vomited, and managed to settle her stomach with an early breakfast of dry toast and small sips of water. Pulling on a warm coat and tying a scarf around her head, she escaped into a morning thick with heavy, silvery drizzle. She carefully picked her way down the path to Etna Creek, where large, wet yellow maple leaves broke and spun heavily to the ground. She breathed in the earthy scent of rain-washed hayfields and crossed the footbridge before passing through a gate into the damp sog of Cocoa Joe McGovern's pastures. A light rain commenced, pattering loudly on her umbrella.

The reality of being a single, widowed mother was beginning to weigh on her. She didn't want to be beholden to anyone. Isabel would likely soon marry and start raising her own family, so she couldn't be a burden to her. She didn't want to be forced to settle down with a husband either, but how could she raise a baby on her own? As soon as she told Mr. McGovern she was pregnant, he'd probably fire her. Working women were already a rarity; pregnant working women were unheard of.

The morning was still a dull, dark gray and Tessie's predictable ghostly form flitted over the field in the distance, galloping bareback on a horse, disappearing and reappearing in the brume. "Vivian!" she cried breathlessly, sliding to plant her feet on the ground.

"Tessie, you must be freezing with no coat," said Vivian, unwrapping the scarf from her head and folding it around Tessie's shoulders.

"I didn't have time to think about the cold," she panted, placing a delicate hand on Vivian's arm and ducking to share the umbrella. "Someone's lookin' fer ya." Her tone was uncharacteristically quiet, and her eyes flashed with wild urgency.

Vivian jolted. "What do you mean?"

"A fancy man from back east is lookin' for ya." She paused to catch her breath. "His name is Mr. Draven Randall *the Third*."

Vivian weakened and grabbed Tessie's hand. "Did you tell him I was here?"

"No, ma'am," she replied. "I kept quiet and no one else in the saloon seemed to know ya either, 'cause he was askin' everybody for a Vivian Garrett or a Vivian Randall." Vivian's mouth went dry. "Miss Vivian, that Mr. Randall is a bad man. I sensed it right away. He's charmin', wears smart clothes, looks rich, talks educated, but he's a snake, sure as shootin'."

"Yes, he is," Vivian admitted, balling her hands into fists.

"Who is he?" Tessie asked.

"A secret from my past." The words barely escaped her lips.

"Are ya married to him?" Tessie questioned bluntly— and loudly.

"Sh! No, I'm not married to him, but—" Vivian couldn't finish her sentence.

"Ya don't have to tell me, Miss Vivian, but I'm afraid for ya. He seems mighty determined to find ya, comin' all the way across the country." She pulled Vivian toward town. "He's stayin' at the Blake Hotel. It's so close to you and Miss Isabel. You shouldn't be out walking by yourself. I don't think you're safe with that man around. I think he's dangerous."

Vivian's mind reeled. Why was Draven here? And why was he looking for her? What if he told people here the truth about their one-night fake marriage? He would destroy her—and Isabel.

The gas lamps still flickered in the pre-dawn gloom as they crossed Main Street.

"Is he a former beau?" asked Tessie. "Never mind. I don't mean to pry. I guess he must have known ya before you was married to your late husband, Mr. Smith. Do ya think he's still in love with ya? No, never mind. Ya don't have to tell me."

"Tessie, your voice is too loud," Vivian shushed. "Let's not talk about this here." She had so many questions. What if Draven actually did love her? What if he had good intentions? She quickly disregarded that nonsense. Draven had never loved her. No, he wanted something. *Needed* something to come all this way to look for her. She thanked Tessie for the warning. "That's twice you've been kind to me, Miss Blackman."

"It's no trouble. I'm just glad ya don't mind bein' around me with my bad reputation and all."

Vivian laughed wryly. "Have you noticed that my own reputation isn't so pristine either?"

"It ain't so bad, Widow Smith," said Tessie, "even though folks are still talkin' about the clumsy suffragette widow who was nearly killed in a cattle drive."

Vivian shook her head. Folks knew she was Isabel's sister, and they'd soon point Draven to their apartment. People knew her as Widow Smith. Draven would put two and two together. He'd suspect her of being pregnant if she were pretending to be a widow, and he'd know the baby was his. She ran tremulous fingers over her forehead. She needed to find him before he exposed her.

Tessie rubbed her arms and chattered her teeth.

"Go home and get warm," said Vivian.

"I will," said Tessie, "but may I ask you a question, Widow Smith, ma'am?"

"Of course."

"I've noticed that no one has better manners than you and I need me some lessons in etiquette. Will ya teach me?" Vivian nearly choked on her surprise. "The fact is, I can't get a single man to ask me to the ball and I'm guessin' it's on account of my bad manners and bad reputation. Iffen you could help me, I might be able to go back to school, quit my job, get myself an education, and maybe even find a husband."

Vivian felt her sympathies tugging to the poor girl. "Oh, Tessie, of course I'll help you. It would be my pleasure, but I might have to leave town suddenly on account of Draven Randall."

"Oh, I hope not," Tessie said with anger in her tone. "If anyone should leave town, it's him."

"I agree, but I may not have a choice. Let's plan to meet this evening at my place for at least one lesson."

Tessie smiled gratefully and agreed. "How much should I pay ya?"

"Payment won't be necessary but, Tessie, I wonder if we might make a trade."

"What kind of trade?"

"Flirting," said Vivian, lowering her voice. "I'm terrible at it. I wonder if you could teach me a few things."

Tessie's face radiated. "I'd be happy to, ma'am. I have noticed ya could use a little help."

Vivian bit back a retort and waved goodbye to the shivering girl as she flitted away around a corner. Was she really that bad at flirting? And how would Tessie know?

She bent to pick up a bottle of milk left on the stoop and climbed the stairs to the apartment. She had to find Draven. What if he apologized and took her back? Maybe he'd treat her well. She shuddered. No, like Tessie said, he was dangerous. For all she cared, he could go to... Well, he could go back to Philadelphia.

****

"What's wrong with scratch paper and an abacus?" Mr. Cocoa Joe McGovern sputtered.

The morning meeting with her boss was not going as Vivian hoped. "Well, sir, I don't mind using an abacus, but I could do my work twice as fast with one of those new Burroughs calculating machines. My father taught me how to use one. They're very modern and useful."

Mr. McGovern yawned and stretched. "All right. Find out how much they cost and I'll see if me budget can allow for it."

The door opened and a messenger interrupted. "Telegram for Widow Vivian Smith," he announced, proffering a cable.

Vivian crushed a pang of apprehension and muttered her thanks as she snatched the telegram. It was from her friend Sarah and read:

Draven coming to Etna. 3 fake marriages. Heir to gfather fortune if son.

Vivian sank into her chair. She already knew Draven was here, but had he really tricked two other women into believing they were married? What a brute! And what did "heir" mean? Oh—he would inherit his grandfather's fortune if he had a son? This must be why he'd come to town looking for her.

"Is everything all right, missy?" Cocoa Joe asked gently. "Did ye lose a loved one?"

"No, no one has died, but I've had a bit of a shock," she said, folding the telegram and stowing it in her drawstring purse.

"Do ye need to take the rest of the day off?" Cocoa Joe inquired. He asked Li Wei to serve her a cup of tea.

"No, I'll be fine. I just need a moment to collect my thoughts."

Someone knocked and opened the office door. He stood on the stoop, wiping his feet. "Got a minute, boss?" he asked.

"Howdy, Rabbi Ry'," said Cocoa Joe. "Come on in."

Vivian glanced up to see Blue standing in the doorway. She ducked her head and pulled her bonnet down over her eyes, pretending to work. She was in no mood to see or talk to anyone, much less Blue, and he still didn't know she worked here.

"Is Rabbi Ry' your nickname for me, boss?" asked Blue. "The name *Blue* isn't unusual enough for you?" Vivian heard the teasing smile in his voice.

"On account of ye bein' a preacher, son."

"Works for me," Blue chuckled.

The warmth of Blue's laughter somewhat displaced the chill of Draven's ghost. Vivian took a deep breath and listened as the men discussed shipments of hay, calving, and other ranch-related tasks.

"Blue, me boy," said Cocoa Joe, "have ye met me accountant, Widow Smith?"

Vivian bit her lip and lifted her eyes to Blue's face, gratified at the surprise in his wide eyes, yet angry that her pulse was so loud, she could barely hear or think straight. He had a very strange effect on her organs.

"Well, I'll be," said Blue, his face breaking into a broad smile. "Yes, sir, I've had the pleasure of meeting Widow Smith."

"It's good to see you again, sir," Vivian returned, blushing and pressing her lips together.

Blue said goodbye and was about to make his departure when the door opened, and Samantha propelled herself into the office with her mother following close behind. A suffocating smell invaded the room. Vivian blinked back burning tears. Cocoa Joe sneezed, blew his nose, and rose to greet them, introducing his wife to both Vivian and Blue as "me Sally Sweet Pea." Vivian watched as Samantha cocked her head, touched Blue's arm, and twittered playfully and brazenly—right in front of her own parents. It was appalling.

"Father," Samantha said charmingly, "do you mind if I hang a Harvest Ball poster in your office window?"

"Don't mind at all, Sassafras."

"Will you be attending the ball, Mr. Ryan?" Samantha asked too sweetly.

"I hadn't heard of it…but…well, I suppose," he answered haltingly. "Sounds like fun."

"Oh, it will be," said Samantha, her face lighting up with mischief. She swung her hips as she pranced across the floor with a poster and a jar of paste. Dabbing the sticky goo onto the corners of the paper, she plastered it to a window, chattering about past balls. Vivian tried to ignore Samantha's obvious machinations toward Blue but was pleased he hadn't asked Samantha to the dance.

Li Wei paced quietly and unobtrusively into the room, laid out a tray of tea for everyone, including Blue, Samantha, and Sally. The servant bowed and retreated as silently as he had entered.

Blue declined the offer of tea despite the invitations. "It was nice to meet you, Miss McGovern; Mrs. McGovern," he said, "but I need to be getting back to work." He jerked his chin at Vivian. "Good day, Widow Smith."

"Good day," Vivian replied, ducking her head and averting her eyes from Samantha's hostile glare.

"You wouldn't attend the ball, would you, Widow Smith?" Samantha asked pertly as Blue opened the door to make his departure. "I mean, it wouldn't be proper for a widow, would it?"

Vivian noticed Blue's pause in the doorway. "I do plan to attend, actually," she said quickly before Blue shut the door behind him.

Mrs. McGovern pulled her husband into the back room for a moment, and Samantha jumped on the opportunity to verbally attack Vivian: "You keep away from Mr. Graver and

Mr. Ryan, you little black widow spider," she threatened. "Do you understand me?" Vivian could only gape. No one had ever spoken to her like that before.

"I...I..." Vivian stuttered. She sucked in her breath and squarely faced the impertinent nemesis. "All's fair, Samantha," she said through gritted teeth.

Samantha huffed loudly and shook a finger in Vivian's face. "This is both love *and* war, Widow Smith." *Yes, it is*, Vivian agreed silently, staring defiantly into Samantha's eyes. "And I won't hesitate to remind every bachelor of your suffragette ways if you try to interfere with their plans to court me."

"Understood," said Vivian.

Mr. and Mrs. McGovern reentered the office, and Samantha caught her mother's elbow. "Come, Mother. We're finished here and we have more errands to run."

Vivian watched her boss's daughter sashay across the farmyard, rocking her hips and making her skirts swing. She looked utterly ridiculous, but that didn't stop every man's eyes from fixing on her—including Blue's.

Isabel stewed. She drew the curtains, paced, and complained that someone might see Tessie enter their building.

"Who cares?" asked Vivian. "If anyone does see her, they'll just think she's visiting the laundry downstairs."

"But what if someone hears her obnoxious voice up here in our apartment?" Isabel fretted.

"They won't," said Vivian. "Look, I need help, and she needs help. The poor girl really does want to better herself."

"I admire your wanting to help her, Vivi. Really, I do. But we must be careful. We can't afford to tarnish our reputations. With your situation and all you've done to embarrass us already, we're on shaky ground as it is."

"I understand better than you know," Vivian grumbled. She'd spent the better part of the afternoon searching for Draven but hadn't found him anywhere. And, of course, she didn't dare tell Isabel he was in town. She'd have an absolute fit. Thankfully, Vivan was pretty sure Isabel wouldn't recognize him if she saw him.

When Tessie arrived, she and Vivian exchanged lessons in flirtation and etiquette, while Isabel busied herself in the kitchen. Tessie learned how to hold back from speaking everything on her mind; Vivian learned more about smiling and making coy eye contact with men.

After their lessons, Tessie shared more about her life and how she'd quit school to work after her father died. Her mother had taken ill, and someone had to care for her. The only job she could find as a woman in this town was as a saloon girl. It was a sobering story, but the subject quickly turned to the upcoming ball and what eligible young men might be willing to escort Tessie. Vivian worried she was raising Tessie's hopes. And, if she was anything worse than a saloon girl, she didn't dare go anywhere in public with her.

"There's Mr. Graver," Vivian suggested.

"Mr. Graver?" Tessie wrinkled her nose.

"Yes," said Vivian. "Don't you think he's nice-looking?"

"I'll agree his *face* is handsome enough, and I simply adore his horse. He rides a lovely Saddlebred named Billie Belle. He bought her from—"

"Tessie, you and your obsession with horses," laughed Vivian. "We were talking about Mr. Graver."

"Oh, yes, well, like I was sayin', his *face* is purty, but he has somethin' wrong with his…you know." Tessie's voice stumbled. "It ain't proper to say, Widow Smith."

"It's all right if we're not in public," Vivian prompted, wondering if Tessie had made a similar observation of Mr. Graver's "gross" anatomy.

"There's somethin' wrong with his backside, Widow Smith. Did ya see him that day when the boys were skinny dippin'?"

"Sh!" Vivian leaned forward and clapped a hand over Tessie's mouth. "Never speak of that horrid day." She slid her eyes to Isabel, who was working in the kitchen, and spoke in a lower tone. "And I did *not* see Mr. Graver's…you know." It was true; she hadn't seen him in the nude. Thank the Lord.

"Well, I did," said Tessie, her nose scrunching. "First time I saw him, I thought he was wearin' an extra-long shirt stuffed in his trousers, but then I saw his hind end when he was swimmin' and—" She shook her head. "Oh, my land, no foolin'! It looked like a woman's buttocks. His conformation is off."

Vivian clapped a hand over Tessie's mouth again.

Tessie lowered her voice a notch. "You look at his face and the rest of his slim physique and ya think he'd make a fine catch and then—"

"And then he turns sideways?"

"Exactly!" said Tessie. "He really is too…I don't know. Too—"

"Well-endowed?"

They giggled till tears spilled from their eyes.

"Poor Mr. Graver," said Vivian.

"Poor *Mrs*. Graver!" snorted Tessie.

Vivian chewed her lip. She tried to imagine being married to Martin Graver with his oversized rump and blew out her cheeks. Whoever married him would have to seriously alter his garments or be so in love as to be content to overlook this singular flaw.

Tessie yawned. "It's late, Widow Smith. I've gotta go."

"Wait, Tessie." Before she left, Vivian had to ask a nagging question. She kept her voice very low. "Please forgive me for asking this, but can you tell me…? You're not a…a prostitute, are you?"

"What! Certainly not!" Tessie squealed. "I'm a saloon girl, that's all!"

Vivian shushed her. "I'm sorry I offended you. I just wanted clarification."

"My ma would skin me alive iffen I was to go and be one of *them*," she protested.

"I'm sorry I asked such an impertinent question," said Vivian. "I just wanted to be certain."

Tessie's lips drew downward, and creases formed between her eyes. "I guess I don't blame ya. I'm sure you've heard awful rumors about me."

"I won't believe any of them," said Vivian. "I just wanted the truth directly from you." She changed the subject. "Tessie, there's one more thing. I want you to attend the ball." She didn't tell her that Martin was her escort. "You teach me to flirt as much as you can until the ball and I'll keep teaching you lessons in etiquette. I'll find an escort for you."

Tessie clapped her hands together. "I wanna go to the ball more than anythin', but…"

"But what?" asked Vivian.

"But would your sister be comin' with us and would she want to be seen with me?"

Vivian saw Isabel jump. Though her back was to them, she'd probably heard Tessie's remark. How could she not?

"Don't worry about Izza," whispered Vivian. "I'll talk to her."

Isabel padded over and raised her hand like an inquiring schoolgirl. "May I interrupt?" She cleared her throat. "I don't know if it would be proper for you to attend the dance with us, Tessie, but I overheard some of what you were teaching Vivi, and the truth is, I think I need to learn some of your flirtation skills. And I can help you with your etiquette, too. May I join you?"

Tessie's mouth dropped open. Vivian's did as well.

"Of course!" Tessie cried. "I'm happy to help ya both!"

Vivian gave her sister a quizzical look, but Isabel refrained from eye contact.

"Izza, what happened? Have you changed your tune about Tessie?" Vivian asked after Tessie left.

"She's actually quite sweet," Isabel admitted. "Mind you, I'm very nervous about ever being seen with her in public, and I'm anxious about gossip, but she seems nice. Even innocent. She needs our help, and the fact that she wants to be in school to finish her education is commendable."

"Ah, I see," said Vivian. "It's her lack of access to education that tugs at your heartstrings."

"And the loss of her father, and the fact that she's forced to work to care for her mother," Isabel added. "It's all too sad."

"And you could use her help too, right?"

"Well, she did say a few things about flirting I'd never considered."

"And her flirtation skills weren't too shocking," said Vivian.

"Yes," Isabel admitted. "I thought she offered very practical advice about how to win a man's heart."

"But the question remains—" Vivian started to say, but Isabel finished her sentence…

"Will anyone ask us to the ball?"

Vivian still hadn't told her about Martin. She would wait to tell her and Tessie. First, she needed to pay Cade a little matchmaking visit. And maybe she could help her sister too.

CHAPTER 16: Fears & Flirtations

After vomiting again that morning, Vivian needed the fresh air to clear her head. Tiptoeing warily out the door, she ventured another walk alone in Cocoa Joe's fields. Though her nerves crackled, she told herself it was silly to fear that Draven would be awake and about this early in the morning or that he'd ever go into a cow pasture.

Slogging through the murky fields, she imagined that she was safe and protected from Draven, or anyone else, amongst the docile, cud-chewing cattle that were no longer fearful enemies but had become more like comforting friends.

Draven. Falling for him revealed Vivian's complete lack of discernment, while Tessie had known right away the man was dangerous. Why didn't she have such discernment? She hoped her judgment wasn't off concerning Blue.

But, back to Draven. Would he want her back for the sake of a baby? Not for a baby, but for his inheritance? Probably. If he took her back and she gave birth to a girl, however, what would he do? Throw them both out? And what if she refused to go back to him and he later found out she had a baby? If it were a girl, he wouldn't care, but if she had a boy, could he take the baby from her? She hugged her arms tightly over her abdomen. If she were pregnant, and she probably was, she must never tell Draven. Son or daughter, who knew what he might do?

Crossing the pasture, Vivian arrived at the far edge near the stile and did an about-face to commence her trek back home. The first hints of daylight painted the haze a delicate violet and she slowed her pace to watch a robin hop its way through the grass and peck at the damp earth.

All at once, the bulky shadow of a man swam into view, disappearing again in swirls of mist. A chill crept over the surface of her skin, and she crouched low, covering her head with the hood of her cloak. Bobbing amongst the cattle, she moved stealthily across the pasture toward home. Hostile or not, she didn't want to risk running into an intruder.

The dark figure reappeared in the fog. Whoever it was, he was close. Too close. Blood throbbed in her ears, and she hunched behind a cow. Peeking over its back, she watched, waited, listened. A muffled rhythm of metal clinked. Spurs. She breathed more easily. Draven never wore spurs. She wasn't even sure he could ride a horse.

But the stranger suddenly gave a terrific whoop and the cows around them spooked, rumbling as they scattered in all directions. For a second, she felt exposed, but she hunched down and jogged alongside a cow as it lumbered across the grass—another jangle of spurs. The man was closer now. She peeked over the cow's back and his black hair, neatly trimmed goatee, hat, and long slicker swam into view. It couldn't be Draven. But it was! She dropped to the moist earth. From her vantage point beneath the cow, Draven was no more than ten yards from her. Had he seen her?

He whooped again, startling the herd and driving them away. He must have seen her. She should face him here and now, but fear strangled her. She didn't want to be alone with him here. It wasn't safe. She ducked and ran, praying he wouldn't chase her, but she'd lost her bearings. Where was the gate? Her hood blew off. Standing on tiptoe, she spied the gate several yards ahead, blocked by a huddle of confused, stomping bovines. She slapped them on their rumps, and they staggered aside, allowing her to weave through their midst.

When Draven's shadowy form appeared to her left, she panicked, but there was the gate in front of her. She propelled over it, stumbled, and continued running. The fog was exceptionally thick above the creek bed, and she hoped she was invisible to Draven as she raced across the footbridge and up the long, steep bank to Main Street. Her pulse flooded and pounded in her head as she listened for the jangling of Draven's spurs and begged God to keep him away.

As she thrust herself over the threshold of her building, she cast a quick look over her shoulder. Draven was nowhere to be seen. She slammed the door and nearly collapsed with relief and fatigue. Panting, she steadied her heartbeat before peeking back through a crack in the door. He was still nowhere to be seen, so she grabbed the bottle of milk on the stoop and sprinted up the stairs, bolting the door behind her.

Isabel rushed to her side. "Vivi, what's wrong? You look like you've seen a ghost and you're soaking wet!" She walked her to the sofa, helped her out of her wet clothes, and wrapped her in a warm blanket. Vivian shook uncontrollably and, at Isabel's insistence, confessed what had happened in the pasture. What she didn't tell her was that it was Draven.

Vivian sipped a cup of hot cocoa and Isabel scolded, comforted, and begged her not to go out alone again. But Vivian wasn't listening. She knew she had to find Draven and speak with him on her terms—in broad daylight in a safe, semi-public location. But what exactly should she say to him? As soon as he saw she was pretending to be a widow, he'd assume she was pregnant. She needed to come up with a convincing story to tell him.

Having completed her work for the day, Vivian opened her umbrella and left Cocoa Joe's office into a sloppy downpour. She trotted up China Hill and halted when she approached Mary's hut. It was time to pay the woman a visit. Climbing the porch steps of the tiny house, she reached out her hand to knock at the same time that the stout woman opened the door and bowed.

"The yonggan come," said Mary. "I am waiting for you. Please." She beckoned for Vivian to enter.

Wariness crept through her. Was China Mary clairvoyant? She crept inside and took in the pungent aroma of sweet and bitter herbs and spices. Clear glass jars filled with dried flowers, sticks, weeds, and gnarled, twisted, shriveled objects lined the shelving that covered two walls of the cabin. A crude ladder and long bench were pressed against one set of shelves. The one-room shelter was sparsely furnished and, for such a small space, remarkably clutter-free. A fire crackled in the woodstove and a teapot steamed on its surface. A table stood against a wall, a stool at one end, a larger chair at the other. Against a third wall was a bed built high above the floor, where boxes, blankets, and linens lay neatly stacked beneath it.

"Sit!" China Mary commanded, pointing to the stool at the table. She chose several jars from a shelf and arranged them on the table. One by one, she opened the lids and removed all manner of oddities, dropping the stuff into a teacup and pouring hot water over the contents. She heaved herself onto the larger chair, slid the teacup to Vivian, and leaned back, her eyes hidden behind the screen of her lashes. "You finally come, yonggan. You have trouble. You drink tea and tell China Mary about it."

Vivian swallowed. "I haven't much time. I have an appointment this afternoon."

"First, you drink tea and talk."

Vivian lifted the teacup and stared into its muddy depths.

"It not hurt you," said Mary, rattling off a string of foreign words.

Vivian took a deep breath and ventured a small sip. The odor of the tea was strong and the flavor sharply spiced, but it was warm and comforting.

Mary's expression was humorless. "I know you have baby."

Vivian's mouth dropped. "What? How?"

Mary smiled wryly. "I have eyes."

"You know for certain?" Vivian asked.

She gave a curt nod. "You trust China Mary, yonggan." Her eyes ran all over her like strokes of a paintbrush. "I hear you are widow."

"Yes, ma'am."

"How many months?"

"About two." Saying it aloud sent a small shock through her body. If Mary was correct, she'd be holding a baby in her arms in a mere seven months.

The Chinese woman examined Vivian's head, face, tongue, ears, nose, hands, and fingernails. "Yes, you have baby, yonggan," she stated firmly," palpating her abdomen.

Vivian closed her eyes and sat motionless for several beats as her fingers gripped the seat of her chair. "What does yonggan mean?" Vivian asked.

"It mean brave. You very brave little lady."

Vivian was skeptical. "How do you know I'm brave? How do you know anything about me?"

"You work in man's world," said Mary.

"Oh, that." Vivian shrugged. "I don't think that's brave. It's pure necessity. I'm glad my father taught me how to balance books."

"Hm." Creases formed between Mary's eyes. "You brave and honest."

Vivian lowered her head. China Mary must not be clairvoyant after all. She was an imposter lying to everyone.

Mary continued her interrogation with a dozen other questions before abruptly changing the subject. "Yonggan, you do big, brave thing to work for Cocoa Joe and you fight to help woman. People little afraid of you and gossip, but they big respect you." She handed a jar to Vivian. "Chinese medicine to protect you and baby." She scooted her chair away from Vivian and narrowed her gaze. "I sorry for you lose husband."

"Thank you," said Vivian, shuddering with dishonesty.

"You look for new man to marry?"

Vivian's chest tightened a little. "I don't know."

"Baby need a father."

"Maybe," said Vivian.

"You will find good, kind man."

"Are you a fortuneteller?" asked Vivian, incredulous.

"No, but you must be very wise when choose new husband. Very wise indeed."

Vivian ate a quick lunch before setting out to look for Draven. On her walk to the Blake Hotel, she questioned China Mary's confirmation of pregnancy and her enigmatic words. Could she trust the woman's diagnosis, and should she take the advice to remarry for the sake of her baby? If she wasn't pregnant, there was no need to hurry to find a husband. If she were pregnant, her widow's scheme was a good one, because it kept pressure off her need to find a husband. However, finding a husband would be best for Isabel's sake—and the baby's.

A quick look through the Blake Hotel registry confirmed that Draven was indeed a guest. Bile rose in her throat, and she barely resisted the urge to retch into a spittoon. If Draven caught her vomiting, it would only fuel his suspicions.

The lobby was a safe, quiet, public place. She took a seat and pretended to read the newspaper while she rehearsed what she would say. She could tell Draven she'd been foolish to worry about pregnancy and laugh it off. She could complain about being stuck in drab mourning clothes in spite of not being pregnant. Maybe Draven would believe her and simply leave town.

But how should she act? If she acted too hurt or angry, she might provoke his temper. If she pretended to be happy to see him, would that make her look weak? Should she ask if he had ever loved her?

For nearly two hours, she fretted over every possibility—until it became clear that Draven wasn't coming. Defeated, she returned home to prepare supper.

After the evening meal, as she and her sister cleaned the kitchen, Vivian entered Isabel's bedroom, rummaged through the wardrobe, and pulled out a pale blue satin gown. She carried it into the parlor with a triumphant smile.

"What do you think, Izza?" She draped the gown over the sofa. "Won't this go perfectly with Tessie's light gray eyes?"

Isabel nodded in agreement as footsteps shuffled in the stairwell.

"Howdy, Miss Vivian and Miss Isabel!" Tessie boomed as she entered the apartment.

Isabel and Vivian winced at the volume of her greeting. It was one thing about Tessie that would have to be remedied straightaway.

As Vivian took their guest's damp coat and hung it by the door, Tessie's gaze was drawn to the gown.

"Oh, I ain't never seen such a beautiful dress in all my life! Fit for a queen!" She cut herself off abruptly, then added, "I got a right fancy dress for the ball too, of course. I'll be wearin' one of my saloon dresses."

Vivian and Isabel exchanged horrified glances. Gently, they explained why a saloon dress simply would not do.

Vivian held out the blue gown. "It's yours to borrow, Tessie. To wear to the ball."

Tessie stared, stunned, her eyes misting. "I might actually look like a real lady," she murmured, for once uncharacteristically quiet.

She took the dress into Isabel's room and returned a moment later, transformed.

"You look pretty as a picture," Isabel said.

"Like a princess," Vivian agreed.

But dressing like a lady did not a lady make. When Isabel asked her to walk across the parlor, Tessie clomped like a bow-legged cowgirl.

Isabel shook her head. "We need to work on your walk, Tessie."

Tessie jammed her fists into her hips. "What's wrong with the way I walk?"

Vivian placed a book on Tessie's head. "Try walking now."

Unsurprisingly, Tessie had excellent balance.

"This is easy," she remarked.

"Good," Isabel said. "Now do it again—without the book."

Tessie obeyed but immediately stiffened. "I feel ridiculous."

"And yet your posture is much improved," Vivian encouraged.

Next came sitting.

Tessie scoffed. "Everyone knows how to sit."

"Not everyone knows how to sit properly," Isabel countered.

"Believe it or not," Vivian added, "you can make people uncomfortable just by how you sit, walk, or stand."

"And talk. And eat," Isabel chimed in.

"And dress," Vivian finished.

Tessie groaned. "I must offend folks all the time."

Isabel and Vivian nodded.

"I was jokin'!" Tessie huffed.

"We weren't," Isabel said.

With a dramatic sigh, Tessie changed back into her day dress, and they continued the etiquette lesson—elbows off the table, legs together, no swinging arms while walking.

"It's all too much to remember," Tessie howled. "Am I doin' anything right?"

"You don't wear too much perfume," Vivian offered.

Tessie snickered. "Ya mean like a certain boss's daughter we all know?"

"Let's not gossip," Vivian chided.

"Arrgh!" Tessie groaned. "I can't remember all this. What's my worst habit? Can't I just fix that?"

"Your worst habit is the way you eat, I think," Isabel began.

But Vivian interrupted: "No, it's the volume of your voice, Tessie."

She looked genuinely shocked. "What's wrong with my voice?"

Isabel hesitated, then spoke carefully. "Your loudness can make you sound shrill… or angry."

"But I ain't mad at all!"

"Exactly," Vivian said. "We know that, but you don't want people to think you are."

"And judging me for it," Tessie added.

"Exactly," Vivian and Isabel replied in unison.

The sisters coaxed Tessie to practice speaking more softly, but she only ended up hoarse. There was no way to effectively tone down her volume overnight. Hopefully, she'd improve enough before the ball.

The final lesson of the night was table manners. They practiced drinking punch and nibbling cookies without waving them around mid-conversation.

"Arrgh!" Tessie barked histrionically. "I need a break from all this. Can I get back to teachin' you two the art of seduction instead?"

"Oh, no!" Isabel gasped. "You can't say that word in polite society!"

Tessie frowned. "What word? Seduction?"

"Yes!"

Tessie threw her hands in the air. "Everything I say is offensive! Fine—the art of flirtation, then."

Isabel exhaled. "Much better."

Tessie smirked. "Now listen. I've watched you two in town, and—" She shook her head, clicking her tongue. "You're makin' some big mistakes. Big, big mistakes."

Vivian tried not to laugh at Tessie's theatrics.

"For one thing," Tessie continued, "you don't smile much. And when you do, it don't look happy or interested."

"Anything else?" Isabel asked dryly.

"Yeah. Eye contact. Always look a man in the eye."

"Even when flirting?" Vivian asked.

"Especially when flirtin'," Tessie said.

Isabel crossed her arms. "Does that actually work?"

"Well," Tessie admitted, "real gentlemen don't fall at my feet on account of my bad reputation. But I can get any saloon man interested in a heartbeat." She winked. "Men don't need much 137ncouraging'."

"What about batting your eyelashes?" Vivian asked.

"Oh, don't never do that." Tessie wrinkled her nose. "You'll look like you got a nervous tick."

Vivian winced. "Oh dear."

Tessie yawned and stretched. "One more thing before I go." She turned to Vivian. "It's about yer women's sufferin'."

"Suffrage," Vivian corrected.

"Right. You can still be a suffragette, but don't talk about it when you're courtin'. You'll scare men away."

"Vivi, she's right," said Isabel. "Listen to her."

"Izza, you believe in suffrage too, or you wouldn't have moved out west as a single, independent woman."

"Beside the point," Isabel argued.

"Yes," Tessie continued. "My point is that men like to feel like knights in shinin' armor protectin' damsels in distress like that hero who rescued ya from the cattle stampede that day."

"Ugh," said Vivian, "don't remind me of that embarrassing incident."

"I thought it was romantic," Tessie sighed wistfully. I'm just sayin' to let a gentleman help ya and let him be heroic like ya did that day. Let men open doors for ya or help ya out of wagons. Stuff like that."

As they bid Tessie goodnight, Vivian turned down the kerosene lamp on the kitchen table.

"I like her," Isabel said. "If I were a teacher, I'd take her as my student in a heartbeat."

She paused. "Vivi… have you seen this hero of yours since he rescued you that day?"

Vivian hesitated. "Once or twice," she said lightly. She wasn't ready to tell Isabel that he worked at Cocoa Joe's ranch.

CHAPTER 17: School

*G*ray clouds hung low, thick with the presentiment of rain, muting the morning light. Not wanting to risk running into Draven alone again, Vivian skipped her usual walk in the pasture in favor of a trip to the local school. She squared her shoulders. Today, she had work to do.

When she arrived, the yard was filled with children. She climbed the steps and entered the medium-sized schoolhouse with its large foyer and two classrooms on either side of a short hallway. She stepped to a door that was open just a crack. Placing her hand on the doorknob, she froze. A soft, low choking moan broke the silence, and she peeked through the crack. Mr. Oswald Davis was kissing Miss Beatty! She backed away from the door, but the canoodling couple's eyes were on her. They knew they'd been caught.

"Stop!" Mr. Davis lunged, his fingers biting into her arm. "Don't tell anyone about this!"

"Let go of me!" She twisted free, her pulse hammering.

Miss Beatty cowered behind Oswald, her face ashen as she clasped her hands imploringly. "Please don't tell anyone," she pleaded.

The head teacher and principal, Miss Hatch, appeared in the hallway just then, demanding to know everything. Vivian stepped aside and watched as Miss Hatch hauled the truth from their mouths. Vivian didn't have to say a word.

A weary expression overcame the principal's face. "Mr. Davis, please remove yourself from the premises immediately. Miss Beatty, I'm placing you on probation and sending you home this instant. I'll call for an emergency board meeting this evening. I request that you attend, Miss Beatty. Due to your impropriety, there will be no school for the upper grades until further notice."

Oswald and Miss Beatty left, and Mrs. Hatch turned her attention to Vivian, asking if she knew Mrs. Barbara Mitchell and Mr. Joe McGovern, whom she did. "Please inform them that there will be a board meeting this evening at seven o'clock in my classroom and that it's an emergency session. Don't give them any details."

Vivian assented and left the school. So much for helping Tessie get permission to rejoin the school. But providence might have just changed Isabel's situation. Her sister might be able to teach at the school sooner than expected—and that would help Tessie too.

She glanced at her watch. There was no time to speak to Barbara Mitchell, nor did she really want to. She headed to work to talk with Cocoa Joe instead.

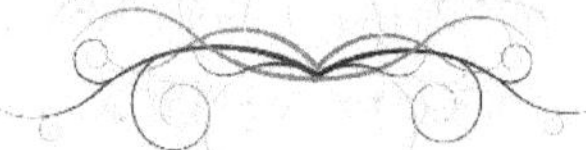

When Vivian told her boss about Miss Beatty and Mr. Davis, he spat into the spittoon before speaking. "Don't tell that nosy gossip, Babs, anything. I'll make sure she's the last board member to know about the meetin' so there's less chance of her spreadin' rumors beforehand."

Vivian nodded perceptively. Though their conversation ended, memories of Draven hunting her down in Cocoa Joe's pasture made it impossible for her to concentrate on work. She watched cowboys and other employees come and go in the farmyard.

"Somethin' is a botherin' ye, wee lass," Cocoa Joe said kindly, removing his spectacles and leaning forward on his desk. "Is it this business at the schoolhouse?"

"I'm sorry," Vivian apologized. She decided to be honest and confess to walking in his pasture and encountering the "mysterious" intruder.

To her surprise, Cocoa Joe was angered. He stood and paced, swearing and scolding. "Ye should not have been a-walkin' in me fields without me permission," he bellowed. She hung her head. He was nice enough to forgive her but warned her to stay off his land. "I don't want ye gettin' into danger, lassie. In fact, just to make certain ye are safe, I want one of me ranch lads to walk ye to and from work every day for at least the next two weeks." She argued that it would be broad daylight, high noon, and perfectly safe to walk alone after work, but he insisted, saying he'd do the same for his own daughter.

"Let me take Bobo with me instead," she begged. "I'll be safe enough with him."

"Ye can take him, of course. He might even sleep on your doorstep, if ye like, but ye must have an escort to walk ye to and from work, lassie."

"But I can't walk in public with a man without a chaperone," Vivian complained.

"Me man *is* your chaperone, Miss Vivi Honeybee!" Cocoa Joe blustered.

"Vivi Honeybee?"

"Ha! Ha! Haaaaa!" he laughed heartily, abruptly changing his tone and slapping his thigh. "I think it fits ye. Vivi Honeybee. Because men buzz to ye like bees to honey."

Vivian shook her head and allowed the hint of a smile to touch her lips.

Tom Kohl arrived at that moment and Cocoa Joe asked him to walk Vivian home. "There was a mysterious man walkin' in me pasture and scarin' our Vivi Honeybee half out of her wits."

"I wasn't scared half out of my wits," Vivian objected indignantly, but neither listened.

At noon, Vivian was gathering her things when Blue stepped into the office. Sparks shivered through her body, and her fingers tightened on her pen before she forced herself to relax.

"Mr. McGovern, Tom Kohl had a change of plans and can't walk Widow Smith home. Do you mind if I do the honors?"

Vivian emitted a small cough as a flood of heat ricocheted through her.

"Thank ye, Rabbi Ry'," said Cocoa Joe. "And take Bobo with ye."

"Tom says a mysterious man frightened you half out of your wits," said Blue as they walked across the yard with the shaggy Bobo in tow.

"I was not scared half out of my wits," Vivian protested with an edge in her tone.

"I suppose you'll be more careful from now on, then?" he asked.

"And stop accidentally running into strangers on my morning walks?" she asked.

"Hm. Good point," he grinned. "I didn't scare you half out of your wits, did I?"

"No one has ever scared me half out of my wits."

"Hm," he chuckled. "Nice of you to let me know we work together at Cocoa Joe's ranch."

"I recently discovered it myself."

They were passing China Mary's shanty, where the Chinese woman sat on her porch, smoking a pipe. Mary waved and Vivian waved back.

"You know China Mary?" Blue asked.

"Yes," she said hesitantly. "Do you disapprove?"

"Not at all," he said. "I consider her a friend."

"Really?" Vivian was surprised.

"She's a good woman," said Blue.

"I think so too," she agreed.

A breeze picked up and it began to sprinkle. Vivian opened her umbrella and Blue offered to hold it for her. She almost protested but remembered Tessie's advice to let a man be chivalrous. "Thank you," she said simply.

They walked a few paces in silence. The nearness of his body, and the press of his shoulder against hers flashed desire through her veins and she struggled to swallow before posing a question. "Why couldn't Mr. Kohl walk me home?"

"Would you rather he did?"

"You're evading my question," said Vivian, frustrated with the tightness in her voice.

"You're evading *my* question."

"Why couldn't Mr. Kohl walk me home?" Vivian persisted.

"Tom told me your story and I asked if I could walk you home instead."

Her heart froze for a whisper of a moment. "So, Mr. Ryan," she said when she was able to speak again, "tell me a little more about yourself."

As they turned onto Main Street with Bobo lagging behind them, she listened to Blue share about his brothers, sisters, and parents. When there was a lull in the conversation, she looked up at him and the hairs of her head prickled under the weight of his gaze.

"Widow Smith, is it too soon for me to ask about your late husband, Oscar?" he prompted sympathetically.

Oh, dear. She had rehearsed a good story, but under Blue's gaze, it felt flimsy. "I don't know if I can talk about him."

"Why is that?" he asked with compassion in his voice.

Vivian bowed her head, avoiding his crisp blue eyes. "The fact is, we met and eloped so quickly, I hardly knew him."

"You eloped?"

She squinted her eyes. "Don't judge me. I thought I was in love."

"*Thought*?" he asked.

Memories of Draven flooded her again. "Oh, don't even ask. I can't talk about Oliver. I'm sorry."

"Don't you mean Oscar?" Blue asked.

Vivian's stomach lurched. "Yes, I mean Oscar." Such a mistake could unravel everything.

"How long did you know him?"

"Believe it or not, only a few days," she said. "I was a complete fool to marry him so quickly. Then again, I have a penchant for making reckless decisions, I'm afraid."

"Well, I can't blame Oscar for wanting to marry you. Any man would easily be swept off his feet by your beauty, but—"

Vivian blushed. "But what?"

"What some may view as reckless may actually be courage."

His words vibrated through her. "It was anything but courage," she said.

"And yet I don't think you're as headstrong and impulsive as you think you are."

"Oh, I was headstrong and impulsive, I'm afraid."

"Do you regret marrying him?" Blue asked.

"Yes, I do," she acknowledged. She wrinkled her forehead and shuddered as her thoughts drifted to suspicions of Draven and his desire to hunt her down. They approached her building. "I thank you for walking me home, Mr. Ryan, but there really is no need. Mr. McGovern is being overly protective." She gestured along the street. "As you can see, I'm perfectly safe to walk home on my own in public in broad daylight."

Blue's ocean eyes pierced hers. "I understand that there's probably no dire need for me to be your escort, but I want to accompany you anyhow, morning and afternoon, if you don't mind my company. I want to know for certain you're safe."

His words both warmed and vexed her. "Contrary to my former antics with the cattle, I'm not your weak damsel in distress."

He chuckled softly. "As I've said before, no one could ever accuse you of being a damsel in distress, Widow Smith." He kicked at a stone on the boardwalk and cleared his throat. "Ma'am," he said, speaking slowly, "I know you're in mourning, but I wondered if you might like to attend the Harvest Ball with me on Saturday evening, even if you don't plan on dancing. Will you allow me to escort you?"

Hot emotion rushed through her. "I'm afraid I already promised another gentleman I'd go with him, but—"

"Ah, of course," he said. "I'm not at all surprised." The corners of his mouth pulled upward, and his eyes twinkled. "I'll bet you've captured the heart of more than a few men in this town."

Vivian reached to take the umbrella from Blue's grasp, and their fingers brushed—the warmth of his skin lingering before she pulled away. She swept her eyes to his. Their faces were only inches from each other as he passed the umbrella to her.

She swallowed. "I…I think he might be courting someone else now, though." The words felt foreign in her mouth, like a lie she almost believed.

His eyes held hers, steady and unreadable. "Impossible," he murmured. His voice was low, certain. "He'd be a fool to court anyone else."

The air between them thickened. If she took one step forward, just one, they would be close enough to…

No, she couldn't. Wouldn't. She was in public! She took a step backward. "Don't be ridiculous," she said, averting her gaze. "Um, Mr. Ryan, I have a favor to ask of you."

"Yes?" he asked.

"I wonder if you might consider escorting my sister."

"Isabel? Doesn't she already have a beau?"

"Not anymore."

"I see." He nodded his head thoughtfully. "Yes. Tell your sister I'd be happy to accompany her." He stepped close to her again and her pulse raced. "But please tell her honestly that my heart's affections are, unfortunately, not for her but for someone else entirely."

Vivian's mouth went dry, and she licked her lips before thanking him. "I…I won't be telling Isabel a thing about you escorting her to the dance," she said. "I mean, I think I'll let you surprise her."

He raised his brows. "I don't know if I like that. I don't want her getting the wrong idea about my intentions."

She nervously pressed her lips together. "I wouldn't worry about it."

"What time should I meet you before work tomorrow morning?" Blue asked.

"A quarter to eight would be fine if you absolutely must come."

"I must."

As Blue made his departure, Vivian's eyes darted up and down the street. It was ironic that Blue was trying to protect her from the very man she was determined to find. She bent to pet Bobo where he lay flopped on the stoop.

After a quick meal, Vivian resumed her quest to locate Draven. She walked slowly past the saloons yet saw no sign of him. At one point, Cade Ranson waved to her from his perch on the roof of the construction site across the street. He looked at her inquisitively. Vivian nodded and shrugged her shoulders. She hoped it was a hint that Tessie might be interested in him. He gave her a wide grin and mouthed his thanks.

She returned to the Blake Hotel and traced her finger through the names in the registry again. Draven's name was still listed as a guest, indicating he had not left town. Once more, she sat waiting for him in the lobby, this time prepared with some embroidery to occupy her time. After three hours, however, she finally gave up and returned home to prepare for another evening with Tessie and Isabel. Where on earth had the blasted man gone?

Samantha stormed into the post office and waited in line to talk to Barbara Mitchell. Earlier that day, she'd seen Blue Ryan walking and talking on the street with Widow Smith— right after she'd distinctly warned the wretched girl to stay away from him.

She huffed and tapped her foot on the wooden floor. What was taking so long? A tall man with black hair stood at the counter. He wore a dark gray, finely tailored wool coat. Only men like Mayor Mitchell and Oswald Davis ever wore such rich attire in a small town like Etna. She took a step to the right and peered more closely at the man's trousers and shoes. He wore brand new, highly polished black cowboy boots with spurs so shiny, they proved he was no rancher or cowboy. He looked like a foreigner trying to fit in. She shuffled slightly to her left to try catching a glimpse of the man's face. When she did, her heart skipped a beat. Piercing dark eyes, perfectly trimmed mustache and goatee. She'd never seen such a handsome man in all her life! And there was no wedding ring on his finger.

The stranger finished his business at the counter and walked past her toward the exit. She simpered at him and batted her eyelashes. He passed without noticing her. She wanted to run after him and make up an excuse to talk to him, but she couldn't think of anything to say.

"Who was that man?" she asked Barbara when she approached the counter.

"I don't know. He just dropped off a letter."

"Find it," Samantha demanded. "I've got to know who he is."

Barbara put her hands on her hips and scowled.

"Please?" asked Samantha, changing her tune.

"Hmph," said Barbara before fishing in the mailbag. "I think his letter was addressed to someone in Pennsylvania. Aha! Here it is." She slid the letter across the counter.

"The return address reads Draven Randall III, Esq," Samantha read. "What does *Esq.* mean?"

"Esquire," said Barbara. "It means he's a lawyer."

Samantha covered her mouth. "Oh! A rich, handsome, bachelor lawyer from Pennsylvania, Babs!" She looked at the letter again. The return address also revealed he was staying at the Blake Hotel.

"Did you come in for anything else?" asked Barbara.

"I did, but it no longer matters." She'd come to vent her frustration about Widow Smith stealing her beaus, but she no longer cared about a lumberman or a poor, dusty cowboy named Blue.

Barbara snatched the letter from Samantha's fingers.

"Barbara, isn't Widow Vivian Smith from Philadelphia, Pennsylvania?"

"Possibly," said Barbara hesitantly. "She's sent letters there."

"I wonder… What are the chances of Mr. Draven Randall III and Widow Smith knowing each other?"

Barbara raised her eyebrows. "You think there's a story there?"

"There might be. Can you look into it?"

A glimmer of mischief danced in Barbara's eyes. "If there's a story, I'll find it. I'll post a letter to my colleague,

Mrs. Hoyle, in Philadelphia. She works for the *Philadelphia Inquirer.* If anyone knows anything in that town, she does."

Samantha's face glazed over with a far-off look. "Isabel's last name is Garrett. See if you can find out more about the Garrett family of Philadelphia and someone named Vivian Garrett in particular. Find out about the Randalls too. I want to know as much as possible."

CHAPTER 18: A Meeting with the Ex

$\mathcal{R}$ain tap-tapped over the eaves as Vivian dusted and tidied the parlor. Isabel had left for the day and Blue wouldn't arrive for another ten minutes.

Blue. Her pulse intensified at the thought of him. She picked up a pair of gloves and a fan left on the coffee table from last night's etiquette and flirtation lessons. Though Tessie's English was still deplorable, and her voice box comparable to a foghorn, the little ghost girl was making rapid improvements in her manners. And Vivian liked to think that she and her sister were making progress in flirtation as well. She was even happier that Tessie now felt confident enough to apply for a job at the Wildwood Café, working for Miss Darcy Meyer. She had high hopes for Tessie's future—especially if she was allowed to return to finish school.

The clock's ticking was particularly loud in the waiting stillness of the room. Five more minutes passed. She opened the window and was alarmed to hear Bobo's deep growl. She heard a voice: Smooth as silk, deadly as a snakebite. Draven. Leaning out the window, she saw him—large black hat, smoke wafting from the cigar in his fingertips.

She jumped back, wincing when she hit her head on the window frame. She dreaded facing him, but she'd have to hurry downstairs to speak to him now, before Blue arrived. She needed to convince him she had feigned widowhood for fear she might be pregnant, and when she realized she wasn't, she couldn't change her act. She'd laugh it off and send him packing before he accidentally divulged anything incriminating to Blue.

She closed the window, threw on her cloak, grabbed an umbrella, and flew down the stairs.

Bobo stood outside the door, frozen as a statue, hair bristling. And there was Blue, standing there beside Draven.

"Good morning, Mr. Ryan," Vivian said to Blue, taking him by the arm and pulling him down the boardwalk, away from Draven.

"Top of the morning to you too, Vivian," Draven said fluidly, smashing the stub of his cigar against the stones of the building. Vivian's blood chilled.

Blue stopped, and his brow furrowed. "Widow Smith, do you know this man?" His eyes were flooded with concern. She wiped a drop of rain from her face and didn't answer.

"Widow Smith?" Draven sniggered softly. "I beg your pardon, *Widow Smith*." He dragged out the words with amusement in his voice. "May I speak with you for a moment, ma'am?"

Vivian increased her pace, practically pulling Blue down the boardwalk to get away from Draven. Bobo remained behind, hackles up.

"I have a small matter of some import to discuss with you, *Widow Smith*," Draven called out, ignoring the dog.

Vivian halted and spun round to face Draven. "Please leave me alone." Her hands trembled as she popped open her umbrella and held it out as a defense shield that made Draven chuckle more.

"Oh, I think you'll want to talk to me sooner or later, ma'am, and I suggest sooner," Draven sneered. Taking a step toward them, he was blocked by Bobo, every muscle tensed in the dog's hulking body.

"Sooner is better than later," called Draven. "Trust me, ma'am."

Blue pushed Vivian behind him and stepped between her and Draven, flipping back his leather duster and placing a hand on the grip of a revolver.

Vivian's breath stopped and Bobo bared his teeth in a snarl directed at Draven who also drew aside his coat to reveal a revolver.

"Oh, no," Vivian cried. "Stop, both of you."

"Sir, the lady doesn't want your company right now," said Blue, "so I'll thank you to leave her alone as she requested."

Draven glanced at Blue's firearm before sliding his eyes to Vivian. "We'll talk later, Widow Smith."

From where he stood, Blue couldn't see Vivian's nod—her secret assent to meet with Draven another time, another place. Without another word, Draven touched the brim of his hat and withdrew.

Blue grabbed Vivian's hand, pressed it into the crook of his arm, and marched her along the boardwalk with Bobo following at a fast trot. Vivian's teeth chattered as she held the umbrella over herself and Blue. By the time they reached School Street, the rain was pelting. Blue halted to lift her over a stream that flooded the road and, though the thrill of his strong hands on her waist fluttered her heart, she could feel the tension of his ire. Was he angry with her or Draven or both? He set her down again and almost pushed her away.

Blue stood in the rain. "Who was that man?" he questioned sharply, after they'd passed Mr. Kappler's brewery. His voice was tight.

Vivian knew he deserved an explanation, but she couldn't give it to him. Not yet. "No one," she answered.

"No one?" Blue repeated, his voice calm but firm. "That man knew your name, Vivian. And he wasn't just here to tip his hat to you."

They remained silent as they trudged down China Hill, sliding now and again in the slippery mush. Vivian was glad he was respecting her reticence, but after some time, he questioned her again with a gentleness in his tone that wasn't there before. "Are you all right, Widow Smith?"

"I will be."

Blue stopped before they reached Big Valley Ranch and lightly touched her forearm. "Please tell me if you're in trouble."

"I'm in no trouble," she insisted.

Exasperated, he spun in a circle. "Widow Smith, anyone with any sense can see that that man is up to no good. What sort of business do you have with him?"

She faced Blue head-on. "If you must know, Mr. Ryan, I had a very brief…um…history with him."

"Did he court you?" Blue asked.

"If you can even call it that," she spat contemptuously.

"Well, it must have meant something to him if he's come all the way out west to find you."

"It's a long, complicated story," she replied, "and not one you need to know. Thank you for walking me to work this morning. I don't expect you to escort me to work or home in the future. Good day, Mr. Ryan."

"I want you to keep your distance from that man, Widow Smith," he said. "I'll see you at noon." Tipping his hat, Blue strode past her to Cocoa Joe's barn.

Her lips parted and snapped shut again before she and Bobo walked to Cocoa Joe's office.

"Yoo-hoo! Samantha!" Barbara Mitchell shouted from across Main Street.

Samantha waved from the post office. "I'm sick to death of that Widow Smith," she grumped to herself while struggling to negotiate the mucky road.

"I have news for you!" Barbara chortled, commanding her to wipe her boots before entering the newspaper office. "First, there's news of Miss Beatty and Mr. Oswald Davis. Widow Smith caught them kissing in the schoolhouse, and Miss Beatty was dismissed on the spot."

Samantha's jaw clenched. "Who cares about anyone kissing in a schoolhouse, Barbara. I want news about Mr. Draven Randall III, Esquire."

"I have news about him too. I wired my friend in Philadelphia, and—" She handed Samantha a copy of a telegram that read:

DR II mayor of Philadelphia. Rich law family. DR III philanderer. Garretts unkn.

Samantha's mouth hung open. "How intriguing! Our Mr. Randall sounds like quite the wealthy, prominent scalawag."

"You'd do best to steer clear of that one," Barbara warned.

"But I think I might like a scalawag," Samantha mused, "and if he's a philanderer, he's probably not married or engaged, which is good for me."

"Your parents would die of broken hearts if you took off after such a rogue," Barbara admonished her.

Samantha's lips tightened. "What I want is dirt on Widow Smith. What is her connection to Mr. Randall? Is your friend going to send any more information?"

"You don't need to know about Widow Smith, and you certainly don't need to know anything more about Mr. Randall. He's a man of bad character and that's that."

But Samantha was more determined than ever to find out all she wanted to know.

Draven lounged in the lobby of the Blake Hotel, one leg crossed so his foot rested on a knee as he puffed idly on a cigar. He held a newspaper in front of his face that went unread. A jagged vein protruded from his forehead. Vivian was as fresh and pretty as ever, but why was the fool pretending to be a widow and why would she risk lying to an entire town, unless… He ground his teeth. Unless she was pregnant with his child, which was exactly what he'd secretly hoped, if such were the case, he'd argue that the child was rightfully his; then he'd threaten to expose her lie if she didn't return to Philadelphia and legally wed him. Or…he could play along with her silly scheme and woo her back gently. He could apologize and feign contrition. She'd easily succumb to his advances just as she had before.

It repulsed Draven to play the part of a lovestruck beggar but, for his grandfather's fortune, he'd do whatever it took. And that meant getting her mind off that stupid gun-toting cowboy, whoever he was.

He folded the newspaper and rested it on the coffee table; then he stood, stretched, and strode to the open doorway, peering out onto the rainy street, where horses, wagons, and people buzzed about like bees darting from place to place. Etna was a rough and muddy town. Vivian would be happy to return to civilization again.

Even if Vivian wasn't pregnant now, he'd make sure she was as soon as possible after a legal marriage. He'd come all the way out here to win her back, and he wouldn't return without her. Vivian was the only woman he wanted for a bride. They looked good together. Both handsome. Both smart.

"Smart," he growled low, his neck stiffening, "and a confounded suffragette." Two things he despised in women. But once he got her back home, he'd get his son, claim his fortune, and put an end to Vivian's uppity smartness and asinine ideas.

The rain stopped and sunlight gleamed through the clouds, lighting up the town. Draven pulled on his coat and hat and tread onto the boardwalk, appreciating the sound his spurs made with each step. He smiled in satisfaction as he thought of Vivian pretending to be a widow. There was no logical reason for her to feign widowhood if she weren't with child, and the baby could be no man's but his.

An Indian man rode up to a hardware store and tied his steam-blowing horse to a hitching post. Draven spat in his direction. He hated Indians.

"Howdy, there, stranger!" a man called from somewhere nearby.

Suddenly a man was in front of him and standing far too close. Draven extended his hand to block him.

"I'm Hiram Planter!" the intruder declared. "You look like you're new in town, mister. Let me welcome you to Etna, California."

Draven didn't shake the man's outstretched hand. His eyes were fixed on the Indian. He wanted to see if their kind was allowed to enter establishments in this town.

"Let me tell you about Etna," Hiram babbled. "If you haven't been here before, this here's Main Street. We've got a few saloons and hotels, and—"

"I don't have time for you, mister," said Draven, brushing Hiram aside like a pesky gnat.

"That's very rude of you!" Hiram shouted after him. "Other folks in this town are nicer to me than you are."

"They shouldn't be," Draven muttered. Ambulating along the street, he passed a small clique of dirty, rough-looking men. He caught the name "Widow Smith" in their conversation and slowed to listen.

"I want to ask her to the ball, but do widows attend balls?" a lumberjack asked.

"But I was plannin' on askin' her," said another extra-large man, punching the lumberjack in the shoulder.

"Nope, I'm askin' her," argued a cowboy. "A widow woman's fair game and I aim to play."

"Gambling's more like it for you," said the lumberjack.

Some lighthearted pushing and shoving ensued, and a gurgle caught in Draven's throat. The idea that the civilized, proper city girl, Vivian Garrett, could have an abundance of suitors in this vulgar, backward town was hilarious. He ran his tongue over his teeth. He was a prize compared to Blue or any of Etna's unsavory rabble. If his money and sincere apology weren't enough to win back Vivian, his charisma would be. It wouldn't take long—a quick, easy triumph.

A pretty little skirt waltzed along the boardwalk across the street and his head snapped to attention. It was the same curly-haired brunette he'd seen in the post office the day before. He'd disregarded her then, but he couldn't deny she was a looker—maybe even more beautiful than Vivian. If the girl would drop her silly Southern belle act and lighten up on her perfume, she'd be worth pursuing—if he changed his mind about Vivian.

He fondled his mustache and goatee. Forget Vivian for now. Judging by the swing of her hips, this little filly was accustomed to attracting the attention of men. He waited till she was almost directly across from him before traversing the street. Sliding in mud and dodging horses and a logging wagon, Draven landed casually on the boardwalk and stood before her, blocking her path.

"I beg your pardon, ma'am." He bowed gallantly, touching his hat. "How rude of me." It was all he said. His smile usually took care of the rest.

"Why, sir, you surprised me," she tittered, batting her eyelashes. He had her nibbling at his line now. All he had to do was set the hook and reel her in. "You're not from around here," she continued. "You new in town?"

"I might be."

"Are you just passing through or are you staying here in Etna?"

"That depends," he said.

Her lips puckered into a delicious pout. "On what?"

"Is there anything fun for a man to do around here?"

Her cheeks colored prettily. "Well, there's our annual Harvest Ball. I don't suppose you'd want to attend such a small-town function with humble country folk like us?"

"I'm sure a darling little thing like you already has an escort to the ball, or I'd ask you myself," he said smoothly.

"I can always tell my escort that someone else is taking me," she said. "I have no strong attachments."

Too easy. He loosened the string under his chin and brandished his hat with a flourish. "Draven Randall the *Third*, at your service."

"Samantha McGovern, the *First* at your service," she replied coyly.

He arranged the time and place to collect her in a hired buggy for the ball. Now that he knew where Vivian lived, he could corner her at any time. In fact, if she was fool enough to attend the ball as a widow, and she likely was, he'd talk to her there.

He stood watching Samantha saunter along the street. She turned back and waved to him, and he gave her a magnanimous bow. Who needed Vivian when he could settle for this sweet little morsel?

After a stop at the post office, Vivian traipsed to the Parker Campbell Store, where she pulled out a chair from a small table on the covered porch and sat to read her mail—one letter from her parents: another from her friend Sarah. She enjoyed her father's descriptions of everyday life back home, but shock and dread hammered through her gut when she read of Sarah's encounter with Draven, followed by details of how he'd eloped—not with two, but with three other ladies. Each marriage was a complete lie. His false marriage to Vivian had been his fourth conquest. Sarah's letter confirmed what she'd surmised from her earlier telegram. Draven's grandfather had left him a fortune, but he could inherit the estate only after he'd married and had a son. The letter ended with a dire warning that Draven was possibly already in Etna looking for her. She was right about that. He only wanted her for financial gain. And now that Draven had seen her widow's act, he must suspect she was pregnant. She was apprehensive, but knowing Draven's motives gave her some power. She only had to figure out how to use her knowledge to her advantage.

She folded the letters and replaced them in her purse before popping into the Parker Campbell Store. She waved to her sister who was helping another customer.

"Hello, Vivi," Isabel called to her. "Go up to the balcony. You'll find the most cunning little fans there."

Vivian reached the second floor and located the fans on a pretty display shelf. She chose a fan bedecked with pale blue ribbons. It would make a charming gift for Tessie, and it would match her blue gown perfectly.

She ran her fingers across the blue ribbons. Blue. Funny how the color always reminded her of him now. Despite her objections, he'd walked her home again at noon. Their conversation had been stilted as they stuck to light topics, such as the weather and Etna's architecture in comparison to that of Philadelphia's. She was surprised Blue had bothered to walk her home at all, since he must suspect Draven of courting her in the past. He was a minister, though. Maybe he was just doing his Christian duty, walking her home.

The shop bell tinkled, and Vivian pitched a glance over the balcony to see the dark shadow of Draven Randall block the doorway as he slammed an angry boot over Bobo's fluff. She jumped back and dropped behind the railing. Bile crept up her throat at the sight of his ruthlessly handsome face. Had he followed her here? She wanted to talk to him, but not here. Not now. Certainly not in front of her sister.

She lost sight of him as he walked beneath the balcony, and she snapped the fan shut. Plunging beneath a table, she listened for the sound of his spurs. Clink. Shuffle. Clink.

Shuffle. Her breath cracked as Draven's heavy footfall began climbing the creaking stairs. She pulled herself further into the shadows of the table and tucked the hem of her skirt out of sight as the top of his black head appeared. He reached the top of the stairs and scuffed his boots across the groaning boards, shuffling closer and closer. Then he stopped.

He muttered an expletive aimed at her.

All right, that's it! She thought, almost climbing from her hiding place to speak the words aloud. *He's the reason women need the right to vote to protect themselves.* She was so angry, she barely resisted the temptation to jump up and confront him then and there. But, no, she'd follow him and speak to him in the lobby of his hotel as previously planned.

As Draven's boots lumbered down the stairs and across the floor, Vivian cautiously emerged to watch him leave. He kicked Bobo before slamming the door shut behind him, and a new wave of rage shot through her. Draven Randall was a selfish son of a gun, and she couldn't wait to confront him. She'd have to be cunning and tactful, and she hoped her planned speech would work on him.

Taking deep gulps of breath, she steadied her nerves, went downstairs, paid for the fan, and crept warily onto the covered porch. When she captured a glimpse of Draven heading to the construction site, she darted through traffic to follow him at a safe distance. This time, she'd finally corner him in that hotel lobby and make him talk with her there. And she'd stop being afraid of the brute.

A half-hour later, Vivian sat facing Draven, displaying what she hoped was a peaceful, cheerful countenance. She'd followed the blackguard for thirty minutes before he finally returned to his hotel. "Imagine my surprise when I saw you here, Draven," she said, clenching her jaw to force the tremor from her voice. "Surely you haven't come hundreds of miles just to see me."

"I have, my dear." His voice was coarse in her ears.

When he leaned closer to her, she felt a rise of triumph knowing his wheedling charms would never work on her again.

"Wronging you and casting you aside was the most despicable thing I've ever done in my life, my dear Vivian, and I've come all this way to beg your forgiveness." She cringed and forced herself not to pull back her hand as he reached for her. "I am deeply and sincerely sorry for all the pain I've caused you, my sweetheart." What a smooth liar he was.

The man was a narcissist, and she had to play to his weakness. "You don't know how I've longed to hear you say those words. I'm—" She hiccupped, resisting the urge to squirm away from the touch of his hand. "I'm overwhelmed, Draven. I thought you'd forgotten about me. I thought you never wanted to see me again."

"No, my darling," he said obsequiously, drawing her hand to his lips. She prayed no one would see them together—especially not Blue.

"You broke my heart. I loved you."

"I know, my dear. Could you ever find it in your heart to love me again?"

She jerked away from him and pressed both hands to her breast; then closed her eyes. "I don't know." Somehow, she had to get the next subject out in the open. "Do you know why I'm dressed as a mourning widow, Draven? I was afraid."

"Of what, my pet?"

She opened her eyes and fiddled with the chain attached to her watch. "I don't dare to say. I'm so ashamed."

He leaned so close, the air from his nose puffed on her cheek. "You can tell me, my love."

Her eyes darted about the room. Thankfully, the lobby was empty, and the bellhop was nowhere in sight. She licked her lips. "I was afraid I might be pregnant," she said, her voice barely audible.

"Oh, my darling." He took both her hands in his. "Are you?"

"Thankfully, no," she said, snapping her eyes at him, "but I wasn't sure at first, so I pretended to be a widow, just in case. I was afraid to be alone and single with a baby and no husband." She laughed. "Now look at me. I'm stuck pretending to be a widow and having to wear these ugly mourning clothes, not to mention lying to everyone." She took his hands in hers and caressed them, even though it made her stomach churn. Draven jerked and she thrilled at his reaction. "The fact is, I rather like all the freedom I have as a widow. I'm independent, free, and single. And I don't really need a husband. People respect me in a different way than when I was single." Draven's body stiffened and Vivian knew he was realizing his scheme had failed. That he'd come all this way for nothing. She wanted to scream with relief.

"Vivian, what if you come home with me? We could be married properly, and no one would know a thing about our past. Your honor would be protected, you'd have more money than you could ever need, and I'd even let you continue with your suffrage meetings."

Let me? She jolted and adjusted her skirts to cover the reaction. She didn't want to be with any man who could choose to allow or deny her to do what she wanted. Why wasn't he giving up and going back home? He couldn't possibly want her now that he knew she wasn't pregnant. Did he not believe her story? Ice chilled her blood. And could he make her go back with him? Was the law on his side? Probably. He was a lawyer, after all.

"Well?"

"You want me to marry you?" she asked lamely. "Again?"

"Yes, I do," he said.

"I…I don't know," she faltered. She had to be careful not to anger him or he could get forceful.

"How could you not know, Vivian?" You know you still love me." His tone was tight. "Would you rather go back to your cowboy?" His true colors were showing—impatience and jealousy.

"What cowboy? Oh, you mean the dusty, uncouth man who walked me to work this morning?" She laughed lightly. "You're funny. No one could ever compare to you, but—"

"But what?" The irritation was there again.

"First of all, I'm not interested in jumping back into another courtship, but he did ask to escort me to the Harvest Ball."

"Forget the ball. Let's leave town together tonight."

"I'm going to that dance," said Vivian with a little too much determination in her tone. "My sister and I have been looking forward to attending together."

"Save a few dances for me, then," said Draven.

"You'll be there?"

He shrugged. "Why not? I'll get a taste of backwater cow town culture before we head back to civilization."

"You'll make the other girls jealous," she said as flirtatiously as possible, disregarding his insinuation.

"You're the one I want, darling."

"How can I trust that our marriage will be real next time around?"

"I said I was sorry, and I am." He was unable to keep the anger from creeping into his voice. "Come back to me. We'll have a proper courtship and invite all of Philadelphia society to attend a grand wedding—with a real minister. Then I'll set us up in a mansion in the best district of the city."

"It's very tempting, but you can't rush such an important decision. I still haven't gotten over the shock of our fake marriage, and now I'm experiencing another shock seeing you again—all the way out here."

"What is there to consider? I made a mistake, I've apologized, we're in love, and I'm begging you to come back to me. Could you ever find it in your heart to love me again?" His voice softened but sounded forced. "I think about you every day, Vivian. Wondering if you're safe. If you're happy. If I ruined your life."

She nearly scoffed aloud. Draven Randall, feeling remorse? Hardly. But she let her lower lip tremble, just a little. Let him think he had an edge.

"Draven, I can't decide so quickly. I'm settled here. I'm living with my sister, and I know it's an uncivilized town in the middle of nowhere, but I'm beginning to like it here."

"I want you back, Vivian, and I need an answer by Sunday evening." There was gravel in his tone. "I have to go back home. I have work to do. You must understand."

"I see," Vivian nodded. Was he really giving her an ultimatum?

Draven studied her with a slow smile, like a cat watching a trapped mouse. "Then you'll consider it?"

Vivian swallowed. This was supposed to be the part where he gave up. Why wasn't he giving up?

"I'm leaving town by stage Monday morning," said Draven. "The train east leaves Tuesday."

"I'll let you know by Sunday," she promised. Of course, she had zero intention of telling him yes.

CHAPTER 19: Prelude to the Ball

Sunlight filtered through a chilly haze into the Garrett sisters' apartment. The day of the long-awaited Harvest Ball had arrived. Vivian stirred, groggy from a restless night of sharing a narrow bed with Isabel, while Tessie dozed on the parlor sofa.

The trio had talked late into the night, trying on dance slippers and gowns, styling their hair, practicing their etiquette and flirtation skills—dreaming of what the night ahead might bring.

Vivian shook Tessie awake and invited her to join her and Isabel in a buttermilk pancake breakfast. After the meal, Tessie went home to complete a few chores and care for her mother before returning to Isabel's apartment in the afternoon, while Vivian went up the street to run a few errands.

When she returned to her building, Vivian was greeted by the laundry brothers in the foyer. Zhang Wei rattled off something in Chinese and surprised her with a bouquet of violet chrysanthemums. She accepted the flowers and gave him a quizzical look. Why was he giving her flowers? He pointed to a note attached to the bouquet. "Card," he said, smiling and nodding excitedly.

Vivian peered at Zhang Wei, momentarily surprised. He was nice-looking, his muscular build no doubt a result of long hours at the laundry. He also appeared to be around her age. Was he asking to escort her to the dance?

"Card, card," Zhang Wei said again, poking at the bouquet.

Vivian found a card tucked into the bouquet and opened it. The note read:

Dear Widow Smith, do I still have the honor of escorting you to the Harvest Ball this evening? Please leave your reply with the concierge at the Schmitt Hotel. Sincerely, Martin Graver

"Oh!" Vivian exclaimed. "These flowers are from Mr. Graver?"

Zhang Wei nodded and smiled. "Nice gentleman say flowers for you. Must read card."

So, Martin hadn't forgotten her! She thanked Zhang Wei with a polite bow, then hurried upstairs. After placing the flowers in a vase, she grabbed her shawl and dashed off to the Schmitt Hotel. Martin's note required a prompt reply. She also added one small yet urgent request. Finally, she wrote one more note—this time to Blue, confirming that he would be Isabel's escort to the ball that evening. He had asked Isabel, Isabel had hesitated, and now Vivian was replying for her.

Next, she paid a quick visit to Widow Fitzgerald to make sure she would still be her chaperone for the dance, and added that she might need to chaperone two other young ladies and their escorts. The widow hadn't forgotten her chaperone commitment, and she was amenable to taking on two more girls—as long as Vivian paid her extra. Widow Fitzgerald was both kind and shrewd, and Vivian approved. Her respect for the widow was growing.

Plans were coming together at last!

Tessie returned to the apartment early in the afternoon. With several hours to kill before needing to dress for the ball, Vivian suggested a walk with Bobo across town. Perhaps they could hike up to the Johnson Creek swimming hole.

Armed with umbrellas, they inhaled a rain-soaked breeze and marveled at the beauty of the valley, now fully transformed from a summer palette to one of autumn's vibrant tapestries of red and gold. Vivian scrunched her knit hat over her ears and clapped a hand over her nose.

"My nose is cold too!" Tessie bellowed. Vivian threw her a stern look. "Oh, all right," Tessie relented, lowering her voice. "Lord knows I don't wanna offend nobody. I was just statin' a fact." They walked along apace before she spoke again. "I swear that dog has come back to life since he started bein' your bodyguard, Widow Smith. Just like you come to life since Blue Ryan started walkin' you to and from work." She giggled and cast a wink at Vivian.

"That's enough nonsense," Vivian retorted. She was torn with ambivalence—happy she and Isabel had escorts to the dance tonight but agitated that she'd not been able to find a date for Tessie.

Tessie rubbed her mittened hands together and grinned. "You're a grumpy Gertie this morning, Widow Smith."

"Oh, I'm sorry if I seem glum," Vivian apologized. "I have a lot on my mind. And don't you think you should start calling me by my name instead of Widow Smith?"

"If you think it's all right," said Tessie.

"I do."

"Well, Miss Vivian, what's on your mind? Or should I say *who's* on your mind?"

"Mr. Randall, for one."

"Have you seen him since I warned ya about him?"

Vivian allowed a pulse of hesitation to hang between them as she wondered how much to divulge to her friend. "Yes," she finally admitted.

"Have ya talked to him?"

"A little," Vivian admitted, aching to tell Tessie the whole truth about her relationship with Draven but she wasn't sure she could keep a secret. She changed the subject and asked Tessie about the boys she liked. That got her chatting about Matthew Wright and Harvey Winslow.

"I wonder if they'll be at the ball and what escorts they'll bring," Tessie mused. The fact that she had no escort didn't seem to bother her.

"Tessie, have you ever considered Earl Boyce?" Vivian asked. "I hear he's single now."

"That dusty, gangly string bean?" Tessie scoffed. "I ain't interested. Besides, he's courtin' a girl over in Fort Jones."

"What about Maxim Artois, then?"

"Max? The Frenchman?" Tessie wrinkled her nose. "He's all right, I s'pose. Plenty handsome. I tried talkin' to him a couple times and couldn't tell if he was listenin' or if he don't understand English too good. Nothin' against foreigners, but I think his lack of English speakin' would be too difficult."

"I know you called Cade Ranson a 'bump on a log' but, if you don't mind the quiet type, what do you think of him?" Vivian asked, holding her breath in anticipation of Tessie's reply.

Tessie exhaled sharply, and her whole body seemed to slump. "No chance."

Vivian frowned. "Why not?"

"Cade would never look twice at me. He's too handsome, refined, and civilized—a real gentleman."

Vivian clamped a hand over her mouth. "So, you do admit you like him?" She resisted the urge to divulge Cade's interest in her.

"Guess what man I think is real purty."

"Cade Ranson?"

"Obviously, but I mean what other man?"

"Who?" asked Vivian.

"Blue Ryan." Vivian's pulse quickened. "But mainly because of his horse." Tessie whistled. "What a perfectly gorgeous bay mare!"

"You and your horses." Vivian laughed. "I've never even noticed his horse."

"Because you're too busy noticin' the *man*." Tessie waggled her eyebrows. "You can see his muscles right through his shirt. That boy's built like a prize-winning stallion."

Vivian rolled her eyes. "You do realize he's not actually a horse? And why did you change the subject? We were talking about Cade Ranson."

Tessie ignored the comment and jogged on ahead, shouting back, "We're at the swimming hole! It's so beautiful this time of year with all the yellow maple leaves."

They sat on a smooth stone beside the creek, enjoying the peaceful murmuring of water as it flowed over mossy stones, and watching Bobo wade into the shallows, lapping noisily.

"You know what I've noticed, Widow Smith—I mean, Miss Vivian? You have a lot of beaus followin' you around."

Vivian grimaced. "That's not true. There aren't so many."

"At least three," said Tessie. "I'm just sorry ya still don't have an escort to the ball." Vivian refrained from telling Tessie she was now going with Martin. Tessie shrugged. "But neither do I. Guess you and me is going to the ball tonight without escorts."

Bobo emerged from the water and shook, compelling Tessie and Vivian to jump up out of the spray.

"I hope you don't like that Mr. Draven Randall," Tessie prodded. "You wouldn't go with him if he asked you, would you?"

"Certainly not."

"Good."

A giant, spiraling, yellow maple leaf twisted and whirled to land and float on the surface of the pool.

"Remember when we saw those boys here?" Tessie sniggered.

"It haunts me still."

"Haunts you?" Tessie's grin beamed in her spritely face. "It warn't a hauntin'. One of my best memories, more like."

"Tessie, that's not proper or ladylike to say," Vivian scolded. Her face burned at the memory of seeing Blue's naked body, his wet skin—

"You gotta admit it was one of the most funnest and funniest things a person could ever see."

"It was utterly mortifying," Vivian argued; then sighed. "But I guess it was a little bit fun and funny."

Tessie slapped her thigh. "Heavens to Betsy and glory be!" she roared. "The tight-laced, prim and proper Widow Smith actually has a sense of humor!"

"Shush, Tessie. Someone might hear you."

"Way out here in these woods?"

"People can hear your voice all the way to Canada, Tessie. And I'm not so tight-laced and prim and proper."

"Are too," said Tessie. "But it ain't a bad thing. It just means you have a good reputation." She exhaled through a frown. "I wish I had a good reputation like you."

"Izza and I are helping you with that, and you're improving quickly." But Vivian knew her own reputation hung in a precarious balance. If Draven said the slightest thing about their history together to anyone in this small town, Vivian's reputation would be ruined, and so would Isabel's. And would Draven possibly be at the dance? She shuddered. She'd stick close to Martin and Widow Fitz. They'd offer a semblance of safety.

Gowns, undergarments, gloves, jewelry, purses, hairpins, ribbons, bows, and myriad other accoutrements were laid out on the sofa and coffee table in Isabel's parlor.

"Borrow whatever you like," said Isabel.

"Really?" Tessie asked with skepticism in her tone, and she figeted nervously.

"Really," Isabel replied.

"And we have a gift for you," said Vivian, handing her a long, narrow white box.

Tessie opened the box and lifted out the white lace fan with blue ribbons. "Oh," she whispered her volume uncharacteristically quiet. "I never saw nothin' so purty in all my born days."

"It's yours to keep," said Isabel, "from Vivi and me."

Tessie's eyes brimmed with tears as she hugged Isabel and Vivian. "Thank you so very much. It's the best gift I ever had."

As evening approached, the three young ladies shivered in their cotton chemises after bathing, grateful for the fire in the woodstove as they pulled on their silk stockings.

"Thank you again for lettin' me wear this ball gown, Widow Smith," said Tessie, sliding her fan open. "And this fan will help me charm a man like a proper lady."

"I'm Vivian, remember."

"Oh, yes, Miss Vivian." Tessie pursed her lips and clasped and unclasped her hands.

"Tessie, is something wrong?" asked Vivian. "You're awfully fidgety."

She shifted from one foot to the other and back again. "I have somethin' to tell ya both—and I'm not sure you're gonna like it."

"What is it?" Vivian asked as she attached supporter hooks to her stockings.

"I quit my job at the saloon today—even before I know if Darcy Meyer will hire me at the Wildwood Café." She smiled tentatively at the sisters' astonished faces. "Did I do the right thing? I'm not sure. But Mama's fully recovered from her illness now, and her strength is back, and she's seeking work in town."

"I think it's wonderful," said Isabel, hugging Tessie.

"And brave of you," added Vivian, taking her turn to hug Tessie. "I'm so happy your mother is better too!"

"She says I can even go back to school if the school will let me, even though I dropped out."

"That's wonderful news!" Vivian cried.

"If I can help you return to school, I will," said Isabel.

"How could you help?" asked Tessie. "I know you're a teacher, but I don't know what you could say to convince the school board to accept me back."

"Well," Isabel hesitated, "I have something to tell you both too. I spoke with Barbara Mitchell yesterday. She's on the school board and she's arranged for me to have an interview on Monday about replacing Miss Beatty. If I get the position, I'll not hesitate to let you join my class, Tessie."

The three ladies joyously laughed and hugged one another.

"We really are blessed, ain't we?" asked Tessie.

"We most certainly are," Isabel agreed, winking at Vivian.

As twilight fell, the trio ate a light snack before changing into their gowns. Vivian did a little spin in Widow Butler's drab heliotrope frock. It wasn't flattering, but at least she had something decent to wear. And she was excited to attend the ball, even if she couldn't dance.

The clock struck six. Widow Fitzgerald and Martin Graver would arrive at any minute.

"I'm so happy and nervous," said Tessie. Her pale skin was smooth as cream against the soft blue of the gown, and her hair was skillfully plated, thanks to Isabel's touch.

"I admit I'm nervous too," said Isabel. "I feel bad saying yes to Mr. Ryan, Vivi, when you'd like him to be your beau."

"It's all right, Izza, and we have Widow Fitzgerald for a chaperone," said Vivian. "She's better than any escort."

"I don't know about that," said Isabel. "I wish you both had escorts."

"I don't care a whit," said Tessie, twirling. "I feel like a princess and you two look like queens."

Vivian stood before Isabel's mirror and squinted. She didn't look or feel like any type of royalty. She passed a fleeting hand over her abdomen, glancing in the mirror behind her to Isabel and Tessie to make sure they hadn't seen the gesture. Only Isabel had noticed. She stared back and raised an eyebrow.

"No queen would wear this puce," said Vivian, "but I'm happy just to have the chance of being at this dance."

"You should see how snappin' green your eyes look, Miss Vivi," said Tessie, "and your big brown eyes look prettier than ever next to your yellow silk, Miss Isabel."

"Thank you, Tessie," said Isabel.

"Do you think anyone besides Mr. Ryan will ask me to dance tonight?" Isabel fretted.

"Just remember how I taught ya to flirt, and you'll have plenty of men askin' ya," Tessie assured her.

Footsteps beat on the stairwell, and they opened the door to admit Widow Fitzgerald. "There are three gentlemen waiting on the boardwalk outside for each of you," she panted.

"Three?" Tessie practically shouted. "How can that be?"

"I'm sure the boys outside will explain," said Widow Fitz.

"Who could they be?" asked Isabel, wide-eyed.

"I don't know," Vivian lied. She knew there would be two escorts. Had Martin come through for her?

Tessie grabbed her cloak and settled it over her shoulders. "Let's go find out!"

Isabel and Vivian scurried down the stairs after Tessie, and Widow Fitz followed, clomping slowly behind them.

Blue was there for Isabel, and he treated her sister like a true lady.

"Good evening, Widow Smith," Martin Graver bowed, offering her a corsage of dainty, pink dianthus flowers.

"Thank you, Mr. Graver. And thank you again for the bouquet and for being my—" She broke her sentence upon seeing Cade Ranson. "—escort…and for finding Mr. Ranson and asking him to escort Miss Blackman," she said in a softer tone.

"It was no trouble at all finding him or convincing him to accept the opportunity," said Martin. "I'm honored you accepted my invitation." He offered his arm to Vivian. "Shall we?"

"Miss Blackman," said Cade, bowing awkwardly to her and proffering a small corsage. "May I escort you to the dance?"

Tessie took the corsage and fumbled with the pin, whimpering a high-pitched cry when she accidentally stuck her finger with it. "Um, yes, yes, of course, Mr. Ranson."

Vivian quickly stepped in and helped Tessie pin the corsage to her dress and, stepping back, she waited for Cade to offer his arm to his date, but he appeared too flustered to think of it for himself, so Vivian gently pulled his arm toward Tessie, placed Tessie's hand on his arm, and nudged them forward.

Tessie, for once in her life, was speechless to be escorted by Cade. It was funny to see the two of them walking side by side with absolutely nothing to say for at least five minutes.

"Widow Smith," Widow Fitzgerald whispered into her ear, "I agreed to chaperone Tessie Blackman, but let me remind you that I am *not* responsible for the embarrassment of her social disgraces, which are inevitable and already quite apparent for all to see."

"Yes, so you told me before, Widow Fitz. I told you not to worry. Remember, I'm paying you to do your best to protect us from disgrace and smooth over any mistakes we make."

Isabel pulled Vivian aside for a brief moment as the group of friends began their jaunt to the Beehive. "Are you sure I should be with Mr. Ryan? I know you like him."

"It's all right, Izza," whispered Vivian, "I'll let you borrow him for the evening."

Main Street was awash with lamplight, gaiety and laughter as they joined streams of people headed to the Beehive. Bobo stuck close to Vivian, guarding her as she walked beside Martin. And, though Martin looked dashing and, mercifully, wore a long coat that covered his ample backside, her mind and eyes were not on Martin Graver. She only had eyes for Blue.

The Beehive was a building owned by a Dr. Furber. The lower floor served as his medical clinic, while the second floor was one giant and magnificent dance hall. Although the Beehive was less than half a mile away, Draven Randall hired a horse and carriage and instructed the driver to park on the street outside the McGovern home. Bouquet of roses and corsage in hand, Draven mounted the steps to the expansive porch and rapped the brass knocker on the door. A housekeeper opened the door and led him through the foyer to the parlor, where Samantha, her parents, and Mrs. Mitchell stood to greet him. With a flourish, he presented the bouquet to Samantha's mother and the corsage to Samantha. He was glad Mr. McGovern wasn't there. For some idiotic reason, fathers generally disapproved of him.

Samantha looked stunning in a very modern black and white gown. He was proud to be attending tonight's event with the belle of the ball—and possibly the belle of the entire county.

Mrs. McGovern introduced Barbara as her daughter's chaperone for the evening.

"Of course, Mrs. McGovern." *That's all I need,* thought Draven, *a busybody poking her nose into his private business.* But he knew how to behave himself. He'd be as cool and polite as ever. "It's a pleasure to meet you, Mrs. Mitchell. I apologize for not bringing a second bouquet of flowers for you, ma'am," he added to Mrs. Mitchell.

"Don't try to butter me up, Mr. Charmer," Barbara sniffed. "I'm not as gullible as I look." She nodded to Mrs. McGovern. "Samantha's safe under my watch, Sally. You and Cocoa Joe can attend the dance and enjoy yourselves." Back to Draven: "There'll be no shenanigans with you, my boy. I know more about you than you think."

"I wouldn't dare to cross you, Mrs. Mitchell. Aren't you a newspaper woman, ma'am?" What did the old bitty mean by knowing more about him? "I've read a couple of your very nice articles," Draven gushed, changing tactics.

Barbara's countenance switched from critical to slightly more accepting, and Draven trusted they were back on the right foot.

Draven strolled with Samantha to the carriage and helped her into the rear seat, where he intended to sit beside her on the short jaunt to the dance hall. He offered his hand to Mrs. Mitchell to sit on the front seat with the driver, but the interfering chaperone thrust Draven's arm aside and crammed into the back seat with her charge. Outwardly, Draven maintained an unruffled façade, but he was close to a boiling point.

Etna's downtown block was jammed with pedestrians and horse-drawn traffic, and Draven's carriage had to slow to a crawl. As they approached Isabel's stone building, he spied Vivian, talking and walking with a merry huddle of friends. His jaw clenched and the veins in his neck throbbed. He hated seeing Vivian adapting to this rugged western country life. Was that the flaxen-haired whore from the saloon walking with Vivian and her friends? He did not approve. Vivian could ruin her reputation here in the middle of nowhere, but he wouldn't allow such behavior back home in Philadelphia. Vivian was also carrying on with other men. He didn't approve of that either. If she was expecting his child, and she might be, both Vivian and the baby belonged to him.

He opened and closed his fists. Tonight, his goal, even if he had to grovel, was to get Vivian alone and get the truth out of her—to admit whether or not she was indeed pregnant with his child. The thought of ingratiating himself with her soured his stomach, but he'd gotten her to fall for him before; he'd do it again.

He twisted In his seat and winked back at his date. Forget Vivian for now. Tonight was his chance to be with the belle of the ball—Samantha McGovern.

CHAPTER 20: The Harvest Ball

*B*obo stretched, yawned, and plopped onto a comfortable spot on the covered porch outside the Beehive. A sudden flash of lightning split the sky, followed by a thunderclap. A ripple of gasps and hoots rose from the guests shuffling into Dr. Furber's building. A cold wind sent a shiver of foreboding through Vivian. Still, she shook it off when she and her merry assembly checked their coats in the foyer, talking excitedly amidst the discordant wail of an orchestra tuning their instruments upstairs on the second floor in the ballroom.

Climbing the stairs, Vivian was delighted to find the dance hall festooned with colored ribbons and garlands of fall leaves that flickered in the light of dozens of lanterns casting shifting shadows across the polished wood floor. The room was rapidly filling with guests from all over Scott Valley, Callahan, and even as far away as Yreka and Gazelle. Samantha McGovern was there too—with Draven, of all people.

"Heavens above! Would you look at Samantha's gown?" Tessie declared in her typically over-loud voice.

"Sh!" both Isabel and Vivian warned simultaneously.

But Tessie's awe was warranted. The stunning gown of bold stripes and black ribbon curly cues was worth a double take and Vivian admired Samantha for having the courage to wear such an avant-garde costume. Vivian recognized the design as a copy of a Frederick Charles Worth gown she'd seen in *Godey's Lady's Book.* Widow Butler was a very talented seamstress indeed. Not surprisingly, however, the gown's neckline plunged dangerously low and revealed far too much of Samantha's décolleté. Men flocked to her, but Vivian hid a smirk when they wiped their eyes, sniffling and sneezing from her cloud of perfume.

"It's an amazin' frock," Tessie gawped.

"I've never seen anything like it," Widow Fitz agreed with a slight wheeze. "I know Widow Butler sewed it. How could she create such a low-cut gown?"

"Looks kinda like she's wearin' a wrought iron gate," said Martin.

"No one asked you, Martin Graver," Isabel reproved him teasingly. "You have no eye for modern women's fashion."

"I prefer your gown, mademoiselle," Martin returned.

Vivian raised a brow at her sister. What was going on between those two? She smiled as she surveyed Martin's black tailcoat that covered his ample backside, and his clean-shaven face and dark hair smoothed to one side. He looked stylish and handsome.

While their dates withdrew to an adjoining gentleman's room to talk, smoke, and imbibe, Vivian, Isabel and Tessie excused themselves to the dressing room, where they changed into dance slippers—all except Vivian, of course. No dancing allowed for her. Eager young ladies clad in gowns, laces, crinolines, and bows took turns in front of the full-length mirror. Samantha was not among them.

"Did you see how all the men are staring at Samantha?" Isabel whispered to Tessie and Vivian.

"I think they're paying more attention to her assets than to her, if you know what I mean," Vivian whispered.

"I wish I had her assets," Tessie moped, tugging down on her bodice.

Vivian gave Tessie's hand a little slap. "Stop that, Tessie. Remember, you're a proper lady now. You don't need tricks to turn heads."

"Do you think I'm pretty enough to attract a real gentleman?" Tessie queried.

"What about Cade?" asked Vivian

Tessie pouted. "You set him up to ask me to the ball."

"I have a little secret to reveal to you, Tessie. I've known for a while now that Mr. Cade Ranson is smitten with you," said Vivian, "and he seems to like you just the way you are."

"Really?" Tessie's eyes popped. "How do ya know? Are ya sure?"

"He told me himself."

"Am I not just the luckiest girl in the world?"

"Yes, you are," smiled Isabel, laughing lightly with Vivian.

This was certainly Tessie's time to shine, and the sisters reveled in her reversal of fortune.

As the music of violins began to swell, Vivian urged Martin to dance while she was compelled to plant herself at the side of the room like a pitiful wallflower. Tapping her toes and swaying her hips, she watched as Matthew Wright's rakish hands slipped too far down his partner's waist. She watched Harvey Winslow flirt with Tessie until Cade came and heroically swept her away. She watched her sister staring dreamily into the face of a young man with a boyish face.

"Who's that man dancing with Isabel?' she asked Widow Fitz.

"Don't worry, Widow Smith. He's a decent fellow if you don't mind the fact that he's a Frenchman." She wheezed and gestured toward Samantha and Draven. "I don't trust

Samantha's Prince Charming, though. Looks like a scoundrel to me."

"What do you know about him?"

Widow Fitz shrugged. "That man's got trouble stitched into every seam of that fancy coat." She looked sharply at Vivian. "Don't you even think of flirting with that scalawag."

"Don't worry. I have the same sense about him," she grumbled.

The soft scuff of leather boots and satin slippers slid around the creaky wooden floor, and the rustling whisper of petticoats and hoopskirts swished beneath silks and satins. And there was Blue, waltzing with a beautiful young lady with brunette locks that sparkled with rhinestone hairpins. They laughed as though they were long-time friends.

"That's Penelope Archer with Mr. Ryan, in case you're wondering," said Widow Fitz, interrupting her thoughts.

"I wasn't—" Vivian didn't finish. There was no use defending herself. Her chaperone had a sharp eye.

"Penelope's famous in these parts," Widow Fitz continued. "A soprano from Yreka. Wait till you hear her voice. It's positively gorgeous. We're lucky to have her as our guest of honor. She's like our own Lotta Crabtree."

The orchestra began playing a new song. Martin asked Samantha to dance, while Draven turned and bowed to Isabel.

"That wicked man is dancing with your sister," panted Widow Fitzgerald.

Draven caught Vivian's eye and winked—a slow, deliberate signal. An uninvited chill prickled down her spine. The nonverbal expression and Vivian's reaction were not lost on Widow Fitz. She gave Vivian a strange look, but Vivian saw no reason to indulge her curiosity.

"Would you like me to fetch you a drink or refreshment?" she asked Widow Fitz.

"Yes, please," her chaperone panted. "How about a glass of punch and one of those little chocolate and vanilla cookies I saw someone else eating? Don't be long, dear. I don't want to lose track of you."

But when Vivian returned with a glass of punch and a cookie, Widow Fitzgerald was nowhere in sight. She peered around and froze at the sound of her name being spoken nearby. Peering through the crowd lining the dance floor, she discovered her chaperone with Mr. and Mrs. Mitchell, Mr. and Mrs. McGovern, Mr. and Mrs. Bowman, and the Millers. Vivian edged closer, stopping to listen when she heard her name mentioned a second time.

"She's a mighty fine bookkeeper, laddies," said Cocoa Joe, "and I'm glad I hired her."

"It's a pity when a lady is born with beauty, a strong personality, *and* brains," said Mayor Mitchell, stroking his long, impeccably waxed mustache. "An utter, complete waste." His wife Barbara socked him in the shoulder. "Ow!" he exclaimed.

Barbara was defiant. "*I've* got beauty, a strong personality and brains."

"You've got the strong personality," he gruffed.

Laughter rippled through the group.

"More's the pity when God has given a *man* good looks, strong personality, no brains, *and* he ends up in government," said Silas Bowman.

"I know you didn't vote for me, Silas," Mr. Mitchell blustered, "but ya don't need to hurl insults—"

"What made you think I was talkin' about you, Mayor?" Mr. Bowman asked.

More chuckles.

"I'm sure Silas is talking about our country's higher-up elected officials," Cocoa Joe interjected. "We have plenty of strong personalities without brains in Congress, and I don't think any are very good-looking."

"At least we haven't legalized votes for women in this state," said the mayor.

Vivian raised a glass of punch in an unsuccessful attempt to capture Widow Fitzgerald's attention.

"As I see it, we'd do well to vote in favor of women's suffrage," said a voice that made Vivian's heart skip a beat. "Maybe then we wouldn't be stuck with so many unfit politicians." The astonishing remark was made by Blue Ryan, and it prompted snorts and snickers from the other men in the group. Coming from a man the bold, feminist statement was impactful—and admirable.

"If you had your druthers, Mr. Ryan, I guess the fairer sex would all be wearing trousers," Mayor Mitchell teased.

"Agreed," said Cocoa Joe. "Tell me you're not serious, me boy."

"Women wearing trousers doesn't concern me as much as peace on earth, honest constitutional government, or saving souls," said Blue. He turned in Vivian's direction, and his gaze held hers, making her mouth go dry as he continued. "But I think even you'll have to admit that much female sensibility is wasted, due to our society's unwillingness to allow a woman to use the brains God gave her. I'd be more willing to back the leadership of one intelligent woman than a hundred male leaders with no common sense."

Stunned, Vivian sipped Widow Fitzgerald's punch and stared at the back of Blue's head long after he turned back to engage in his conversation. Why did it feel as though he'd said all that directly to her—as though he could see into her soul?

"Show me one woman with common sense and I'll be seein' pigs fly," Vivian heard Mayor Mitchell say to Blue. Barbara punched her husband in the shoulder again. "Ow!" he cried. "I ain't talking about you, dear."

"I have more common sense now that I've gone and married you," said his wife, "so watch out. You should be seein' those pigs fly any day now."

Exclamations and guffaws resonated.

"It looks like we have another suffragette in our midst, gentlemen," Mayor Mitchell growled.

"If you're ever posted as minister of a church, it'll be filled with females," laughed Mr. Bowman. "Folks might mistake you for bein' too feminine."

Blue grinned, unabashed by the teasing. "Well, seein's how I can spit and belch with the best of you gentlemen, I don't think there can be any doubt as to my masculinity. Not to mention I'm ugly and—" he sniffed under an armpit, wrinkling his nose, "—kinda stinky too."

"Well, I didn't want to say anything," laughed Cocoa Joe.

"I've got me some Cherokee warrior blood in these veins too," Blue added.

Mayor Mitchell whistled. "Ya don't say."

"I wouldn't go tellin' folks about any Indian blood," said Mr. Bowman. "You want to make friends around here, not enemies."

Cocoa Joe gave Blue a slap on the back. "This lad is a darned good cowboy. That's manly enough for me."

"A cowboy and an Indian in one," laughed Mr. Bowman, roughing Blue's hair. "No wonder you're a little confused."

"I don't speak disparagingly about Indians," said Blue.

"He's joking about being an Indian," scoffed Mayor Mitchell. "Look at his blue eyes."

"Funny thing about my eyes," said Blue. "When I was just a tiny papoose, my indigenous mother was eatin' a blueberry pie at the table in our kitchen and a rattlesnake curled up on the floor right beside her. It started rattlin' his tail, and my ma was so scared, she grabbed me and jumped up onto the table, screaming. Pa came in and killed the snake, but when my mother looked back down at me, my face was all smeared with blueberry pie and some of the blueberry juice had gotten into my eyes and turned them blue. They've been blue ever since."

"Oh, for pity's sake," said Mrs. Bowman.

More laughter.

"If you tell such tall tales in public, I can't imagine what tales you'd tell from the pulpit," scolded Barbara.

Blue grinned boyishly. "That is a problem, Mrs. Mitchell. You never know what might come out of my mouth on a Sunday mornin'."

"Ye might keep folks awake in church, though," said Cocoa Joe under his breath and clearing his throat, "which would be welcome indeed, laddie."

Vivian marveled at Blue. His jovial self-deprecation caused everyone to like him despite his bold, contrary opinions. With a straight face, he looked up and winked directly at her. She swallowed and felt a rush of heat burn her cheeks.

He made his way over to her.

"Thank you for your gracious words on behalf of women, Mr. Ryan," said Vivian, noticing how white his teeth looked in his tanned face. Goodness gracious, he was handsome.

"You heard that, did you?"

Vivian nodded.

"I see you've been occupying yourself at the refreshment table."

Vivian would have elbowed him if her hands weren't full. "These are for Widow Fitzgerald."

She finally had a chance to offer the half-drunk punch and cookie to Widow Fitz, after which Blue invited her to join him on a bench. They sat side by side, so close that it turned her insides to jelly.

"Are you really in favor of suffrage for women, Mr. Ryan?"

"I am," Blue nodded.

"Would it shock you if I told you I want to be mayor of a town someday?"

"Nope. And if you stick with me, I'll make sure you do all you were born to do in this lifetime."

Vivian coughed and nearly choked. "Don't you think you're being a little too forward, Mr. Ryan?"

"Widow Smith, I've been in these parts only two weeks and I've heard an awful lot about you already."

"First of all, you're changing the subject," she said sharply. "Second, what have you heard?" she demanded.

"That you're the most beautiful, intelligent, courageous, and desirable woman in all Scott Valley."

She choked as she cleared her throat. "Nobody says that."

"I'm telling the truth," Blue disputed.

"What makes you think I'd believe anything you say?"

"I deserve that," Blue conceded. "But I'm being serious now. They say other things too."

"Like what?"

He leaned so close that the warmth of his breath caressed her ear. "Men want to tame you, Widow Smith."

She jolted. "I don't need to be tamed," she protested. "What do they think I am, Shakespeare's shrew?"

"Your words, not mine."

She paused a beat. "Do *you* think I need to be tamed, Mr. Ryan?"

"Not that my opinion matters, but no. Why be tame when you can be wild?"

"I'm not wild!" she exclaimed.

"Aren't you?" he asked, mischief seasoning his tone.

"I never know if I can take you seriously, Mr. Ryan."

"You should take me very seriously, Widow Smith. In my perception of you over these past weeks, I've concluded that there's no other woman in the world who interests me more than you."

She nearly choked again, her mind swirling. Her whole body felt paralyzed, as though it had been dipped in warm honey. His eyes held hers, unflinching, unwavering—and far too close. Close enough that she thought of kissing him.

The orchestra began playing a new waltz. "You should dance, Mr. Ryan," she suddenly urged, angry at the quavering of her voice.

"I want to dance with *you*, Vivian," he said, the huskiness in his tone sending a shiver through her.

"Well, you can't," she said quickly, "but I'm sure there are plenty of girls who'd like to dance with you."

"I'll ask your sister, then, if Mr. Martin Graver will yield her for a dance."

"You noticed them too?" asked Vivian.

"Hard to miss," Blue chuckled. "By the way, I talked with Miss Garrett, and she and I have an understanding. I explained that I only have eyes for you."

Vivian felt her mouth pop open, and Blue chuckled. "I hate to leave your side, but I did promise at least one waltz to my companion for the evening, if you'll excuse me." He stood and winked at Vivian. "I look forward to spending more time with you, Widow Smith—and dancing with you at future balls." He left her side, winding his way into the crowd.

"I could use some air," a man's whisper hissed above her, making her hair stand on end. She glanced up to see Draven. "Care to step outside for a chat?" He sat beside her in the spot Blue had just vacated. She withdrew from him, but he edged closer. "I need a moment with you, Vivian."

The auditorium buzzed with a cacophony of music, dancing, and conversation, and no one noticed Draven as he seized her wrist, yanking her to her feet and steering her toward the exit, his grip tightening when she tried to resist. His breath was hot on her cheek. "Unless you want to cause a spectacle, I suggest you cooperate."

Her heart pounded. If she screamed, would anyone hear over the music? Would they even care? As he dragged her down the stairs, her mind raced for an escape.

"I miss you, Vivian," he continued. His words grated on her entire being like rocks in a coffee mill.

The waltz in the dance hall above them ended, and the master of ceremonies' voice rang out, announcing that Penelope Archer and her cousin would be gracing them with a song. Eager guests hurried up the stairs past them as they returned to the dance hall, leaving Draven and Vivian alone on the stairwell.

A lone fiddle struck a familiar tune, and a duet began:
Once in the dear dead days beyond recall.
When on the world the mists began to fall…

Vivian tried again to pry her arm free from Draven's grip, but he held her fast.

"You're hurting me." Her voice rose, sharp and urgent.
…And in the dusk where fell the firelight gleam
Softly it wove itself into our dream.

His voice was slick and oily. "I need you, Vivian," he said as if her protest meant nothing.

"You said you would give me more time to think, Draven. You're pressuring me."

"I'm not pressuring you; I'm *begging* you." He pulled her another step down the stairs. "We need to go someplace we can talk—in private."

She didn't know if she was more angry or scared. "We can talk right here," she said firmly.

Boisterous shouts and applause broke out as the duet ended.

"It's too loud to talk here," said Draven, putting an arm around her waist and practically carrying her down the stairs.

When they reached the bottom of the stairwell, she clung to the banister. "I'll make a scene if you don't let go of me, Draven."

A group of young men shambled past them, joshing one another as they tumbled down the stairs and out onto the front porch to smoke cigars.

"I won't hurt you," said Draven, "but it's important that I speak with you. I can't do so with all these people around." His voice was low, almost coaxing, but there was a steel edge beneath the words. His grip on her hands was firm—too firm. She tested his hold, but his fingers only tightened, the pressure causing her to shake with anxiety.

She let him lead her into the busy, well-lit vestibule, where he took both of her hands in his. "Vivian, my sweetheart, my darling." His obsequiousness repulsed her. More people crowded past, and Draven tugged her out of the way until they were at the edge of a dim corridor.

Vivian hugged the wall for safety. "I thought we were going outside to talk," said Vivian struggling again to pull her hands from his sturdy grip. She had a sudden urge to scream but didn't want to look like a fool in public. Before she had a chance to form another thought or plan, Draven yanked her into a pitch-black room, shut the door behind them, and leaned against it, barring any passage back into the hallway. She thought through a dozen things to say, but nothing felt safe enough until…

Her first reaction was panic, but she forced herself to remain calm. "Draven, you silly goose," she said, impatient with the quaver in what she intended as a nonchalant giggle. "You opened the wrong door. We're not outside; we're still in the building."

A sudden burst of light shone on Draven's face as he lit a match. "There's a candle on that shelf," said Draven pointing. "Fetch it for me."

Draven's match sputtered out. She stepped slowly, carefully in the dark to the shelf where she'd seen the candle, just as the room lit up again with the light of another match. She darted her eyes about the room for a separate entrance or a weapon she might use in an emergency, but there was neither. Reluctantly, she handed the candle to Draven. "Where are we?" she queried in as strong and bold a voice as she could muster.

"A place where we can finally talk without constant interruptions."

Candlelight illuminated the room. It was a small kitchenette with only one very tiny window that offered no hope of escape. There was a woodstove, a countertop, a table and chairs, and shelves filled with canning jars, plates, glasses, cooking utensils, and several medical books. It was probably where Dr. Furber prepared meals for himself during long workdays at his clinic.

Draven set the candle on the woodstove and, with his back turned, Vivian took the opportunity to leap to the door. She placed her hand on the doorknob, but—

Draven flew past her, peeling her hand from the knob and turning the lock. "What are you trying to do?" The words slithered like a snake as he shoved her aside.

"You made a mistake coming in here," she said. "Let's go outside to talk."

"I need to speak to you in private," he said in his oily voice.

"I don't mind a private conversation, Draven, but not here. You'll ruin my reputation."

"You're not going anywhere," he said, taking a step toward her.

Her blood turned to ice and her thoughts spun in all directions. She could scream, but with the orchestral music and all the racket in the hallway, who would hear her? She could try reaching for the door again to unlock it but even if she managed to unlock and open it, she wouldn't have time to squeeze through before Draven stopped her.

She decided on a third tactic. Feigning boredom, she drew in air through her nose and shuffled casually to the counter. Portraying what she trusted was a placid façade, she said, "We have only a few minutes before someone comes looking for me, so if you have anything to discuss with me, please do it quickly."

"I came all this way for you, Vivian. The least you can do is hear me out."

She hoped he'd stand across the room from her or seat himself at the table. Instead, he swept across the floor to stand within inches of her, deliberately blocking any escape she had in mind. The intensity in his eyes burned a chill into her scalp. She didn't know what he might do to her in that closed room, and she didn't want to find out. Screaming was too risky. If no one heard, she'd enrage him. Fighting was useless. He was too strong. Letting him sense her fear was also not a good idea. Her only option was to play along until she could slip away.

"The fact that I'm here should be enough for you to see that I'm giving you another chance to come back to me," said Draven.

She fought the bile that roiled in her throat. He was giving *her* another chance? Like she had jilted him instead of the other way around? How narcissistic could he be?

"I need you, Vivian." He leaned so close that she could smell the whisky on his breath.

That's true, she thought internally. *You need me so you can get your hands on your grandfather's money.*

"What do you say?"

"About what?"

"Come back with me to Philadelphia. It's your home, Vivian. It's where your family is. We'll have a grand wedding."

She knew she'd have to play dumb to get away from him. Fluttering a hand before her face, she faked a gasp. "Mr. Randall, are you asking me to marry you…again?"

"I'm giving you another chance," he said with gravel in his tone.

He wasn't even pretending to make a romantic proposal. "I'm flattered, Draven, but it's too soon for me to give you an answer. The truth is, we hardly know each other. I was far too hasty in marrying you the first time."

"What do you mean, we *hardly* know each other? We were married."

"Illegally," Vivian argued.

"Not true," Draven grinned, his teeth white in the candlelight. "I have a copy of our marriage certificate with me as proof."

Vivian sucked in her breath. "That's impossible. You said we weren't married."

"I never said that. You left me, Vivian. Ran out on our marriage."

"What are you saying?" Vivian was genuinely shocked and confused.

"I'm saying we're legally married."

"You're *saying* we're married, but we're not really married, right? That's what you told me."

"I have our marriage certificate."

"If you do, it must be counterfeit."

"I'm a lawyer, Vivian. I know a legal document when I see one."

Vivian pursed her lips, forcing herself to keep from yelling a retort at the wretched man. "You're joking, of course," she said.

"I'm not joking. Our marriage certificate is in my hotel room, signed by witnesses. Even signed by you, my dear."

"But I never signed anything."

"I recall that you did," he practically sneered.

She felt sick to her stomach. She knew he was lying because she never signed any marriage certificate, and she never saw any witnesses sign such a document. "You forged my name?"

He shrugged.

Her head swam. She couldn't faint. Not here, not now. Oh, how she despised this man! This was entrapment. If such an incriminating—and obviously counterfeit—document truly did exist, she must find it and destroy it. And she knew a little about counterfeit marriage certificates herself, because she had one of her own—with her fake late husband's signature—and his death certificate too.

"I don't know, Draven," she faltered. Her throat was dry. "This is all such a shock to me. First you tell me we were never legally married; now you're telling me we're married. It's too much to comprehend all at once."

"I never said we weren't married, Vivian. That's a lie you made up and told yourself."

What a bald-faced lie! He was deliberately confusing and manipulating her.

She watched the muscles in his jaw tense. "I'm leaving on the train Monday morning. I want you on that train with me."

That sounded demanding. She'd have to appease him if she wanted a chance to make her getaway. "I do miss Mother and Father and all my friends back home."

"And me."

"Of course, you," she croaked. How could she make him lose interest in her? She looked down at her skirt. "There's a part of me that wishes I was pregnant. I'd come back to you in a heartbeat then. I could picture us a happy family. But, honestly, I have my sister here. She's family, and being a widow isn't all bad."

His eyes flashed with what looked very much like hatred. "If you're not pregnant, I came all this way for nothing."

She wasn't expecting a confession from his own lips! "What do you mean, Draven?"

"I mean, I—we're married. I came out here to get my wife back, and I look forward to your being the mother of my children, Vivian."

"What do you mean you came all this way for nothing if I'm not pregnant?"

"You misunderstood me, Vivian."

There he was lying again—the snake! She knew it was useless to debate him. "If we're married, why are you here at this dance with Samantha? She's probably wondering where you are."

"When a husband comes into town to take back his wife, he doesn't want to make a scene, of course. I decided to preserve your honor and give you the chance to return without anyone knowing we're married and that you ran away from me. But if you refuse to come back, I'll expose you for the fraud that you are."

She knew he'd make good on that threat. Things had just taken a turn for the worse. Now she was trapped—in more ways than one.

"I will return to Philadelphia with you," she conceded, "But until we leave on Monday, we have to continue pretending not to know one another. That means you'll go on pretending to court Samantha, and I'll keep pretending to be a widow for a while longer."

"Excellent. I agree. I knew you'd come to your senses, Vivian."

His face broke into a grin, and he spun on his heel, raising his fists above his head in triumph, giving Vivian the opportunity she needed to leap to the door, unlock it, turn the knob, and dart out of the room to freedom. She ran down the hall to the foot of the stairs, her eyes scanning, darting in search of anyone who would make her feel safe.

"Vivian!" Draven shouted, chasing after her. "What game are you playing?"

Her blood pulsed so loudly in her ears that she could barely think. "Do I know you, sir?" she asked, turning to face him, fighting to keep her voice steady.

A familiar figure appeared at the top of the stairs.

"Samantha!" Vivian called breathlessly, gripping the handrail and nearly collapsing as she stumbled up the stairs to be by her side on the landing.

"That's it," said Samantha, grabbing and twisting Vivian's arm. "I'm sick and tired of you stealing every unattached man in town from me," she shouted in a whisper. "First Mr. Ryan, then Mr. Graver, now Mr. Randall! He is *my* escort to the ball. *Mine.*" She said all this as Draven climbed the stairs toward them. "I know some things about you and Draven Randall, Widow Smith, and when I tell Mr. Ryan, I guarantee he'll lose interest in you. That's right. I'm going to make sure you never have any prospective suitors in this town."

Vivian clutched at Samantha's hand. "Samantha, please don't! What do you know?"

"Good evening, my dear Miss McGovern," Draven said languidly interrupting their hasty conversation.

"Where have you been, Mr. Randall?" Samantha declared saucily. "I've been looking for you everywhere."

"May I have the next dance?" he asked Samantha.

"Excuse us, Widow Smith." She took Draven's arm and gave Vivian a hard shove that slammed her head against the doorframe of the dance hall. Dizzy and disoriented, she stumbled and lost her balance. Her head ached and she began to shake uncontrollably. The strain of her encounter with Draven and then Samantha was too much for her.

"Widow Smith?" It was Blue Ryan.

She caught a glimpse of his face as the room tilted, and strange halos formed around the lanterns on a nearby refreshment table. The room faded into darkness and Blue disappeared. A jostling woke her for a moment, and she felt herself being lifted and carried, her cheek pressed against

Blue's solid chest as she inhaled the scents of pine, leather, and soap.

The next thing she knew, she was lying on a sofa, covered with blankets, still trembling. A fire roared in a woodstove and Widow Fitzgerald was coaxing her to sit up and drink a cup of chamomile tea.

"Where am I?" asked Vivian.

"Oh, dear," said Widow Fitz. "You don't know where you are?"

"What happened?"

"Oh, dear," Widow Fitz whimpered, wringing her hands. "You don't know what happened?"

"Where's Mr. Ryan?" Vivian asked.

"Blue's still waiting outside the door," Mabel Fitzgerald replied, agitated. "He gave me his card to give to you—an official offer to come calling on you tomorrow morning to check on you." Her chubby hand pressed the card into Vivian's palm. "Mr. Ryan is waiting to walk me back to the dance hall to chaperone Tessie and Isabel. But maybe I should stay with you instead. I'm worried about you, Widow Smith."

"What?" asked Vivian. She couldn't seem to make sense of anything Widow Fitz had been saying.

"I'm here," came Blue's voice from the other side of the door. The door opened and he peered inside, his eyes on Vivian. "I heard you say my name."

"Did you carry me, Mr. Ryan?"

"I did, ma'am."

"I'm so embarrassed," said Vivian.

"Don't be," said Widow Fitz. "He was only trying to help."

"Did I faint?"

"Yes, ma'am," Blue answered.

"In front of everyone at the dance?"

"Not many people saw you, dear," Widow Fitz assured her. "You fainted near the doorway. Mr. Ryan caught you and carried you all the way here."

"Am I at home? Where's Bobo?"

Widow Fitz patted her head. "Yes, you're home in your apartment, Widow Smith."

"Is she going to be all right? I can fetch Bobo for her," she heard Blue say before the voices grew muffled, and Vivian closed her eyes.

When she awoke again, she was alone in the apartment. She turned her aching head to see Bobo snoring softly on the rug by the door and breathed a sigh of relief. She felt something in her hand and squinted in the low light of the kerosene lamp on the kitchen table.

It was a calling card printed with the words: *Mr. Blue A. Ryan.* She flipped it over and read a neat scrawl on the back: *I'm praying for you.* She closed her eyes and drifted off to sleep again, pressing the card to her heart.

CHAPTER 21: Confessions

The morning after the Harvest Dance dawned bright and cold. After stoking a roaring fire in the woodstove, taking hot baths, and dressing for the day, Vivian and Isabel sat at the table, eating breakfast and discussing the details of Vivian's ordeal with Draven the night before.

"How frightful!" It was the first time Vivian had told Isabel about Draven's coming to town to find her, and she wanted to know every detail. "Why didn't you tell me he was here?"

"Oh, how could I be such a poor judge of character?" Vivian wailed. "I thought I could get him to leave town or at least leave me alone. I was wrong. I'm afraid to leave this apartment, Izza."

"I completely understand," said Isabel, "but you'll be safe with Mr. Ryan."

Vivian swallowed. "That's true, but I must explain everything to him. I can't let him develop feelings for me."

"Because you have feelings for him?" asked Isabel. Vivian's cheeks flushed as she nodded. "He confided in me and asked my permission to court you, Vivi. He really likes you."

Vivian exhaled as a tear ran down her cheek. "I could never let him court me. I have to tell him the whole truth." She patted her abdomen. "The *whole* truth."

"Oh, dear, Vivi." Isabel reached across the table and held her sister's hand. "I hope Mr. Ryan has the moral decency to keep all this news to himself."

The teakettle whistled, and Isabel jumped up to pour cups of tea. "Tell me more about this marriage certificate Draven says he has in his hotel."

"I never signed a marriage certificate, Izza. I never even *saw* a marriage certificate."

"You can't let Mr. Randall show it to anyone, Vivi. That man is dangerous. Fake or not, the law will force you to go back to Philadelphia with him."

"I think you're right," she replied.

They washed and dried dishes together as they continued a conversation about all that Vivian had missed after she left the dance. As they were putting dishes away, Isabel glanced at the clock. "Oh, my! I forgot that Mr. Graver and Mr. Ryan said they'd stop by to visit at nine o'clock!"

"What?!" Vivian exclaimed. "It's quarter of nine now! Why are they coming?"

"Mr. Ryan said he wanted to check on you, and Mr. Graver offered to join him."

"Izza! I'm not decently dressed. And my hair!"

"Go get ready. You still have fifteen minutes."

"Izza?" Vivian called out from the bedroom. "Do you like Mr. Graver?"

There was no answer, so Vivian peeked out the door. "Well?"

"I do." Isabel's entire face turned a bright pink. "He walked me home last night. And, Vivi, he told me he likes me too."

"Really? Oh, Izza, I'm happy for you!" She gave her sister a quick embrace.

"Hurry, Vivi. They should be here any minute."

Vivian finished primping and jogged to the window. Pushing it open, she peered out, leaning to get a full view of the street below. Outside the Schmitt Hotel stood Blue with

Samantha McGovern. She heard her name and Draven's. Then she heard the words "eloped" and "marriage." Weak with a rush of dread, Vivian ducked back inside and slumped into a chair. Shame enveloped her like a grave. She deserved to be rejected by everyone in town. And Isabel did not deserve the shame she'd brought to her.

"I heard," whispered Isabel, rushing to kneel at her side. "Vivi, I'll go down and talk to Mr. Ryan and Samantha. Wait here." Vivian heard the clatter of her footsteps on the stairs as Isabel ran.

Vivian stood on shaky legs to close the window. Wiping tears from her eyes, she watched as Blue stood with Samantha hanging on his arm. How would Samantha know about her marriage to Draven? Did Draven tell her? But why? And poor Izza. She was innocent in all this, and scandal would destroy her.

Though she shook uncontrollably, she managed to descend the stairs to join her sister. She couldn't let Isabel defend her honor. She needed to confront her own problems.

Blue slowly peeled Samantha's fingers from his arm as he stood rigid and still, his eyes boring a hole into Vivian's. "Is it true, Widow Smith?" he asked, his voice tight.

"I owe you both an explanation." Vivian wrung her hands, pleading.

"Why don't you both come inside so we can talk," said Isabel. Martin arrived as well, and he was invited to join the discussion.

Samantha jabbed her hands into her hips and stood her ground. "I refuse to be part of this scandal. Joining the Garrett sisters in their apartment could ruin my reputation." She flashed angry eyes at Vivian before she stomped off, nearly running into Tessie.

"What's she so hornet mad about?" Tessie hopped up onto the boardwalk. "Howdy, everyone!"

Time froze for a second.

"Samantha just told Mr. Ryan some things about Vivian's past," said Isabel.

Tessie clapped a hand over her mouth.

Isabel took charge. "Let's all go inside." She grabbed Vivian's hand and pulled her into the building.

Blue and Martin followed the sisters and Tessie into the modest apartment, the silence amongst the group thick as fog. Vivian's hands trembled as she poured tea into cups with barely concealed nerves. She felt Blue's eyes on her where he stood near the sofa. His face hid his emotions.

Martin stood near the window, arms crossed. He glanced at Isabel as she served tea and withdrew to the woodstove, her fidgety fingers and knitted brows betraying her worry.

Vivian stepped over to her sister and squeezed one of her hands before taking a deep inhale. She faced the gentlemen and Tessie. Her voice was barely above a whisper. "Mr. Ryan, what you heard outside from Samantha—it's not the full truth. But I can't pretend anymore. You deserve to know." Her eyes flitted to Martin. "And, Mr. Graver, you're welcome to hear what I have to say, but I ask that you please not repeat it to anyone. I know I can't make you keep this confidential, and I can't keep Samantha quiet, but I ask you to please not tell anyone for the sake of my sister. She doesn't deserve the scandal."

Martin moved away from the window and seemed torn between whether he should leave or stay.

Tessie dragged a chair from the table to the sitting room area and sat down. "I think you should hear Miss Vivian speak. She's innocent, and you deserve to hear the truth as much as she deserves to be heard."

Blue crossed the floor and lowered himself onto the couch, resting his elbows on his knees. "I'm listening," said Blue, his gaze steady.

Martin took a seat beside Blue. "I'll listen too."

Vivian swallowed hard. Isabel remained at her side, offering silent support.

"Mr. Draven Randall III was a man I trusted," Vivian began. "I was young, naïve, and gullible when we met in a park in Philadelphia. He charmed me, professed his love for me, promised me love and a future." She paused, tears threatening. "I agreed to elope with him. No big wedding. My parents didn't know. We married in a small chapel. No witnesses."

"He faked the wedding," Isabel added.

"A fake wedding with a minister?" Martin asked.

"A friend posed as the minister," said Vivian.

"No witnesses?" asked Blue.

"None," said Vivian.

"That's important to remember," said Isabel.

"Like I said, I..I trusted him," Vivian stuttered. "The morning after our wedding night..." Isabel nodded her encouragement to Vivian, and she dropped her eyes to the floor. Nervously rocking one foot, she went on: "The next morning, he told me I didn't please him and that our wedding was a sham." She heard a gasp from either Martin or Blue but kept her eyes lowered. "He'd tricked me. He said we were never married at all. But..." She tapped her foot nervously and pushed back the cuticle of a finger.

"Would you like me to tell them?" asked Isabel.

Vivian bit down hard on her lower lip and shook her head. "I didn't tell Mother and Father anything until…until I feared I might be with child."

Gasps from Martin and Blue sucked the air out of the room.

"Are you?" Blue's whisper was hoarse.

Vivian pressed her eyes closed and held tightly to her sister's hand to steady herself. "I'm not entirely sure yet, but I confess it is a possibility."

Isabel spoke this time: "Our father met with a lawyer who helped create a falsified marriage certificate and false death certificate for Vivian; then they arranged for her to come out here as a widow so that, in case she was with child, she and our parents could avoid scandal and shame in Philadelphia." She put a comforting arm around Vivian's shoulders.

Martin shifted awkwardly in his seat and swallowed. "Is that all?"

"No, there's more," said Isabel. "Mr. Randall came all the way out here to find Vivian. He wants her back because his grandfather passed away and left him a lot of money—but he can only inherit it if he marries by the end of the year and has a son."

Martin raked his fingers through his hair. "I'm not sure I should be hearing all this."

Vivian finally tilted her head up a little. "I know. I'm sorry, Mr. Graver. You're welcome to go, if you'd like." But Martin made no move to leave.

Blue furrowed his brow. "Widow Smith, er, Miss Vivian, I am terribly sorry for all the trauma, grief, and betrayal you have experienced. I can see you don't deserve any of it."

Vivian's eyes brimmed with tears. "Thank you, Mr. Ryan." Isabel squeezed her hand.

"You have my sympathies too," Martin added. "You and your sister have both suffered a great deal."

"Miss McGovern told me Mr. Randall had faked other marriages?" asked Blue.

"We found out the same thing just recently," said Isabel, "from a friend back in Philadelphia who did some investigating for us."

Blue's jaw tightened, fists clenching. "Did he hurt you, Miss Vivian?"

She hesitated, then nodded. "Emotionally, yes. He threatened me last night at the dance. Said he has a copy of our marriage certificate in his hotel room and that he'll use it as proof of our marriage and force me to go back with him to Philadelphia if I don't go with him peacefully."

"But it's a forged marriage certificate?" asked Martin.

"Yes," Vivian answered.

A heavy silence followed, broken only by Blue's sharp inhale as he stood and paced. "This man needs to be put in jail."

"I wanna slug the varmint!" shouted Tessie, slamming a fist into her palm.

"I'm so afraid," said Vivian, "I don't dare to leave this apartment." She gave Blue a sheepish look. "Which reminds me: Mr. Randall's the reason Cocoa Joe asked you to walk me to and from work. He's the man who frightened me when I was walking in Cocoa Joe's pasture."

Blue shook his head, his face slowly registering surprise, then recognition, then compassion.

Martin drummed his finger on his knee. "If Draven Randall presents that certificate to the law…"

"They'll force me to go back with him," Vivian whispered.

"No," Blue said, standing abruptly. "They won't."

Vivian's eyes widened.

"I don't care what paper he claims to have." Blue's voice was steady, but anger flickered in his eyes—not at her, but at Draven. "I won't let him take you away, Miss Vivian."

Tears streamed freely now, and Vivian hid her face behind a hand. Isabel stepped in, holding her tightly.

Martin cleared his throat. "Blue's right. You're not alone in this. We won't let Mr. Randall kidnap you."

Vivian looked up, hope mingling with fear. "You believe me?"

Blue's eyes were filled with pity and sympathy. "Vivian, I don't doubt your motives, but I admit I doubted your honesty when you told me your late husband was Oscar Wendell Smith." One corner of his mouth twitched upward. "I knew an Oscar Wendell Smith back in Chicago. He was killed in the street by a horseless carriage in New York about six months ago." Vivian clapped both hands over her mouth. "The chances of you being married to a deceased man by the exact same name seemed pretty slim, but I knew you must have your reasons. That you were in some kind of trouble."

"You knew I was lying all this time about being a widow?"

Blue nodded. "I don't judge you. You're the victim of a villain's terrible crime, Miss Vivian."

"That's right. She is," Tessie practically hollered.

"I just hope you weren't trying to entrap an innocent bachelor into marrying you and making him believe Draven's baby was his," Blue said hoarsely.

"Never," said Vivian. "Hence the widow's garb. There's no need for me to hastily marry anyone as a widow with a baby—my former husband's baby."

"But other people are too quick to judge," said Isabel. "That's why we'd like to keep as much of this a secret as possible."

Both Martin and Blue promised never to tell a soul. And, before they took their leave, they agreed that, if they couldn't come up with enough evidence against Draven to have him arrested and thrown in jail, maybe they could work together to make plans to make him leave town.

Vivian breathed a long sigh and dabbed at her eyes with a handkerchief. "Thank you both for being here to support and care for me," she said to Tessie and her sister as she collapsed onto the sofa and closed her eyes. "I'm exhausted."

Tessie waited until she heard the entrance door close downstairs before she broke a weary silence. "I think your Mr. Ryan might be in love with ya, Miss Vivian."

Vivin's eyes popped open, and she blew her nose on the handkerchief. "Don't be ridiculous. There's no chance of that now he knows the whole truth."

"I think Tessie's right," said Isabel, kneeling to add another stick of wood to the stove, "but it doesn't mean he'll ever act on it."

"I think now he's just being kind," Vivian sighed.

"May I?" Tessie asked, gesturing to the tea service on the coffee table.

After Tessie boiled more water and served tea to everyone, she cleared her throat and stared at Isabel. "Well, have you told Miss Vivian about you and you-know-who?"

She smiled wanly. "As a matter of fact, I have. I just hope he still likes and respects me after all he just heard. I wouldn't blame him if he feels overwhelmed by all of it." She tilted her head and squinted. "The question is: Do you have anything to share about you and Mr. Ranson?"

"Well… Oh, I can't wait to tell ya!" Tessie squealed. "As a matter of fact, Cade asked to court me. Can ya believe it? He knows all about my bad reputation and he loves me anyway!"

"Loves?" asked Vivian, lifting her head from the back of the sofa.

"I know. That's what he actually said: *Loves!*"

"I can't believe he could say anything, much less *loves*," Vivian chuckled softly. "It's really wonderful, Tessie. I knew the two of you should be together."

Tessie exhaled happily and yawned.

Vivian broke the quiet. "Girls, I need to get that marriage certificate away from Draven."

"How?" asked Isabel.

"I need your help. I need to get into Draven's hotel room, find it, and destroy it."

"I'll help ya," said Tessie, "but I don't know if you should destroy it. Ain't it evidence that Draven is a forger?"

"I don't know," said Vivian. "All I know is I need to steal that document from him and hide it someplace safe so I can use it if and when I need it."

"I'll help you too," said Isabel. "What do you need us to do?"

CHAPTER 22: Intrigues

"Where do you think Mr. Randall might be on a Saturday afternoon?" asked Isabel, pushing up the window and leaning out. Isabel scowled. "Vivian, if you want to go through with this dangerous scheme, you need a better disguise." She scanned the street and the boardwalk below. "Bobo's back. It's rather sweet—like he knows when to be here to protect you, Vivi."

Vivian stood on her toes to crane her neck over her sister's head. "I wish you hadn't kicked him out, Izza."

"I didn't know you were so fond of dogs." Isabel shut the window

"He's growing on me. Oh! I have an idea! I'll be right back." Vivian grabbed a pair of scissors and dashed out of the apartment and down the stairs.

"I wonder what that's about." Tessie picked up a ball of yarn from Isabel's knitting basket. She fumbled, dropped the yarn, and chased it across the floor, winding a long line of wool that had laid itself out across the boards.

Vivian popped back in the door again holding a tuft of Bobo's dark yellow fur in her fingers. "Bobo to the rescue," she declared, panting.

"What on earth?" Isabel exclaimed. "Don't bring that in here, Vivi."

"He spends a lot of time in saloons," said Tessie.

"Bobo hangs out in saloons?" asked Isabel. "Why am I not surprised?"

Vivian ducked into Isabel's bedroom and called out, "I think she means Draven."

"Oh, of course," Isabel muttered, biting the inside of her cheek as she watched Tessie pick up another ball of yarn. "I didn't see Draven anywhere on Main Street. Tessie, what are you doing?"

Tessie was tucking two balls of yarn into the bodice of her dress. "I'm sure I could work my magic on him again."

"Cade is happy with you the way you are, Tessie. There's no need for knitting enhancements in your bodice," said Isabel.

"I think she's talking about Draven," said Vivian.

"Tessie, no!" Isabel protested. "Don't you dare do anything that could put your reputation in jeopardy after all we've done to repair it."

"How's the costume coming along, Miss Vivian?" asked Tessie, changing the subject.

"Fine." She emerged from the bedroom wearing trousers, shirt, suspenders, and jacket borrowed, with permission, from Zhang Wei's laundry downstairs. Her hair, tied back into a ponytail, was tucked into the back of a man's shirt.

"You don't look at all like a man, Vivi," Isabel wailed. "You look like a lovely young lady wearing trousers. You'll attract more attention rather than less."

Vivian hovered in front of the mirror for a few seconds, then spun round. "How do I look?" she asked.

"Like a handsome young gentleman!" Tessie exclaimed.

Vivian made a bow wearing the tuft of Bobo's fur glued to her upper lip.

Isabel shook her head. "I admit it looks rather convincing. Very clever, Vivi."

"It's a perfect match to your hair color!" said Tessie.

Vivian sneezed and the "mustache" floated to the floor.

"Oh, dear!" Isabel whined. "How is this charade going to work if you're allergic to your own mustache, Vivi?"

Tessie picked up the dog hair caterpillar from the floor, barely suppressing a snort. They all enjoyed a good laugh.

"I tried using flour paste," said Vivian, "but… Oh, I know!" She swiped a bead of sap from a log beside the woodstove and dabbed it on her upper lip; then pressed the "mustache" to her skin. It worked!

Tessie popped a black felt derby—also borrowed from Zhang Wei—onto Vivian's head.

Isabel bit her lower lip and wrung her hands. "What if someone recognizes you?"

"As long as Draven doesn't recognize me, that's all that matters," said Vivian.

"I'll try to make sure he don't see ya at all," said Tessie. "I'm sure I can keep him occupied in whatever saloon he happens to be in."

"The hotel corridors are also quite dim," Vivian reassured her sister. "No one will recognize me."

"Well, are we ready?" asked Tessie.

"Let's take one more peek outside," Vivian suggested. All three poked their heads out the window.

Tessie pointed across the street. "There's Samantha and Barbara Mitchell outside the newspaper office."

"What's Samantha up to?" asked Isabel.

"Iffen I know her, she's lookin' for a man," said Tessie.

"Probably Blue or Draven," Vivian agreed.

"Looks like she's headin' to the Wildwood," said Tessie.

They watched Samantha McGovern sashay along the boardwalk and dart across the street, making a beeline for the Wildwood Café.

"I wish she were with Draven now," said Vivian.

"Maybe she's meetin' him at the Wildwood," Tessie suggested. "I'll check there first."

They backed away from the window. "So, the plan again is…?" Isabel questioned.

"Tessie scouts out the Wildwood and the saloons first," said Vivian. "Isabel, you wait on the boardwalk. Tessie will signal to you if she finds Draven anywhere. Then you'll signal to me, Izza. I'll get into Draven's hotel through the back door while you distract the bellhop at the front of the hotel. I'll tiptoe up to the lobby, sneak behind the front desk, get Draven's key, and search his room for the marriage certificate."

"All right, and I'll wait outside and keep a lookout for Draven," said Isabel. "I'll run back to warn you if I see him coming.

"I'll signal to you, Isabel, if I can't detain him or maybe he moves really fast and ends up back at the hotel," said Tessie.

"If I see him enter the lobby, I'll try to distract him," said Isabel. "But what should I do?"

"Ask if he's seen Mr. Graver," Vivian suggested.

"Tell him he looks handsome and use some of the flirtation skills I taught ya," said Tessie. "And if I see anything's going wrong, I'll run around to the back of the hotel and warn ya, Miss Vivian."

"Exactly," Vivian nodded.

Isabel held out her hands. "Look at me. I'm nervous as a cat."

"I think it's excitin'," said Tessie. "I think it's gonna work."

"And if it doesn't? If Vivi gets caught?" asked Isabel.

Tessie winked. "Then we claim it was all for a bet—and that she lost."

"Not bad," Vivian agreed.

Isabel gave a firm nod. "And one or both of us will be ready outside, whatever happens. No matter what, you have to find that marriage certificate, Vivi."

Vivian stood in the doorway of the stone apartment building watching Tessie and Isabel carry out the first leg of their mission.

Isabel came running back up the boardwalk to Vivian. "He's in the Wildwood with Samantha," she wheezed. "Tessie's keeping an eye on them. She'll distract Draven if he looks like he's planning to leave. Go round to the back of the hotel now! I'll sit on a bench out front and keep watch. Hurry!"

Samantha smoothed her gloved hands along her apricot wool coat, feeling smart in the new, shapely fashion trimmed with an extra row of buttons trailing down the bodice. A wide, ostrich-plumed hat crowned her head, and her perfume was lavishly applied. She'd been across the street talking with Barbara Mitchell about how Draven had seemed to lose interest in her. She was so angry, she wanted to do as much damage to Vivian Garrett as possible. She'd already succeeded in ruining her chances with Mr. Ryan. Now she had to win back Draven's attentions.

"He must want her back," Barbara had deduced. "Why else would he come all this way to find her?"

When Samantha saw Draven enter the Wildwood Café, it was her chance to try her wiles on him again.

Draven Randall beckoned to her from a nearby table. "Would you care to join me for a cup of coffee or tea, Miss McGovern?"

"Thank you kindly," she said, unbuttoning her coat and casually tossing her head so that a brunette curl swung precociously over her eyes. She hung her coat on a hook beside the door as Tessie entered.

"Afternoon, Samantha," said Tessie in her loud voice.

Samantha ignored her, turning up her nose and swinging her hips as she weaved through the tables to where Draven stood holding a chair out for her.

"You look pretty as a peach this fine afternoon, Miss McGovern," Draven drawled, touching his napkin to the corner of an eye and stifling a sneeze. "I beg your pardon. It must be the dust in this town."

"I daresay we're seeing too much of each other lately, Mr. Randall. People might start to talk." She said coyly, though slightly annoyed at Draven's sniffling. Why were people always sneezing and sniffling around her?

He walked around to his side of the table after seating her. "And what might they say about us?" His teeth gleamed white behind his mustache.

"Impolite things, knowing this town," she snapped, removing her gloves.

"Improper things?" he queried.

She leaned toward him across the table. "Salacious things," she whispered impishly.

He chuckled and, as he ordered a cup of tea for her, Samantha wondered what it would be like to be married to this rich man. If she moved to Pennsylvania, she'd miss her parents, but wealth would make up for her homesickness. Even if he were once a notorious philanderer, she'd make him fall in love with her, repent of his sinful ways, and all other ladies would be pea green with envy.

"There's something different about you this afternoon," Draven remarked, examining her slowly and carefully, as though admiring a work of art.

She batted her eyes and twirled a finger in her ostrich feather. "My new hat perhaps?"

"It's very nice, yes, but there's something else," he said. "I sense a grown-up shrewdness in you, my dear."

Samantha shook her curls. He was a perceptive devil. She hoped he didn't suspect her of trying to trap him in marriage. "I'm as shrewd and grown-up as I've ever been," she said saucily, aware that every word she said could make or break her chances of a future with him.

Draven laughed aloud. He flirted mercilessly, admiring her cheeks, hair, and lips. He even commented on her perfume, but she wasn't sure his words were entirely complimentary when he described the scent as "redolent of leather, musk, and tobacco."

Suddenly Draven's hand was on her knee, hidden beneath the tablecloth. She froze before trying in vain to pull back from his tightening clasp. She cast her eyes about the restaurant, alarmed yet excited at the same time.

Mr. Randall laughed lightly and slid his fingers further along her thigh. She didn't know whether to be flattered or outraged. She remained stiff and still, wondering what reaction he wanted from her. "Mr. Randall, you are very naughty," she scolded in a shrill whisper.

"But I think you like naughty, Miss McGovern," he said in a cavalier tone, "because I think you're a little naughty yourself."

She lifted her head. It wouldn't do to let him think she was loose. What a delicate balancing act this was. "Mr. Randall," she said, her voice low, "No man will know how naughty I can be until after I've married him—and that man *won't* be you."

She slid back her chair, thanked Draven for the tea, and walked away, swaying her hips as she crossed the room and donned her coat. She tossed Draven a smug parting glance and withdrew from the café, the forbidden touch of his hand still tickling her thigh. Had she left too soon? No, she'd stick with her feminine instincts. She knew how to entice a man. By telling Draven what he *couldn't* have, she knew he'd want her all the more. She was counting on it.

Vivian darted out the back door of her apartment building and into Pig Alley, dashing furtively to the Blake Hotel. Slipping through the back door, she tiptoed slowly along the darkened hallway. She froze with each creak of the floor as she stepped until she realized she had no reason to be so stealthy. She should behave normally, as though she were a guest. She raised her head, squared her shoulders, and padded up the corridor to the lobby, where she spied Isabel and the bellhop bent near the front door, searching the floor.

"It fell off right about here," said Isabel. "Oh, I hope I find it. These ear drops were a gift from my grandmother. I just can't lose one."

"I'm sure we'll find it," said the bellhop.

Isabel was splendid! Vivian dropped close to the floor and crept behind the counter to where the room keys hung in neat rows along the wall. She located one with a small tag that read "Randall." On the key chain was the number 14. She snatched the key, snuck back to the hallway, and forced herself to walk slowly around the corner.

"Here it is!" Isabel's voice carried from the lobby. "Thank you ever so much for helping me find this little ear drop. I would have been so sad to lose it forever."

Vivian scurried up the stairs to the second floor. It would make for a more difficult escape if there was any danger, but she couldn't think of that now. She passed another couple on the stairs and tipped her hat. The couple took no notice of her.

The moment Samantha exited the Wildwood, Tessie pinched her cheeks and made sure her hips were swinging seductively as she wound her way to Draven's table.

"Mr. Draven Randall the *Third*," she gushed.

"Well, if it isn't the little pixie from the saloon," said Draven. "Haven't seen you there lately."

Tessie seated herself across from Draven. "That's because I don't work there no more, Mr. Randall. But let's talk about you and Miss Samantha McGovern. You two certainly make a charmin' couple."

Draven lit a cigar. "What did you say your name was again, sweetheart?" He blew out a puff of smoke.

"Miss Blackman," she answered, walking two fingers across the table to stroke his arm. "But you can call me Tessie."

"Are you lookin' for male companionship, Miss Tessie Blackman?" he asked, squinting at her.

"I might be." She reached out a toe against his leg beneath the table.

Draven stood, sauntered over to the counter, and paid his bill, leaving Tessie alone and wondering what he was planning next. He took a few steps toward the door, turned his head toward her, and tilted his head as a signal to come with him.

She hurried to his side. "Where to, Mr. Randall?"

"A place where you can get the male companionship you seek," Draven whispered into her ear.

She shivered. "The saloon?" she asked innocently, knowing full well what he meant.

He laughed, threw on his coat, and opened the door for her. When they were alone outside on the boardwalk he said, "To my hotel." He turned and strode up the street, leaving her behind, which was just as well because, with his back to her she hopped up and down, gesticulating wildly, trying to get Isabel's attention where she sat on a bench outside the Blake Hotel.

Tessie shouted and pointed to the sky. "Look! Look! Those birds! Oh, I love those birds," hoping Draven would turn around. He did. "Oh, goldarn, you missed them. They flew away."

"I wonder if you could possibly be any louder, Miss Blackman." His eyes were simmering with displeasure. "How absurd can you be?"

"Let's get a little drunk at the saloon first, darlin'," Tessie drawled, giggling. "I could use a drink."

"Looks and sounds like you've already had a drink or two."

Tessie skipped to Draven and tugged his arm. "I ain't drunk nothin'," she pouted. "Please? One pint of beer?"

Draven hesitated; then shook his head. "You are the strangest little imp," he said, shaking her from his arm. "Walk behind me. I don't want anyone thinking we're together."

"Understood," said Tessie, letting him walk ahead as she giggled loudly and jumped up and down, waving to Isabel.

Vivian arrived at Draven's room and unlocked the door. She slipped inside, locked the door behind her, and quickly surveyed the room. There was a trunk beneath the bed. Sliding it out, she tried to open it, but it was locked. Hopping up, she ran to the wardrobe. Searching pockets, she located a small key in the pocket of a pair of trousers, and when she inserted the key into the trunk lock, it fit and opened!

Carefully lifting the clothing within, she felt along the bottom. Nothing. She searched the inside seams all around the sides, but there were no papers of any kind. She relocked the trunk, replaced the key in the trouser pocket, and dug deeper into the wardrobe. Locating a small briefcase, she opened it, but it was empty. She replaced it, closed the wardrobe doors, and scurried over to a desk. Rifling through it, she again found nothing. She was beginning to panic. Draven wouldn't carry the marriage certificate with him, would he? No, it had to be in this room—if it even existed.

Maybe he'd been bluffing the whole time. Arms akimbo, Vivian stood in the center of the room, running her eyes across every inch of the small space.

It was time to deepen her search. She lifted the mattress of the bed and sifted through all the bedding as well as beneath the pillows and inside the pillowcases. She opened a hatbox and felt along the top of the wardrobe. She scoured the interior of the wardrobe from top to bottom.

In consternation, she sat on the bed and stuttered out a prayer for help. "It's not stealing if the document is rightfully mine, Lord. Please help me find it." From where she sat, she discerned a gap beneath the wardrobe, where something lay hidden in the shadows. Heart pounding, she dropped to the floor and pulled out a leatherbound portfolio. Unfastening the buckle, she opened it, and there it was. The marriage certificate lay on top of a stack of legal-looking documents. She lifted out the papers and thumbed through them in search of other possible incriminating documents. But they slipped from her trembling hands, scattering across the floor. The marriage certificate was lost amongst them.

As she frantically gathered the papers, glancing quickly at each one, a tap sounded on the door, and she froze, holding her breath. Hearing no further tapping or noises outside the door, she continued gathering the papers and replacing them in the portfolio as fast as she could. When she found the marriage certificate again, she stared at her name on the signature line: *Vivian Garrett.* But it wasn't even close to her signature style. She folded and stuffed the paper into the waist of her trousers; then she crawled on the floor in search of any other escaped papers. Finding none, she closed the portfolio and slid it back under the wardrobe.

There was another sharp "tap, tap, tap." She placed her ear on the door.

"Vivi!" someone whispered. It was Isabel! She opened the door and found herself being pulled from the room and down the hallway.

"He's coming!" Isabel shouted in a whisper. "We have to hurry downstairs and go out the back."

"I must lock the door!" Vivian shook herself from Isabel's grasp, ran back to Draven's room, and locked the door with clumsy fingers.

Isabel ran to Vivian and tugged her back to the stairwell. "Tessie led Draven to the saloon," she whispered in her ear. "She says he drank a couple of whiskeys, but he said he was going back to his hotel, and she couldn't detain him anymore. He's coming, Vivi. He may already be here." They came to a halt and jumped back when they spied Draven and the bellhop at the foot of the stairs. They flattened themselves against the wall, peering frantically up and down the corridor. There was no way out!

"You'd better find it," Draven ordered. "I'm not paying you to rent a room I can't get into." His words were slurred.

"Yes, sir," said the bellhop, jingling a handful of keys. "I promise we'll locate your key, but I have the copy here and I'll be happy to let you back into your room."

With no place to hide, Vivian pulled her sister into her arms and pretended to kiss her. Draven and the bellhop glanced their direction but turned away, ignoring them. Vivian watched until Draven stumbled into his room, slamming the door behind him while the bellhop was apologizing to him mid-sentence. The moment the bellhop turned and went back down the stairs, Vivian released Isabel and the two followed behind him.

"Don't rush, Vivi," said Isabel. "Stay calm and walk slowly like normal hotel guests."

The sisters reached the landing and made a quick survey of the lobby. A couple stood at the counter, and the woman's hand hovered above the bell. Vivian leaped to the counter and snatched the bell away before it could be rung. "Welcome to—" she began; then cleared her throat and lowered her register. "Welcome to the Blake Hotel. I'm afraid the bellhop is busy assisting another guest at the moment. May I be of assistance to you?" Vivian handed the key to Isabel as the dumbfounded couple blinked, looked at one another, muttered something unintelligible, and left the hotel.

"It's your mustache," said Isabel, ripping Bobo's fur from her upper lip.

"Ow!" Vivian cried.

"It was off kilter," Isabel explained as she pushed Vivian out the door and onto the boardwalk.

"Where's Tessie?" Vivian asked.

"I don't know. Hurry!" she cried in a whisper, pulling Vivian up the walk toward their building. "Let's get home as fast as we can and hope Tessie's there."

Thankfully, Tessie was back at the apartment and, after each shared her story of the afternoon's capers, Vivian gave the marriage certificate to Tessie, who took it home with her for safekeeping. It put Vivian's mind at ease knowing the document would be hidden in a place where Draven could never find it. Though it was a forged marriage certificate, it was also evidence against him, in case she needed it in the future.

"I need a nap," Isabel exhaled, collapsing onto her bed without even closing her bedroom door.

Vivian sat on the sofa, head in her hands, tapping her heel on the floor in an attempt to control her nervous shaking as a blast of wind hit the window, shuddering the pane. After several minutes, she changed out of her masculine garb and into a dress, and then donned a long wool coat, scarf, knit hat, and gloves.

Only once she was walking the path alongside Johnson Creek, drinking in the earth-spiced aroma of mushrooms, moss, and damp earth did Vivian's heartrate finally slow to normal. She paused to turn her eyes skyward to watch a "V" formation of Canada geese flying below the gathering storm clouds, then plodded onward, enjoying the bright splashes of glittering autumn leaves that quaked and danced as they fell upon the gurgling current of water.

On the walk back home, a brisk wind gusted from tall cornflower-blue peaks iced with a fresh layer of snow. She prayed she'd never be forced to leave this beautiful place with her dear sister and new friends.

CHAPTER 23: The Cold of Night

An icy wind blew in shuddering blasts against the apartment windows as Vivian stoked the fire in the woodstove, jabbing at the coals as though she could fend off the solitude of the room. She was happy her sister was keeping company with Martin for dinner with Tessie and Cade at the Wildwood Café. Vivian tried to smile, imagining Isabel's laughter, the clinking of cutlery on china, the warmth of friendly company. Meanwhile, the fire's flicker cast long shadows on the walls, and cold dread seeped into her bones, unshaken by the blaze.

She opened the door and called Bobo inside from the landing. The dog continued to faithfully guard her, somehow sensing her need for protection and, since another storm was on its way, she couldn't let the poor thing stay outside on a night like this. Besides, she needed his company and didn't care how Isabel would protest. Bobo came willingly, wagging his tail and sniffing about from room to room. When he concluded his investigations, he flopped onto the floor at her feet, and she reached down to scratch his fluffy head. He really was the sweetest, most unselfish soul. With Cocoa Joe's dog there to comfort her, Vivian felt safe and, selecting a copy of the latest issue of *Strand Magazine*, she stretched out to comfortably recline on the sofa.

"Do you want to hear a story, Bobo?" she asked. "How about Sherlock Holmes' *The Adventure of the Naval Treaty*?"

She cleared her throat. *"Then I heard a gentle creaking as the window was very slowly opened,"* she read aloud dramatically and laughed at the perk of his ears and the tilt of his fuzzy head. "…*he had some weapon in his hand,*" she read on.

A log in the woodstove crashed, and both Vivian and Bobo jumped. "It's nothing, Bobo," she laughed uneasily. "Maybe we shouldn't read scary stories late at night." She continued anyhow. "…*It looked to me like a long knife….*"

Bobo sprang uncharacteristically to his feet and the hair on his neck and back stood on end. Vivian held her breath and listened. A slow, steady clinking and shuffling on the stairwell sent chills up her spine. She slowly set the magazine aside and tiptoed to the door. Crouching low, she jiggled the knob. It was locked. Thank the Lord. Then she watched in horror as the lock slowly twisted before her very eyes. She grabbed the knob, attempting in vain to hold the lock in place. The door opened and Draven appeared in the shadows of the landing.

"Hello, Mrs. Randall," The haunting words slithered from the darkness, and she could smell the alcohol on his breath. "You broke into my hotel room today."

She lunged and threw her whole body against the door. "Get out!" she cried, fear catching in her throat, making her voice crackle. She managed to shut the door, but it slowly opened again, pushing her, sliding her backward on the smooth, polished wood floor as it swung on its hinges.

Bobo stood on all fours, bristling with his hackles up, growling at Draven with teeth bared. Vivian tried to stand and take steps to hide behind him, but Draven reached behind the door with a black-gloved hand, seized her arm, and rammed her to the floor. The impact of the fall knocked the breath from her and shot pain through her right arm. "Or was it your sister or maybe that harlot, Tessie?"

"I don't know what you're talking about," Vivian panted.

There was a low snarl and snap as Bobo lunged at Draven's calf. Vivian took the moment to half crawl, half stumble to the kitchen, where she opened a drawer, grabbed a knife, and spun round to face her intruder.

He stood less than a yard from her, pointing his Smith and Wesson at her chest. "Where is the marriage certificate, Vivian?"

She gasped and dropped the knife, clattering it to the floor as her eyes went to Bobo lying motionless by the door. "What did you do to him?" she whispered, her voice shaking uncontrollably. Something warm and moist made her eyelashes sticky, and she couldn't see out of her left eye.

"Forget about the dog," Draven rumbled. He took a shuffled half-step toward her, still pointing the gun. "Where's the marriage certificate you stole from me?"

She swiped at her eye with the back of her hand and blinked dazedly at the crimson smear on her knuckles.

"Answer me!" he roared. He swept his arm across the kitchen countertop, sending pots, pans, and bowls crashing to the floor.

She sucked in her breath sharply. "I…I don't know what you're talking about," she stammered, her voice shaking and barely audible.

"Yes, you do, Vivian. Find it and give it back to me now."

"Draven…" She fought hard against the panic. "I know about your grandfather's will, and that you need to marry before the end of the year, and you don't inherit your fortune until after your wife gives birth to a son. You must think I'm pregnant or you wouldn't have come all the way out here to find me and take me back to Pennsylvania."

A flicker of something crossed Draven's face—fear? Desperation? But it vanished as quickly as it came, replaced by cold fury. "Shut up. You think you have me all figured out now, don't you?"

"Draven, I don't think I'm pregnant, but if I am, the way you're treating me would cause a miscarriage."

He snarled. "So, stop fighting me, and I'll treat you more carefully."

"And what if you have only girls? What would you do with me? Divorce me like King Henry VIII divorced Anne Boleyn?"

"You think you're so smart, Vivian," he hissed. "You're coming with me to Philadelphia, and you'll come peacefully, or I'll make sure you don't make it out of here alive."

His chest heaved, breath coming fast and shallow, hands trembling with rage as he stepped closer. He poked at her chest with the barrel of his revolver. "Pack your things and get me that marriage certificate. We're leaving a little sooner than planned. We'll take the next train out of Yreka in the morning." He withdrew the gun from her and shoved her out of the kitchen and into the parlor. "Hurry before your stupid sister gets home."

Her hands trembled at her sides, legs rooted to the floor as if they no longer belonged to her. He shoved her again, and she lurched into Isabel's bedroom. And he at last uncocked and re-holstered his revolver. "Don't be long."

Vivian shivered. The apartment was warm, but she felt almost hypothermic. She opened the wardrobe and pulled out a couple of dresses, stopping to stare again in shock at the blood smears left by her hand. She grabbed a few other items of clothing and stumbled back to the parlor, dropping a skirt and blouse on the floor in her haste. She opened her trunk, stuffed the clothing inside, then stood to face Draven again, trying to think of a way to stall him until Isabel came home. But she couldn't do that. What if she came home alone without Martin? What would Draven do to her?

"I'm getting some magazines and books to read," she said, treading carefuly to a bookshelf near the window.

"Forget about magazines and books," Draven shouted, making her jump. "Get that marriage certificate."

"All right, all right," Vivian gasped, backing toward the window, watching Draven warily.

Bobo whined and when Draven looked down, Vivian yanked open the window a crack and dropped to the floor. Putting her face to the small opening, she screamed, "Help! Help! Above the laundry! Help me!"

"Shut up!" Spurs and boots stomped across the floor. "Scream again and I'll shoot you, Vivian," he bawled, pulling out his gun and striking the butt of it against her head. Her consciousness wavered and she slumped to the floor. She faintly heard Draven's swearing as he slammed the window shut and rolled her onto her stomach, wrenching her arms behind her back. "I can't trust you to stay quiet," he growled as he bound her wrists and grabbed her by the hair before stuffing a handkerchief into her mouth. He jerked her to her feet. "Get the marriage certificate. NOW!"

She tried to think. The certificate was at Tessie's house, and she didn't dare go there to retrieve it. And, even if she did, she didn't know where Tessie had hidden it. She had to pretend to find the marriage document and hope Draven wouldn't look at it. She tried to speak, but the gag blocked her words.

Draven grabbed her arm and shook her hard. "Get the marriage certificate, and let's go!" He shoved her again so hard that she stumbled, catching her fall on the back of a chair.

Her mind raced. What paper might pass for a legal document? She kept her writing stationery in a paper portfolio on the bookshelf behind the dining table. Stumbling her way around the table, she used her foot to pull out a chair from the table, climb onto it, dropped the handkerchief from her mouth, and used her teeth to pull the portfolio from where it was tucked amongst other books. From the corner of her eye, she watched Bobo slowly, painfully rise to his feet, eyes unfocused but determined.

Draven strode over, grabbed the folder, stuffed it into his coat, and yanked Vivian off the chair and onto the floor, where he tied the handkerchief around her head again. She bit his finger as he was securing it between her teeth, and he slapped her across the face. Her head snapped sideways, white-hot pain exploding behind her eyes before everything went black. "Let's go," he said, propelling her toward the door.

Bobo stood there on all fours, teeth bared, blocking their exit.

"Get outta the way, you stupid mutt!" Draven shouted, waving his gun.

Vivian attempted a scream behind her gag. Bobo snarled as Draven kicked him, digging the spur of his boot into the dog's rib cage and slamming the poor creature against a wall, where he collapsed in a heap on the floor. Vivian moaned in horror.

"You care too much about that cursed dog," said Draven. "You want a dog? I'll buy you a dog when we get back home to Pennsylvania." He wrapped Vivian's cloak around her body and wrenched the hood over her head, dragging her down the stairs. Once outside, he lifted and carried her to his wagon, tossing her onto the seat and climbing up beside her. She made a move to lunge from the wagon, but Draven grabbed her coat and yanked her back. "Oh, no you don't," he said, raising up and stuffing a few yards of her coat beneath his derriere and dropping his full weight onto the fabric, making it impossible for her to move.

But as Draven rose from his seat for those brief seconds, Vivian had seen her portfolio on the wagon seat beneath him.

Draven clucked to his team of horses and made a U-turn, heading north on Main Street; then wound more of her dress around his leg and slammed his boot onto the hem of her skirt, tethering her to his side. "So you don't try to jump again," he growled.

Vivian was desperate to catch sight of someone she knew on the street as they drove away, but there were very few people out on a blustery night like this. As Draven slapped the reins again, she shook her head in an attempt to remove the hood from her face and head, but when the hood finally slid to the back of her neck, Draven jerked it back over her head again. "Don't even think about it," he snarled.

It was then that she saw Blue from the corner of her eye, walking along the boardwalk toward her apartment building. She threw her head back again, trying to capture his attention, but Draven reached over and held the hood over her face, swearing low. Vivian struggled to turn in her seat and look back at Blue, but he wasn't looking in her direction. He stood beneath the window of her apartment, flinging pebbles. She heard them plink against the glass. If only they'd delayed leaving just a few minutes…

Blue gazed up at Vivian's window, anticipating the appearance of a lovely face framed with golden locks. He knew she'd had a harrowing evening and having to tell her delicate story to Blue and Martin had certainly been emotionally challenging for her. He wanted to know how she was recovering.

He waited patiently before slinging another pebble at the glass. Still no response. The lamps inside were lit, so she must be home. She was probably resting, poor thing, and he shouldn't bother her.

"Did you hear those screams?" a man asked Blue, sauntering out of the Schmitt saloon.

"What screams?" Blue asked in alarm.

"Those screams a few minutes ago."

"Was it a woman screaming?"

"I think so."

"Did you see anyone?"

"No, I heard someone scream something about laundry. It was strange."

"Laundry?" It didn't make a lot of sense, but Blue didn't want to wait to try to figure it out. He pulled open the door to the Garretts' building and vaulted up the stairs two at a time. The door to the apartment was wide open and there were blood-smeared clothes strewn about the room, as well as a half-packed traveling trunk. All went silent, and his ears rang. In slow motion, he leaped inside and nearly tripped over Bobo who lay unconscious on the floor. He called for Vivian and searched the apartment, but it was empty, except for an injured and bedraggled dog. He ran back down the stairs and outside just as Martin, Isabel, Tessie and Cade were walking up the boardwalk after their meal at the Wildwood.

"She's gone!" Blue shouted.

"What's wrong?" asked Isabel. "Who's gone?"

"Vivian," said Blue, "Bobo's inside and badly injured. The door to your apartment was wide open, and there's a mess of clothes scattered around the room. There's blood, too."

Isabel bolted toward the building, but Martin jogged up and caught her arm, blocking her path. "Don't go in there. It might not be safe."

"Martin's right, Miss Garrett. We need a sheriff or deputy," said Blue.

"There aren't any lawmen here in Etna, except for a justice of the peace," Isabel shouted as she ran. "I saw him in the Wildwood."

"Martin, Cade, are you armed?"

"Of course," said Martin, pushing aside his coat to reveal the handle of a revolver.

"Same," said Cade.

"I need help finding Vivian," said Blue.

"We'll help," said Martin. Cade nodded.

"I'll help too," said Tessie.

"All right," said Blue. "Cade, check out the Blake Hotel and Saloon. See if Vivian or Draven Randall is there. Martin, do the same at the Schmitt Hotel and Saloon. I'll search the Wildwood and talk to people on the street. Meet back here in five minutes."

The men took off in different directions.

"I'll run to the livery stable to saddle up some horses!" Tessie boomed as she sprinted down the street. "I know Cade's horse and yours, Blue! Which horse is yours, Martin?"

"Blue roan gelding, stall four," he yelled, dashing into the Schmitt Saloon.

Tessie flew down the street. In less than five minutes, all four men regathered in front of Vivian and Isabel's apartment building.

"Folks saw Mr. Randall and Tessie in the Blake Saloon earlier today," said Cade, "and the Blake Hotel bellhop saw him enter his hotel room this afternoon. But no one saw him leave the hotel or town—and no one has seen Widow Smith."

"Someone in the Schmitt Saloon saw a man and woman ride out of town in a wagon just minutes ago," Martin panted as he jumped off the boardwalk and jogged over to the group.

"Let's get our horses," said Blue. "We'll make a plan on the way. I'm guessing Vivian's with Draven, and they're headed out of the Valley to Yreka."

They sprinted to the livery stable, where Tessie already had a few horses saddled and ready to go. When they'd finished readying their horses, the three men and Tessie swung into their saddles.

"Tessie, you stay here!" Cade ordered sharply.

"Not likely," she snorted. "I can ride better than all of ya."

The small posse tore out of town, headed north.

The wagon rumbled past a farmhouse. Vivian swiveled on the seat to watch Etna's lights fading behind them, struggling to free herself from the strip of cloth that bound her wrists. A quarter mile past the Methodist chapel, Draven pulled back and forced the wagon to a sudden stop, vaulting Vivian backward over the seat and into the wagon box. "Nothin' personal, but you were gettin' in my way," he sniggered. "Stay down and don't do anything stupid," he said, smacking the reins again.

Vivian lay stunned on the hard wooden floorboards, wincing from a bruised hip and shoulder. As the wagon bumped along at an alarming speed, she rolled onto her stomach and worked to push herself up to a kneel before she was thrown backward and hit her head on Draven's traveling trunk. She slumped to the floor and lay panting and exhausted, groaning in pain.

After closing her eyes to take a few ragged breaths, she gathered enough energy to resume her fight against her wrist restraints. It didn't work. She squinted, her eyes searching for something she could use to pry off the tight band of cloth that bound her wrists. At last, she discovered a protruding nail on the wall of the wagon box. Struggling to kneel, she hooked her wrists over it and yanked, pulling and scraping the cloth on the nail's head, using it to tear through the fabric. She cut herself a few times but eventually unraveled the cloth enough to tug her hands free, leaving the cloth hanging on the nail.

She tugged the gag from her mouth, gasping for breath and massaging the bleeding corners of her mouth and working her jaw. She lay back, massaging her wrists and staring up at the moon that played peek-a-boo in the stormy clouds. Shuffling to rotate on her back, she also cast a sharp eye to Draven who was still urging on his team of horses at an unhealthy pace—and paying no attention to her.

She crawled to the rear of the wagon. Setting her jaw, her heart pounded in her ears as she glanced back at Draven. She climbed over the backboard and placed one foot and then the other on the narrow rail, hanging on tightly. She bounced down the pot-holed road. Untangling a foot from her skirt, her other foot slipped off the rail and she clutched the backboard, hanging, dangling inches above the ground. She looked down at the road racing beneath her, panting before she held her breath and let go, landing hard and tumbling on the frozen ground.

Vivian lay in the road, watching the wagon rumble off in the dark. She still wasn't safe. She had to get to the side of the road where she could hide, in case Draven looked back. She crawled, dragging herself to a grove of trees. She rolled into a ditch and lay hiding in a patch of tall, damp grass, staring up at the sky and thanking God that Draven hadn't seen her or noticed she was gone. At least, not yet.

She must have fallen asleep or fainted, because the thundering of hooves startled her, and she opened her eyes, disoriented, shivering, aching all over.

The hoofbeats grew louder. She heard the creaking of leather saddles and the snorting of horses. She propped herself onto her forearms, straining in the dark, watching the riders appear on the road. They shouted to one another as they galloped closer. One of the voices was unmistakably Tessie's.

"Help!" Vivian cried out with every ounce of her strength.

The riders tore past without slowing their pace. Vivian laid her head down on her arms and let the tears soak the sleeve of her cloak. Lightheaded, she knelt on one knee and pushed herself to stand on unsteady legs. Her head and body throbbing, she staggered to the road and began her long walk to Etna, nearly sure she would pass out before Tessie or anyone else found her.

It was a hard ride for Blue's horseback posse. They were nearly to Patterson Creek by the time they overtook Draven's wagon. Galloping on either side of the wagon, Blue, Cade and Martin readied their guns and commanded Draven to stop. Instead of complying, he held the reins in his left hand, stood joltingly to his feet, cocked his revolver in his right hand, and aimed at Blue.

At the same time, Vivian's stationery portfolio slid across the wagon seat and flipped open on a breeze that carried the papers into the air, scattering them onto the road.

A shot cracked. Draven had fired at Blue and missed. Barely. A stray piece of paper blew into Draven's face and stuck there, and as he raised his hand to flick it away, he lost his balance and landed with a hard thump onto the wagon seat. Still urging the horses onward, he again raised his right hand, this time sitting and twisting on the seat and aiming the shiny black barrel of his gun behind him toward his pursuers. His gun gleamed with a cool hint of silver in the night, making it an easy target for Blue and Martin. They shot simultaneously at the revolver, knocking it from his hand.

Draven roared, swearing and using his unwounded hand to slap the reins even harder onto the backs of the wearied horses. Blue edged closer alongside the wagon, posting in his stirrups and balancing dexterously as he pulled himself to a kneeling position in the saddle. Positioning one foot beneath his body for leverage, he jumped off his horse and leaped onto Draven, nearly knocking him off the wagon. Cade jumped onto the wagon seat beside Blue, and they both tackled the villain.

"Help me tie him up," Blue shouted, grabbing hold of the reins and drawing the horses to a halt.

Cade set the brake. Martin dismounted and sprinted over to help.

"Get those papers!" Draven's voice was raw and strained.

Tessie dismounted to retrieve Draven's revolver from where it lay on the road.

"Fetch me the papers!" Draven shouted again.

Climbing into the wagon box, Tessie trained the gun on Draven's head as she glanced down to look for Vivian. "She's gone!" Tessie screamed. "Where is she?"

Blue turned Draven onto his stomach and held him down with one knee while he and Martin secured his wrists with a bandana.

"You shot my hand!" Draven swore furiously.

"Where is she?" Blue demanded, ignoring his blustering.

"And you let all those papers fly away!"

"Where's Vivian?" Blue shouted close to Draven's head, pulling him up to sit on the wagon seat.

"What do you mean?!" Draven grunted, turning to peer back into the wagon box. "Infernal she-devil!"

"Tell me where she is!" Blue twisted Draven's collar in his fist and shook him.

"She must have escaped." Draven's words were low and gravelly.

"We must have passed her on the road," panted Tessie.

"Martin, you and Cade bind this varmint's ankles with a couple of handkerchiefs and toss him into the wagon box," Blue barked.

"What are you gonna do for my hand?" Draven growled. "And you have to fetch those papers. They're important."

"No one cares about your papers!" Martin shouted.

Martin removed the kerchief from his neck.

"I'll go back and look for Miss Vivian," Tessie panted.

"Wait," said Blue, jumping off the wagon and landing on the ground. "Tessie, you and Martin take this blackguard back to the jailhouse and fetch the magistrate from Callahan. Don't let him out of your sight, and keep your guns trained on him. Don't let him get away. Cade, as soon as you finish here, join me to search for Vivian."

"Yes, sir," said Cade, tying two handkerchiefs together.

Draven kicked and fought hard against Cade and Martin but while they worked to restrain him, Blue took off at a gallop in search of Vivian.

****

"Vivian!" a voice shouted from behind her, and hooves pounded in the darkness. Panic slammed Vivian's heart, and she stumbled off the road, dropping to hide in some tall weeds.

"Vivian, it's me, Blue!" He jumped off his horse while still in a gallop, and ran to Vivian, where she sat crouched, forearms lifted to protect her head.

"Vivian." Blue's voice was gentle and soft now. "I'm not going to hurt you. It's me. It's Blue Ryan."

Vivian nearly collapsed with relief. Blue scooped her up, and she lay baby-weak in his strong arms. He lifted her onto his horse, settled her in the saddle, and removed his coat, wadding it around the pommel to make her journey more endurable. Swinging up behind her, Blue wrapped one arm around her waist and reached for the reins. Cade rode up and, with a firm arm around Vivian, he galloped back to town with Cade following close behind.

"Her breathing's irregular, Doc," a voice spoke in the dark.

"Lay her on the bed," another voice replied.

Vivian felt herself sinking and Blue's blurred face wavered above her. "Don't leave me," she spoke in a faint whisper.

"I won't," said Blue as her vision and consciousness failed.

CHAPTER 24 – New Uncertainties

*V*ivian awoke on the sofa in the parlor with a cloth bag of ice on her bandaged forehead. She tried to move but her entire body ached. She squinted to see China Mary in the kitchen. "What happened?" Vivian asked faintly.

"You lie down and rest, yonggan," China Mary commanded.

Bobo lay on a blanket nearby. A large white bandage was wrapped around his middle. Though he looked dead as ever, his soft breathing revealed he was alive.

"Is Bobo all right?"

"Yes, dog is fine." Mary washed her hands and poured a cup of tea. "You drink this," she said as she tottered to Vivian's side and positioned herself on the coffee table beside her. Vivian lifted her heavy head, sipped, and lay back on the pillow, too weak, stiff and sore to drink more. "You drink little more soon," said Mary.

Clothes hung from a clothesline between the kitchen and dining table. "Did you wash my clothes?" she asked.

"No," said Mary. "Zhang Wei and Zhang Ying wash. I dry."

"Oh, thank you. Please tell them thank you," Vivian murmured, pressing her fingers to her forehead. "Was Mr. Ryan here, Mary?"

"He stay all day and all night, yonggan," Mary answered. "I make him go home to sleep."

"What? What day is it? What time is it?" asked Vivian, blinking at the muted sunlight touching the window.

"Half past twelve Monday," China Mary answered. "You sleep long time."

Vivian pushed herself onto her elbows. "Oh, no, that means Blue is missing work, and I'm missing work. I have to explain to Cocoa Joe—"

"He know already," said Mary. "Not to worry. And not to worry about Mr. Ryan. Cocoa Joe make him stay home to rest. He say he come back to see you and dog in evening." She lifted the teacup to Vivian's lips. "Drink more tea." Vivian took a small sip.

"What happened to Draven Randall?"

"When others come back, they tell you," said Mary. "Now you rest."

Vivian touched her eyelids to catch any tears on the brink of spilling. "I've been a naïve fool."

"Maybe," Mary nodded.

"You don't have to be so agreeable," Vivian retorted, "but it's true. I've made reckless, impulsive decisions. I'll be wiser in the future."

"I know you will," said Mary.

That evening, Isabel and Tessie walked into the apartment, each looking a little worn, yet concerned about Vivian's wellbeing.

"You're awake!" Tessie exclaimed. "How are ya feelin'?"

Vivian sat up straighter, clutching the blanket. "How are you two?"

"We're fine," said Isabel. "Are you feeling any better?"

"Aching everywhere and a bit groggy, but I'll mend. Izza told me you had an interview with Miss Darcy Meyer today, Tessie. How did that go?"

"I got the job!" Tessie beamed, giving Isabel a quick side hug that said *thank you*. "I thank ya both. I couldn't have gotten this job iffen ya all didn't help me with my manners and all." She plopped onto a chair. "Unfortunately, I can only work there part-time, afternoons and evenings, but that's a good thing iffen I get to go back to school."

"We're working on that," said Isabel, sitting to unbutton her boots and lean back on the sofa beside Vivian.

"All right. So…" Vivian swallowed. "You haven't told me what happened to Draven. Does anyone know? Did he leave town? Did he come back to look for me? What has happened?"

Tessie licked her lips and pressed them together, raising her eyebrows.

Isabel cleared her throat. "Um, Vivi…" She looked down at her hands in her lap.

"What's wrong?" Vivian demanded.

"Um…" Isabel's eyes pleaded with Tessie.

"I'll tell you, Miss Vivi. Mr. Ranson, Mr. Graver and Mr. Ryan, and I all rode out in search of ya, and we caught up to Mr. Randall's wagon, but you weren't there. Your Mr. Ryan fought Mr. Randall for ya, and my Cade joined him and tied him up. Then Mr. Ryan rode back to look for ya, and Cade followed him. Mr. Graver and I drove Mr. Randall back to the Etna jailhouse, where Mr. Denny, our justice of the peace, slapped him in jail for assault and kidnapping," Tessie said excitedly.

"But—" Isabel interjected.

"But?" Vivian urged.

Tessie frowned, crossing her arms. "Yeah, the sad thing is that, bein' a lawyer and all, Mr. Randall somehow wiggled out of jail and a trial."

"The viper!" Vivian gasped. "Does that mean he's still roaming free in Etna? Am I safe?"

"He left town," said Tessie.

"And you're safe," said Isabel gently.

"Just like that?" Vivian blinked and breathed a sigh of relief. "After everything?"

Vivian glanced at Bobo where he stretched and gave a soft whimper, as if echoing her confusion. "Why hasn't Cocoa Joe come to check on Bobo?"

Isabel shifted uncomfortably. "Oh, dear…that's a sad, sad story, Vivi." She looked at Tessie, who nodded. "When Draven left town, he took Samantha with him."

"What?!" Vivian's eyes widened. "No!"

"They left together on the train today," Tessie said as quietly as she possibly could.

"They plan to be married in Pennsylvania," said Isabel softly.

Vivian's lips parted, but no words came. Finally, she said, "I can only hope and pray Draven will treat Samantha better than he treated me."

"And better than he has all his other women," Tessie muttered.

Vivian stared down at her hands, her thoughts swirling. "I need to warn her somehow."

"It's too late, Miss Vivian," said Tessie. "She's gone."

After a long silence, Vivian nodded, her jaw clenched. "I should have warned her."

Isabel clutched one of Vivian's hands. "She wouldn't have listened to you, Vivi. She was so jealous of you."

"She really didn't like you," Tessie added, then winced. "Sorry."

Vivian offered a tired half-smile. "It's fine." She sighed. "What do I do now?"

"Nothing," Isabel replied. "I think you should wait to see what Mr. Ryan has to say to you. He cares for you, Vivi."

"Not enough to ask a pregnant single woman to marry him," said Vivian. She lay back and the room fell silent. Shadows from the woodstove flickered on the walls. Her heart ached—not just from bruises and betrayal, but from uncertainty. "I'd like to believe Blue likes me, Izza, but I can't get my hopes up. Anyhow, I'm an independent woman—and don't forget a suffragette."

Isabel's lips twisted into a smile. "That's you, all right."

"And everyone but Cade and Mr. Ryan and us know you're a widow," said Tessie.

Vivian let out a weak laugh. "As long as I can trust all of us to keep my secret, I think I'll be all right."

"You still need a husband," said Isabel. "You can't keep working for Mr. McGovern and care for a baby."

"I'll pray and try to figure it out," said Vivian.

"And we'll be here for ya, Miss Vivian," Tessie promised.

Isabel squeezed Vivian's hand. "We're not going anywhere."

Vivian glanced at Bobo, then at the friends beside her. Her voice was stronger now. "I think we're here for each other."

CHAPTER 25 – Beginning and End

$\mathcal{V}$ivian spent the next few days cocooned at home, her body aching with every movement, her heart heavier still. The bruises on her arms faded from purple to yellow, but the ache of betrayal throbbed fresh beneath the surface. Each morning, China Mary arrived with a basket of pungent herbs and steaming teas that tasted like boiled twigs and pepper yet somehow dulled the pain. She was also thankful for the surprising outpouring of kindness from Etna's townspeople who dropped off meals and get-well cards. She wrote several thank-you notes to everyone who helped her, including Blue, although she tried not to fawn all over him and make him sound like her hero.

Still, Vivian's thoughts strayed again and again to Samantha. She hadn't heard a word since the kidnapping, and an uneasy dread coiled in her chest, tightening each day. At the same time, she struggled with guilt at her relief that she could now walk down the street without scanning every shadow now that Draven had left town.

Cocoa Joe dropped by to check on Vivian and Bobo one afternoon. He also dropped off a brand-new Burroughs calculating machine, along with ledgers, receipts, and invoices, asking her if she could work from home during her convalescence. She agreed. He cleared his throat, then pointed through the door to the landing. "There's one more thing—a gift from Mr. Ryan."

Vivian followed his gaze to a handcrafted oak rocker in the shadows. Cocoa Joe dragged it inside. Its polished arms gleaming in the firelight. "He hopes it will speed your recovery."

She trailed her fingers along the smooth wood, her throat tightening. "Please… tell Mr. Ryan thank you. It's very kind of him." Her voice caught, and she swallowed hard. "Mr. McGovern, I want to know if you've heard anything from Samantha. Do you know how she is?" But tears suddenly welled in his eyes, and he abruptly excused himself.

Autumn storms brought more rain. Feeling stronger, Vivian bundled up and ventured out with her umbrella for short walks, happy for the fresh air and soaking in the divine feeling of safety she knew now that Draven was gone.

A few evenings after the kidnapping, rain tapped on the window as Vivian sat in her rocking chair by a warm fire, reading a book. Isabel was working late at the mercantile, and China Mary busied herself in the kitchen, grumbling about the unhealthy meals neighbors had brought.

Mary chopped an onion and grated sweet potatoes. "You need soup and vegetables, not bread and cheese."

Both she and Vivian were startled at a knock on the door. Mary wiped her hands on her apron and told Vivian not to get up.

The door opened, and there was Blue. Vivian's breath caught. She laid her book on a table beside her and smoothed the blanket across her lap.

"Hello, Mr. Ryan," China Mary greeted him, and he gave a slight bow to both Mary and Vivian.

"Come in," Vivian called, gesturing.

"Good evening, ma'am," he said, stepping inside and removing his hat. He ran his fingers through his hair. "I wondered if you're feeling well enough to take an evening stroll with me."

She hesitated only a second. Blue was all she'd hoped for in a man—morally upright, God fearing, humorous, hardworking, and brave—not to mention devilishly handsome. She stood and tossed the blanket behind her. "I'd be happy to, Mr. Ryan." She stroked the smooth arm of the wooden rocker. "As much as I love this beautiful chair, I don't mind taking a break from it."

China Mary shook her head. "Be warm and don't stay too long. I wait for you?"

"There's no need," said Vivian. "Isabel will be here soon. Thank you so much for the delicious meal you've cooked, Mary."

"Don't forget eat meal, yonggan. It is not good cold."

"Yes, Mary," Vivian complied as she buttoned her boots.

Blue held her coat for her, and she donned hat and scarf before walking slowly and carefully down the stairs behind Blue as he held her hand, steadying her along the way.

The rain subsided and the air was damp, cool and fresh on their leisurely promenade. Even Bobo felt recovered enough to join them, limping faithfully by their side. As twilight wrapped itself around them, Blue stroked Vivian's hand, sending a sizzle up her arm to her chest. She longed to return his gesture and stroke her thumb over his knuckles, but didn't dare to be so forward.

"Miss Garrett," Blue said, his voice gruff, "I have something to tell you." He stopped, turned, and faced her. A deep ache suddenly throbbed in her bosom. "I've fallen in love with you, Vivian."

His words soaked through her like warm honey, sweet and slow. At the same moment, a gentleman propped a ladder against the streetlamp beside them, breaking the magic. Blue grinned and greeted the lamplighter, who lit the wick that cast a splash of golden light around them.

The lamplighter moved on, and Blue gently tugged Vivian closer. Placing both hands on her face, he tilted her head to the light, and Vivian inhaled the scents of rain, horse leather, and pine. Her insides collapsed and liquefied with anticipation. He leaned in, bringing his mouth to within an inch of her lips. Her spine met the lamppost behind her, and he pressed his body closer.

"Mr. Ryan, you're a minister," she whispered. "How can you court me, a fake widow and a liar who might be pregnant?"

"Because I'm completely, madly in love with you," he whispered. The slight brush of his mouth over hers simultaneously awakened and paralyzed her and, when his mouth finally touched her lips, a pulse of heat threaded through every inch of her body.

"So, what if I'm courting a poor widow who's with child? No one but a handful of us will ever know the full truth. The question is: Do you love me, Vivian?"

She suddenly felt wine-tipsy warm and weak as a kitten. "I do, Mr. Ryan. I love you too." She relaxed into another kiss as he caressed her cheeks with his hands.

Then he dropped to one knee, golden lamplight bathing his rugged face. "Will you marry me?"

The words yanked the breath from her lungs. "What?" she gasped, unsure of what she'd just heard.

"Will you marry me, Vivian Garrett?" She was too stunned to speak and, even when she opened her mouth, no words came out. He smiled and rose, then placed his hands on her arms. "Let me rephrase the question. Will you allow me to love you and take care of you, and any future children we might have, for the rest of my life?"

"You'd be willing to raise Draven's child," she asked shakily.

"More than willing," he replied. "No one will suspect it's anyone's child but mine. And I say we get married soon." There was a twinkle in his eye.

She hauled in a breath and looked away. Lamplight flickered in myriad puddles on the street and a robin trilled its goodnight song. "If I say yes, am I being a reckless, impulsive fool again?"

"Maybe," he said, "but then so am I."

Her breath came faster. After the multiple traumas she'd experienced with Draven, she should be more wary of this man. She'd never felt anything like this for any man before.

"Yes," she said, decisively.

"Yes, you'll marry me?"

"Yes," she nodded firmly.

Blue folded her against him until their bodies melted into one another. Vivian's heart thudded in her chest. After everything, she should be cautious. But wrapped in Blue's arms, beneath the soft lamplight, all she felt was peace. And something more—*desire*.

He kissed her again—first softly, then with surprising urgency. For a preacher, Blue sure didn't repress his passion.

Epilogue

August 1894

The sun ducked low behind the peaks of the Marble Mountains, and the cooling shadows offered a welcome transition from the afternoon's stifling August heat as the wheels of the baby carriage crackled in the gravel. Vivian's parents strolled beside the buggy. Their faces softened with pride each time they glanced into the carriage. Grandma Garrett brushed a finger across Evelyn's tiny hand, Grandpa beamed like he'd won a prize, and they couldn't be happier with their cowboy preacher son-in-law.

Blue and Vivian were married in October 1893. They bought a modest home and were ready for Evelyn's arrival in May the following year. Throughout her pregnancy and following the baby's birth, Vivian continued working for Mr. McGovern. Most days she worked at home; on others, she hired a part-time nanny to help.

When Reverend Patterson resigned and moved away in early 1894, Blue was offered the pastorship of the Congregational Church. With his continuing work as a cowboy, most of his sermons included a colorful and humorous ranching story and the congregation loved him.

Vivian and her parents approached the street corner outside the Wildwood Café, stopping to chat with a small group of friends that included Tessie and her new husband Cade, Cocoa Joe and Sally, and China Mary.

"Rabbi Ry' will be mighty tired after work today, Vivi Honeybee," said Mr. McGovern. "He and the boys have been brandin' calves."

"Material for his next sermon, I'm sure," said Vivian.

"At least folks can stay awake in church now that he's preachin'," said Tessie, giving Cade a squeeze.

"But I don't get me mornin' church naps anymore," Cocoa Joe chuckled as Sally elbowed his ribs.

"Have ya told 'em yet?" Cade asked Tessie.

"Not yet," she said before announcing far too loudly, "We're expectin' a baby next February!"

Whoops and whistles echoed.

"China Mary's helpin' me through the awful mornin' sickness. Thank you again, Mary."

"You are welcome, Mrs. Tessie," she replied.

"We heard that! Congratulations, you two!" shouted Martin as he and Isabel approached. They were newly married as well.

Another young woman arrived pushing a perambulator and wearing black widow's garb with a daringly low-cut neckline. A pungent, invisible cloud hovered around her, causing anyone within five feet of her to suffer from sneezing and watery eyes.

"Why, if it isn't me sweet Sammy Sassafras and our wee grand-bairn, Rose," Cocoa Joe bellowed. "Ha! Ha! Haaaaa!"

"Shush, Father, you'll wake the baby," Samantha scolded.

He put an apologetic finger to his lips and took a peek in the carriage.

Draven married Samantha in a rush, and nine months later, divorced her minutes after she gave birth—not to a son, but a daughter. He'd found a loophole in his grandfather's will, granting him freedom to seek a new wife and try again for an heir.

No one questioned the circumstances of Draven Randall's supposed untimely passing or Samantha's sudden widowhood and return to Etna, but Vivian knew Draven was still very much alive back in Philadelphia. Since returning to Scott Valley with baby Rose, Samantha and Vivian formed a surprising friendship, due to their daughters sharing the same father. Local town folk assumed the bond was due to their shared widowhood, a welcome misunderstanding. Samantha's marriage to an abusive husband led her to be an ardent and fearless suffragette and she joined Vivian's popular cause. She also campaigned for Vivian to be the future mayor of Etna, but folks weren't quite ready for such a radical change just yet. Samantha faithfully attended rallies and meetings, motivating folks all over Scott Valley to sign suffrage petitions. And now that she was single again, she was on the prowl for a husband, flirting outrageously with every handsome man she met, and eager to cease her mourning period.

"Oh, no! Oh, no!" a woman cried from the stoop of the Wildwood Café, where she crouched to stroke Bobo's head. "Please, somebody help this poor dog! I think he's dead!"

"He's not dead!" Vivian's cluster of friends all shouted at once, startling the woman before she strolled away with a scowl on her face.

"Vivi!" shouted Blue, sprinting over and waving a bouquet of daisies. "For my beautiful bride," he said, planting a kiss on her cheek. "There's more where that came from."

"What, daisies or kisses?" she asked. Even after all these months, he could make her heart flutter, and he made her feel cherished and beautiful.

"Both," said Blue, bending to scoop up his kicking, wriggling daughter, hugging and kissing her chubby face. No one who saw Blue with his blue-eyed baby Evie would think he wasn't her true father. He was positively devoted to her.

"Howdy, everyone!" a voice rang out from the boardwalk. Hiram Planter.

"Don't worry. I'll talk to him," said Samantha. "I could use the company."

"Are ye that desperate, Sammy lass?" asked her father.

"My time back east only made me miss the folks here all the more—even Hiram," she teased lightly. "We were schoolmates, you know."

"I come with you, Sammy," said China Mary.

They wished everyone a pleasant evening and headed over to Hiram.

"Samantha has really changed," Tessie muttered too loudly.

"Haven't we all?" Vivian added.

"Mostly for the better, I hope," said Cocoa Joe.

Sally chuckled softly. "Change or no change, some things never wait—like the chickens at feeding time. My love, we really ought to be heading home."

"What's that?" Cocoa Joe asked. "Ah, yes, quite right, quite right. The chickens."

At last, only the Garretts remained with Blue and Vivian.

"We'll be back to your place after supper," said Mrs. Garrett. "Your father's treating me to a meal at the Wildwood Café this evening."

"Don't stay out too late, kids," said Blue, waving to his in-laws and carrying baby Evie, while Vivian turned the carriage toward home.

Just past Dr. Furber's Beehive, they stopped to watch the eastern hills blush orange in the setting sun as a covey of quail flew with buzzing wings into a blackberry thicket. Gnats glistened like fairy wings in the golden light and barn swallows dipped and swooped over the pasture's sleepy haze. Evelyn's eyelids fluttered and Blue sang softly....

Way down in the meadow where the lily first blows

Where the wind from the mountains never ruffles the rose
Lives fond Evelina, the sweet little dove
The pride of the valley, the girl that I love.

Blue sneezed, briefly startling the baby before she drifted to sleep again. After gently lowering her into the carriage, he reached into his trouser pocket and pulled out an oddly shaped wad of fabric that looked very much like a bathing cap

"Whatever is that thing?" Vivian interrogated.

"Oh, this? I must have grabbed it instead of a handkerchief by mistake." He stuffed it back into his pocket and sniffled.

Vivian handed him a handkerchief. "It looked like a lady's bathing cap," she said. "Wherever did you find it?"

Blue wiped his nose and pocketed the kerchief. "Funny you should ask," he said. "I found it at the Johnson Creek swimming hole."

"Why on earth did you bother to bring it home?" When Blue bit down on a smile and shrugged, she felt a slight rise of angst in her gut. "Well, for pity's sake, you should take it to church on Sunday and ask if anyone's lost it."

"Found it over a year ago," Blue said casually.

Vivian's heart skipped a beat. "What are you saying?"

His white teeth gleamed in his broad smile. "I never saw you, exactly, but I've always had my suspicions."

Her mouth popped open. "Mr. Blue Ryan," she groaned, "you can't be serious."

"Oh, but I am."

"Why in Heaven's name did you keep the silly thing all this time?"

He lifted his shoulders. "Memories of a particularly humorous situation, my dear Widow Smith," he grinned mischievously.

"Blue, you're absolutely terrible," she scolded. "I can't believe you knew I was there. Did anyone else see me?"

He shrugged. "I doubt it. No one said anything and believe me, if they saw you, I think they'd talk about it."

"Good point," said Vivian, breathing a sigh.

"But there is something that's been troubling me since that day."

"What's that?"

"Did you happen to see—?"

"I'm not talking about this," said Vivian, feeling her face burn as she stomped ahead, pushing the carriage with increased speed.

"Do you know what Shakespeare wrote about protesting too much?" Blue teased. Vivian disregarded him. "I have to say, I found the cap when I first arrived at the creek that afternoon and it seems to me, we'd been swimmin' a good while before you went a-scramblin' over that bank."

"I will not discuss this any further," she said adamantly.

"Were you skinny dipping?" he asked.

"Of course not!"

"Hm. You know, my Cherokee people skinny dip."

Vivian rolled her eyes. "You and your people."

"You know, we could sneak up to that swimmin' hole one of these days and do our own bit of skinny dippin', just the two of us."

"Absolutely not," she said firmly.

He moseyed over and kissed her on the neck.

"Blue, not in public."

"Or you could ask your mother to watch Evie while we take a walk over to Etna Creek tonight," said Blue. "There's a nice grassy spot on the bank, where—"

"Shush!" she reprimanded. "Someone might hear you."

"Like who?" he asked, taking a half-turn and pointing to the empty street. He opened the garden gate for Vivian, and she parked the carriage at the foot of the porch steps, leaving Evelyn for Blue to tend to as she hustled into the house to prepare a light supper.

A short while later, with Evelyn asleep in her cradle, she and Blue were seated at a small table on the back porch overlooking oaks, pines, and a small vegetable garden. At the conclusion of their meal, Blue leaned back in his chair and sipped a glass of iced tea.

"Vivi," he said contemplatively, "when the McGoverns said they had to go home and feed the chickens, I don't think that's what they meant."

"So, what of it?" asked Vivian.

"They have a hired hand to feed their animals and Cocoa Joe seemed mighty eager."

"So?" Vivian repeated.

"So, I think it was a secret message."

"What kind of a—?" Vivian stopped herself. "Oh, Blue, for pity's sake. Your mind goes to the oddest places."

"My mind? Your mind is the one thinkin' things."

"You are utterly preposterous."

Blue gulped another draught of tea. "You know what I'm thinkin'?"

"I know exactly what you're thinking," said Vivian as she stacked the dishes.

"I was thinking of what might have happened to you if I hadn't rescued a certain damsel in distress nigh on about a year ago—the second time I saved your hide, by the way."

"You didn't rescue me, Blue," Vivian reminded him. "I rescued myself—not from the stampede, of course, but from that…certain person who shall not be named."

"And you missed the whole shootout."

"That occurred *after* I made my own heroic escape."

Blue set his empty glass on the table and crossed his arms over his chest. "If Draven had found you, I don't think you could have escaped a second time."

"Once we'd gotten to Yreka, I'm sure I would have figured out a way to escape again."

"I don't know," said Blue. "He would have kept a closer eye on you."

Vivian shuddered. "Probably right," she muttered.

"But I would have ridden all the way there to save you," said Blue.

"I do believe you would have," Vivian whispered. She stretched her hand across the table and lightly touched his arm. "I might have a way of thanking a certain strong, masculine Cherokee warrior who once fought to save a damsel in distress in an epic gun battle."

Blue straightened, squared his shoulders, and took Vivian's hand. "What are you sayin', Vivi Honeybee?"

"I'm sayin' there are some chickens that need feedin'."

THE END

Author's Historical Note

Several real people, places, and historical details are woven throughout *A Widow's Whim* to celebrate the unique heritage of my former hometown, Etna, California. In the 1890s time period, the town was called "Etna Mills," but I shortened to its modern name of Etna.

One of the most memorable figures from Etna's past was a Chinese woman known locally as "Chinee Mary," who lived in the 1890s with her mother, called "Old Susie." They were the only Chinese women in the community, living among roughly a hundred Chinese male laborers. The two women wore traditional Chinese clothing—long, floppy-sleeved tunics over trousers—which caused quite a stir among the townsfolk, who weren't accustomed to seeing women in pants.

Because the nickname "Chinee Mary" reflected the racial attitudes of the time, I chose to rename her "China Mary" in my novel. Historical accounts describe her as kind-hearted, especially toward children. Knowing that many youngsters were frightened to walk past the Chinese settlement—often filled with loud, unfamiliar voices—Mary would kindly escort them along the path.

She was also known for her cleverness and humor. Mary owned two wire-haired terriers who were expert chicken catchers. When they made a "catch," she would scold them loudly for all to hear, then secretly scoop up the unlucky bird and tuck it into the wide sleeve of her tunic.

The top of Callahan Street, branching off Etna's Main Street, is still known today as "China Hill," a lasting reminder of the area where the Chinese community once lived.

Many other true-to-history locations and figures appear in *A Widow's Whim*, including the Parker Campbell Store (later the Denny Bar & Parker Co. and now the Denny Bar

Company restaurant and distillery), the Blake Hotel, the Schmitt Hotel, and early establishments such as the Kappler Brewery and Dr. George Furber's "Beehive" building. You'll also spot nods to the old jailhouse that now serves as the Etna Museum, and to the Congregational Church (now Scott Valley Berean Church) as well as the Crystal Creek Methodist Church, which is no longer standing—though a monument marks its place along Highway 3. I also briefly reference the Lotta Crabtree, a singer-dancer famous in California's Gold Rush days.

A few modern touches appear as well, including the Paystreak Café and Bobo the dog, who is based on a story told by Etna residents Don and Sandra Murphy about their own comical pup.

My heroine, Vivian, was largely inspired by Mrs. Marilyn Seward, a longtime resident of Etna. She was the wife of Pastor Wendell Seward of the Scott Valley Berean Church and also served as Etna's mayor. My hero, Blue, draws inspiration from both my husband, Pete, and Marilyn's husband, Wendell—both true champions of women's rights and personal heroes of mine.

Etna's past and present intertwine beautifully, and I wanted this story to honor both—the people who built our valley and those who continue to keep its history alive.

Bibliographical   **Reference**

Campbell, Loretta M., and Dorice E. Young. *Etna: From Mule Train to "Copter, A Pictorial History of Etna.* Etna, CA: Eschscholtzia Parlor No. 112, Native Daughters of the Golden West, 1965.